PRAISE FOR JENNIFER JA

". . . intricately plotted . . . The action builds to a jaw-dropping conclusion."

—*Publishers Weekly* on *The Stranger Inside*

"Impressively original . . . Jennifer Jaynes has proven herself to be a consummate and consistently entertaining novelist."

—*Midwest Book Review* on *The Stranger Inside*

"Great mystery writing at its best."

—*Fresh Fiction* on *The Stranger Inside*

"Talented Jennifer Jaynes turns up the intensity with her first stand-alone thriller: *The Stranger Inside*, an edge-of-your-seat crime thriller solidifying her place alongside the best of female crime writers out today!"

—*Judith D. Collins Must Read Books Blog*

"Jennifer Jaynes has quickly become one of my favorite writers. Her stories are deep, dark, and twisted . . . I can never turn the pages fast enough."

—Minka Kent, international bestselling author of *The Thinnest Air*

"Jennifer Jaynes writes a smart and twisty thriller that's guaranteed to keep you reading well past bedtime . . . I am anxiously awaiting the next book."

elling author of

n't Say a Word)

MALICE

OTHER TITLES BY JENNIFER JAYNES

The Stranger Inside
Disturbed

Strangers Series

Never Smile at Strangers
Ugly Young Thing
Don't Say a Word

Children's Books

I Care About Me

MALICE

JENNIFER JAYNES

THOMAS & MERCER

Text copyright © 2018 by Jennifer Jaynes
All rights reserved.

No part of this book may be reproduced, or stored in a retrieval system, or transmitted in any form or by any means, electronic, mechanical, photocopying, recording, or otherwise, without express written permission of the publisher.

Published by Thomas & Mercer, Seattle

www.apub.com

Amazon, the Amazon logo, and Thomas & Mercer are trademarks of Amazon.com, Inc., or its affiliates.

ISBN-13: 9781503903913
ISBN-10: 1503903915

Cover design by Scott Biel

For Colton Berrett
A beautiful soul gone way too soon.

PROLOGUE

GOOSEFLESH DIMPLED DR. Daniel Winters's arms as he lay in bed, trying to get his bearings. The room was cool and dark except for a narrow slice of light glowing from the bottom of a door on the other side of the room. But the door was in the wrong place.

What the—? He wasn't in his bedroom.

The room slanted a little as he sat up. Rubbing the goose bumps from his arms, he listened and could hear the pounding water of a shower. Then an air-conditioning unit shuddered on and began blasting more chilled air. Slowly, it all flooded back to him: He and his boss, Teddy, at the hotel bar. Teddy leaving. A woman approaching him, asking if she could sit in the seat Teddy had vacated.

She hadn't been his type.

She'd been far too attractive.

Daniel had never trusted women who were over-the-top beautiful because as a child, he'd seen several of them slowly and systematically destroy his father. In his experience, exceptionally beautiful women also had inferior personalities and intelligence compared to women of average physical beauty. He theorized that was because the beautiful never had to try very hard. People were seduced, even hypnotized, by superficial beauty, no matter what was—or more important, *wasn't*—on the inside. But Daniel wasn't one of those people.

He recalled the woman's long chestnut hair, her blue eyes, and full, heart-shaped lips. Her syrupy voice and the confident way she carried herself.

"Another chardonnay, please," she'd called to the young bartender. Then she'd pointed to Daniel. "And another drink for this gentleman."

"No, thank you. That's unnecessary," Daniel said, a bit surprised. He couldn't remember a woman, especially one he didn't know, ever offering to buy him a drink before.

"I know." She smiled, a dimple dotting her cheek.

"Another ginger ale, sir?" the bartender asked.

"Ginger ale, huh? Wild night on the town, I see," the woman remarked.

She was witty.

Pay the tab and go, the little voice—the one that had talked sense into him his entire adult life, that had protected him and kept him from serious harm—had whispered.

Although he usually listened to the voice without pause, he decided to ignore it this time. He convinced himself that one drink wouldn't hurt. After all, it was within the rules he'd set for himself: three drinks maximum while out and never, ever at home.

He was curious about the woman. Of what she wanted from him. He had no expectations, so what the hell. He had nothing to lose.

"Make it a whiskey on the rocks, please," he said. "Jameson."

Bad things, Daniel, the voice warned. *Alcohol always leads to bad things. You know that.*

Again, he ignored the intrusion. He turned to the woman. "Thanks for the drink."

She gave him a little nod.

He noticed that despite her nearly perfect exterior, the nails at the ends of her slender fingers were bitten to the quicks.

"Here you go," the bartender said, sliding Daniel's drink in front of him. He picked up the glass and took a long sip, the whiskey burning a fiery path down his throat.

Oh, how he missed that feeling.

And *didn't* miss it.

He took another sip.

"So . . . how long have you been a doctor?" the woman asked.

Daniel almost choked on his liquor. Surprised, he turned to her. "What makes you think I'm a doctor?"

She tilted her head toward him, her glossy hair falling like a curtain against her left shoulder. "Well, I'm guessing you came here from work, so the way you're dressed tells me you're a professional, but you're not wearing a suit, so that rules out finance," she said, her eyes sharp, intelligent. "You ordered a middle-of-the-road drink—nothing pretentious—so you're not in the movie business. And you don't seem to have the arrogance of a lawyer."

He felt his brow crease. "That's . . . amazing."

Her lips twitched with amusement. "Also, I overheard someone saying hello to you earlier. He called you Dr. Winters."

Daniel grinned. Witty *and* funny. Despite himself, his interest was piqued.

"So, what is it that *you* do?" he asked.

"I'm a cocktail waitress. I work at Jiminy's, just outside Malibu."

"Cocktail waitress, huh?"

They proceeded to talk for hours. He learned that her name was Mia, that she was staying in one of the hotel rooms upstairs because her apartment was being fumigated. That she had been born and raised in Arizona but had been living in Los Angeles for the last two years. That she wasn't a big people person and considered herself a homebody. She was very articulate and Daniel was surprised to find her to be highly intelligent, despite her looks. She'd also been a bit philosophical, at one point asking him if he thought he was destined for happiness.

The question had seemed to come from left field. "That's pretty random," he said, studying her, searching for signs that she'd had too much to drink. In his experience, that was the only time people broached such subjects. But she seemed fine.

"It's just something I think about from time to time," she said, pushing a lock of hair behind her ear. "You don't?"

"No, never," he lied. "How about you? Do you think you were destined for happiness?"

She shook her head. "Actually, no. I don't."

Her answer had surprised him. Up to this point, she'd seemed pretty upbeat.

"Why's that?" he asked.

She stared at him for a moment, then her eyes slid away and she seemed to focus on something on the other side of the bar. "I just have this sort of *knowing*. Deep down," she said. "Plus, my experiences so far . . . they've really been shit."

Her eyes returned to his, and she watched him for a beat. Then her lovely lips curved into a smile and she changed the subject. As they continued to talk, he studied her closely. He also kept ordering more whiskey and far exceeded his three-drink maximum. He'd gotten drunk. So drunk that he also blacked out at some point. It was something he hadn't done in years.

I warned you, Daniel. But you kept ignoring me.

Blinking himself back to reality, he now felt for the bedside lamp and flipped it on. He looked around the dimly lit room for his clothes and found them neatly folded at the foot of the bed. The air-conditioning unit shuddered loudly again, then went quiet and he could hear the sound of water running again.

The woman was in the shower.

Grab your clothes, and get the hell out of here, the voice instructed.

It was right, as usual. If he left now, before she emerged from the shower, he could avoid the awkwardness that would undoubtedly ensue.

He could just drive home and forget last night ever happened. That he'd ever even met her.

But he didn't move.

He heard the faucet squeak as she turned off the shower. Seconds later, the bathroom door opened. A cloud of coconut-scented steam drifted out and the woman appeared with a fluffy white towel wrapped around her body.

"You're awake," she said, sauntering toward him, her hair damp.

"I am," he said. His voice was gravelly from dehydration. "May I?" he asked, pointing to the glass of water on the bedside table.

She nodded.

He reached for the glass and drank half of its contents. His head pulsing from last night's alcohol, he turned his attention back to her. "Good morning, by the way."

"Good morning," she said, smiling. "I had a really great time last night."

"Me too," he said, setting the glass back on the table and scratching his elbow. And he was pretty sure he had, even though he couldn't remember it all.

Staring mischievously at him, she casually let her towel drop to the floor, then crawled onto the bed and slid beneath the covers with him. When she pressed her soft lips against his mouth, his entire body relaxed.

The voice began protesting again, but he forced it to the back of his mind. He was exactly where he wanted to be. He was also blissfully unaware that his life was about to change in every way imaginable—and within a year's time, one of them would be dead and the other would be on the run.

CHAPTER 1

BARBARA AND MADDIE

Ten Months Later

BARBARA HEMSWORTH WAS roused from a deep sleep a little before 1:00 a.m.

Had she heard something downstairs?

Or had she only been dreaming?

The bedroom was quiet. All she could hear was the gentle ticking of the grandfather clock in the hallway.

She rolled over and reached to touch her husband, Sean, but his side of the bed was empty. *He must have fallen asleep on the couch again,* she thought.

Frowning, she peeled back the covers and threw her legs over the side of the bed. Then she pulled on her robe and stepped into the dark hallway, the hardwood floor cold beneath her bare feet.

Downstairs, she found Sean in the living room on the larger of their two bisque-colored couches. He was fast asleep, still wearing a shirt and tie. His laptop was on the coffee table. A manila folder lay beside it, but half of its contents had spilled to the floor.

Her husband was a pediatrician and often stayed up late charting, reviewing labs, and responding to patient emails. So, finding him collapsed on the couch wasn't odd.

Especially lately.

Things were tense both at work and at home. Yesterday, Sean had told her that he'd received a death threat because he'd spoken out about his concerns about a new drug they were giving kids at his clinic. He'd been instructed to recant his concerns publicly, but Sean hadn't been willing to do so. He'd gone to both the police and the FBI with the threat, but neither had seemed to take him very seriously.

Earlier that day, Barbara had upgraded their home security system and instructed their teenage children, Justin, sixteen, and Maddie, fourteen, to stay inside the house until further notice. There was to be no going out with friends. Not even school. No going anywhere *period* unless they were accompanied by either Sean or Barbara.

Barbara stared at her husband. His mouth was slightly agape, and he was snoring softly, rhythmically. She was reaching out to wake him, to ask him to come up to bed with her, when she heard a rustling sound in the kitchen.

She froze.

Was it one of the kids?

"Justin?" she called. "Maddie?"

Silence.

Had one of them snuck out of the house tonight and was slipping back in? Could that be what had woken her a few minutes ago? Justin had been grounded a month ago for doing that very thing. But she'd caught him sneaking back into his bedroom window upstairs. Not a door or a window down here. Plus, now that the security system—

She spun in the direction of the security system panel and saw that the system had been disarmed. Every muscle in her body went rigid. She remembered Sean engaging it earlier that evening. She'd watched him do it. Who would have turned it off?

A shadow darkened the other side of the room, and a man stepped in, holding a gun. A bolt of terror shooting through her, Barbara screamed for Sean to wake up.

❖❖❖

Fourteen-year-old Maddie was lying upstairs in bed, texting her boyfriend and listening to the band Fall Out Boy when her door swung open, and her older brother, Justin, came bursting into her bedroom.

She jerked to a sitting position and yanked the earbuds from her ears. She was about to yell at him—to ask him why the hell he was barging in without knocking—but stopped when she got a good look at him. His face was pale, and his eyes were round as saucers.

Her heart stuttered. Something was wrong. "What is it?"

"You didn't hear that?" he whispered, his breath ragged.

"Hear what?"

He glanced nervously at the doorway. "I think it was Mom. It sounded like she screamed, but . . ."

The hair rose on the back of Maddie's neck. "Seriously?"

A shadow of doubt crossed his face. "I . . . I'm not sure."

The way Justin was acting was creeping her out. He was usually so calm and relaxed. Maybe even *too* relaxed. She recalled how weird their parents had been behaving earlier. How they'd been whispering between themselves and how insistent they'd been about her and Justin not leaving the house. About keeping the doors locked. Not opening them for strangers. Some guy from a home security company had even been at the house this morning. Their mom said their dad had received some kind of threat at work.

She watched Justin step into her doorway and peer out into the dark hallway. "It's probably nothing, but just in case, stay in here, and lock your door," he said, his voice low. "I'm going to go see what's going on."

Maddie scrambled off her bed. "But I don't—"

"Just do it, Maddie!"

Justin disappeared into the hallway.

As Maddie shut and locked the door, an odor filled her nostrils. A foreign one she couldn't place. But it smelled dangerous.

Could someone be in the house? she wondered. She slowly backed away from the door and grabbed her cell phone from her bed. Her thumbs flying across the keypad, she shot a text to her boyfriend: Something weird is going on here.

She looked up from her phone and stared at the bedroom door.

"Dad? Mom?" she heard Justin's muffled voice call out from the end of the hallway, where their parents' bedroom was.

Her phone dinged.

She looked down at the screen. Ryan had replied: Weird? What do u mean?

She quickly typed: IDK, but someone might be in our house.

Even as she typed the words, she felt as though she was being a little too dramatic. Threat or no threat, people didn't just break into houses . . . not in *their* neighborhood. But she was curious what Ryan's reaction might be. She wanted to know if he would get worried about her. She looked up from her phone and stared at her bedroom door again, her head tilted, listening for anything out of the ordinary. But all she could hear was the grandfather clock outside their parents' bedroom and Justin's footsteps as he walked down the staircase.

She heard a creaking sound.

It was the loose step—the sixth one from the bottom. It had been creaking since she was a little girl. She always tried to avoid it, especially if she was doing something she wasn't supposed to be doing.

Suddenly, she heard a loud crash as though something—or some*one*—was tumbling down the stairs. White-hot terror rose inside her and she clapped a hand over her mouth.

Justin?!

Oh, my God! What just happened?

Panic fluttered like a trapped moth in her chest as she contemplated opening the door to find out what was going on. To help her brother.

Step number six squeaked again. Someone was heading upstairs. Toward *her*.

Her heart thundering in her chest, she sprinted to the other side of her room and crawled beneath her bed.

Call 911! Someone is in my house, she texted.

The phone dinged: Stop messing around.

I'm serious! I'm under the bed! she typed. Call 911 NOW!

The phone dinged again: Stop, M. Ur starting to freak me out.

She tried to reply, to tell Ryan that she wasn't messing around, that she was really in danger, *horrible* danger, but her hand was shaking so badly, she kept tapping the wrong buttons.

She heard footsteps in the hallway, drawing closer. A moment later, she heard the knob to her bedroom door turn. But the door didn't open.

She'd locked it.

The house went silent again. Then something slammed into the door, and she heard wood splinter. Another slam, and the door swung open on its hinges.

Her breath turned to ice inside her chest as the phone clattered to the carpet. She clamped a hand over her mouth again, barely stifling a scream.

A *ding!* pierced the silence as another text came through, but she didn't dare breathe, much less move to pick up the phone. Sweat carving a jagged path along her spine, she listened to the intruder's heavy breathing and tried to stay quiet. She lay still as a statue and watched a pair of large black boots step into the room. Then the person who belonged to them moved slowly past her bed and out of view.

She heard her closet door opening, the squeak of her hangers moving as her clothes were being moved around. Then silence slowly settled over the room. A moment later, the boots reappeared. They were heading away from the bed, away from her. She shuddered with relief as she watched the intruder step from her room, into the hallway.

Ding!

Bile slid up her throat. *No, Ryan, no!*

The boots froze, then turned and faced the bed.

CHAPTER 2

DANIEL

Two Days Later . . .

A LITTLE AFTER 6:00 a.m., Daniel sped down Southern California's Pacific Coast Highway, heading from his beachfront Malibu home to Pacific Palisades, where he worked for a pediatric practice. Healing Hands Pediatrics was one of the most well-respected pediatric practices on the West Coast, with more than half of its patients coming from affluent families, including many A-list celebrities, movie producers, and other members of the entertainment community.

It was a sunny December morning, and the windows were down. The chilly ocean air flooding into the SUV invigorated him. His elderly golden retriever, Bruce, rode shotgun, his thick, yellow coat blowing in the salty wind.

Daniel loved the picturesque drive to work—the dazzling blue waters of the Pacific Ocean on his right side, and the majestic rugged beauty of the Santa Monica Mountains on his left.

Sometimes he felt overwhelmed by the new world in which he'd found himself. The house in Malibu, the swanky clinic, the respect he was enjoying now that he was a physician. Even now, after two years of living this new life, it still seemed a little surreal. As though he was living a life meant for someone else. He was certain that he would never become completely used to it. But that didn't mean he enjoyed it any less.

Today was his first day back at work since returning from his honeymoon. Ten months after meeting Mia O'Brien at that hotel bar, he'd done the unexpected: he'd asked her to marry him. She'd said yes, they'd found a justice of the peace, and then they'd taken off for a two-week honeymoon in the Caymans. Even now, when he thought back to how it had all unfolded, he was still a little stunned.

The whirlwind romance.

The marriage he'd always vowed he'd never have.

Especially to a woman like Mia.

It had been difficult—even painful—to kill a conviction that he'd held and reinforced for most of his life: that beautiful women were bad news. But the more he'd gotten to know Mia, the more he realized his theory about beautiful women didn't apply to her.

When he became too chilled from the brisk morning air, he rolled up the windows, flipped on the radio, and listened to a radio host report the local news.

"Officers entered the Sherman Oaks home after receiving a call from a concerned friend of the family early Saturday morning," the radio host was saying. "The family of four had all died from apparent gunshot wounds, and authorities think it may have been a murder-suicide. Though names haven't yet been released, neighbors say the father was a respected pediatrician in the area and the mother an active member of the community."

Christ, that's horrible, Daniel thought with a shiver. Sherman Oaks was only ten miles from Pacific Palisades. The guy had been a pediatrician. Daniel wondered if he'd known him.

While he couldn't wrap his head around how someone could possibly kill his own family, he did understand suicide. His own family had been handed some pretty crummy DNA, and many of his family members had been addicts. All the males had died before the age of forty, most from suicide. He'd come pretty close to an attempt a couple of times himself in his younger years. That was one reason why it was important for him to stay on the straight and narrow with his health and not start drinking again. Well, at least, not to the point of intoxication.

The talk of murder and suicide was putting a damper on his fantastic mood, so he flipped the radio off and enjoyed the rest of the drive in silence. Reaching Pacific Palisades, Daniel turned onto Entrada Drive, then drove the remaining three blocks to the practice. As he pulled into his reserved parking space, he noticed something was different. Usually, he was the first one to show up in the mornings. But this morning, there were already several other vehicles in the parking lot, including Teddy's. Why would his boss be opening the clinic early?

A *Curious George* cartoon played from the practice's two flat-screen TVs mounted on the walls as he led Bruce through an already half-filled double waiting room. Business was certainly booming these days. Unfortunately, that wasn't necessarily good news in his line of work. As Daniel made his way through the waiting room, children and their parents *ooh*ed and *aah*ed at Bruce. At the practice, the three-legged dog was a celebrity in his own right. Daniel brought him in at least once a week to help soothe some of his more neurodiverse patients.

Daniel noticed a commercial for a new drug was airing on a monitor above the reception desk and frowned.

At the desk, he greeted Margy, the practice's office manager. Margy was in her seventies and had smooth cocoa skin and short silver hair. She'd been with the practice from the beginning, when Teddy had opened it almost twenty years ago.

"Welcome back, Dr. Winters." Margy smiled. She reached down to pet Bruce. "And good morning there, Dr. Bruce. We've missed you."

Bruce set his graying chin in the woman's lap, enjoying the attention.

"So, what's with the clinic opening so early this morning?" Usually, he had at least an hour of quiet in his office before he saw patients.

Margy's smile faded a little. She peered at him over the rim of her glasses. "Oh, those are the Respira patients."

Respira? Daniel shook his head. "Come again?"

She pointed to a 24x36-inch poster on the wall next to her. On it was an image of young boy with his parents. The whole family was smiling and sitting in a green field. The poster was captioned:

PARENTS ARE BOUND TO MAKE MISTAKES. BUT PLEASE . . . DON'T MAKE ONE WITH HIS HEALTH. ASK YOUR PEDIATRICIAN ABOUT RESPIRA TODAY.

Daniel raised an eyebrow. They didn't usually promote pharmaceuticals at their practice, especially with such aggressive fear-based ads. He wondered if the commercial he'd glimpsed a moment ago was for the same drug. "Respira, huh? What is it?"

"The new immunoceutical," she said, her mouth twisting a little.

Immunoceutical? Was he missing something? He didn't even know what an immunoceutical was. "Come again?"

"It's become a pretty big deal around here. I'm sure Teddy will fill you in."

His nurse, Deepali, a bright, ambitious young woman from New Delhi, stopped what she was doing and turned to Daniel. "Married life looks good on you, Dr. Winters." She smiled. "Welcome back."

"Thanks." He beamed, feeling the same warm contentment in his middle that he usually felt when he was at work. His colleagues were like family, and the practice felt like a second home. It was good to be back.

As he made his way down the examination hallway, his nostrils filled with the familiar scent of their signature bubble-gum-scented antiseptic. Right outside his office door, he noticed another large poster for the new drug. He frowned, wondering what the big deal about this drug was. Why the big push?

He walked into his office and let Bruce off his leash. The dog hobbled into his kennel and turned in three tight circles before curling up on the baby blue lambskin dog pillow Mia had bought for him. Daniel grabbed his lab coat from the hook on the back of his door, shrugged it on, and went to his desk. He placed a hand on the back of his curved office chair, surveying the space. Except for a few new files in his in-box, everything seemed just as he'd left it.

Immaculate. Just the way he liked things. When his surroundings were organized, so were his thoughts. He sat down at his desk and, as he waited for his laptop to power up, leaned back in his chair and closed his eyes.

He had never felt so happy and fulfilled. He had the perfect career, the perfect wife, the perfect life. He loved just about everything about his job: practicing medicine, the patients, his colleagues. Even his mess of a boss, Teddy.

Life was really good.

Fantastically good.

But the dark, cynical part of his brain stained the otherwise-perfect picture. It was holding its breath, waiting for the other shoe to drop. For things to sour in some sort of way. There was also the little voice in his head that kept pestering him about Mia, frequently asking: *Why you, Daniel? Why of all the men in Los Angeles did she pick you?*

It's not that he was unattractive. Or that he had trouble with women. He was tall with thick brunette hair and dark eyes. At the age of thirty-seven, he was still in great shape. He was successful. He had a beautiful beachfront home in Malibu—although if he hadn't inherited it from his late uncle, he'd certainly be living much more modestly.

The little voice also whispered that he'd been a fool to ask her to marry him so quickly. He agreed it was an uncharacteristically impulsive move on his part, but the feelings he'd had for Mia had just been so intense, so unlike anything he'd ever felt for anyone before, he'd been terrified to let her slip through his fingers.

Then again, it could also have been that he'd been ready for another challenge. Now that he'd finished medical school, landed his dream job, and successfully quit going overboard on the alcohol (for the most part), maybe he'd wanted to prove to himself that he wasn't too stubborn to change his mind about a belief he'd had since he was a boy: that beautiful women were trouble. Whatever the reasons, he was eager to get past this inner conversation. Eager for the little voice to finally shut the hell up.

Due to the lack of any real parental figures in Daniel's life, a therapist had once taught him the art of self-parenting when he was a teenager, and the little voice had been born. The therapist had explained that it was his higher self. That it was natural for it to want more for him. It had served him well before Mia. Even saved his life a few times. But now, it was being overprotective and unnecessary. And, frankly, it was starting to piss him off.

"Your first day back and asleep on the job already?" a deep voice boomed, lurching Daniel from his thoughts.

Daniel opened his eyes and watched Dr. Teddy Reynolds barrel into his office. The man worked his large frame into the chair that faced his desk.

"So, when am I going to get to meet this future ex-wife of yours? You can't keep her a secret forever, you know."

"Soon." Daniel smiled. It had been his stock answer for everyone the last several months. He just hadn't been ready to introduce Mia to anyone. He was still trying to get used to the relationship. Soon, though, he knew he'd have to make good on his promise.

The large man studied him as if checking to see if married life had physically changed him. Daniel observed his boss, too. As usual, Teddy looked like he'd just rolled out of bed. It was barely 7:00 a.m., and his tie was already pulled loose. His blond comb-over was mussed, as though he'd been running his fingers through it—and his cheeks were as ruddy as ever. It wasn't a healthy look.

Teddy was larger than life in every way and always looked one boisterous yell short of a heart attack. Still, Daniel was glad to see that the older doctor was back to himself. He seemed to have been going through a rough patch in the months before Daniel had left for his honeymoon.

Teddy listened as Daniel gave him the CliffsNotes version of his honeymoon. Of how gorgeous the Caymans were, the amenities the resort offered, the cuisine. When he was done, Teddy smiled. "Seems you left out most of the good stuff."

He'd certainly shared the G-rated version.

"In all seriousness, you look happy, Danny. Happiest I've ever seen you. I'm glad to see it."

"Thanks."

"And you know what?" he said, clapping his massive hands. "You're about to be even happier."

"Yeah? How's that?"

"Did you see the waiting room when you came in?"

Yes, it was practically full. "I did."

"The new posters? The commercial?"

How could he miss them? "Respira, right?"

Teddy nodded. "I'm telling you, immunoceuticals like this one are going to shake up health care like you've never seen."

"Should I be embarrassed that I don't even know what an immunoceutical is?"

Teddy laughed. "A lot of doctors don't. But they will soon. They're a brand-new class of drug. A pharmaceutical rep will be in around lunch to get you up to speed. It's on your schedule."

Teddy's eyes were practically dancing. "It's good to have you back, Danny," he said again. "These are exciting times!"

Daniel grinned. "Sounds like it."

When Teddy had gone, Daniel pulled out his phone and shot off a quick text to Mia.

Wish I was home with you. What are you up to?

He watched the screen, anticipating a flirty reply. Mia never made him wait long.

But no texts came through.

He tried to remember if she'd said she was working today. He had hoped she'd quit Jiminy's once they were married, maybe do something else or stay at home for a while. After all, she didn't *have* to work. But she'd told him that she enjoyed her job and loved the independence. Plus, over the last several months, he'd learned she didn't do well with change. With the marriage, the move into his house, the trip to the Caymans, she said she needed to keep some things the same . . . at least for now. And Jiminy's was one of them.

He texted her again.

And again, there was no response.

Probably in the shower, he told himself, dropping his phone into the pocket of his lab coat. But he could feel the little voice waking up again.

❁❁❁

Daniel walked into Teddy's office at noon.

His boss was sitting behind his mahogany desk, talking to a man Daniel had never seen before. Noticing Daniel's arrival, Teddy stood up.

"Danny, I want you to meet Thomas Blackwell. He's a pharmaceutical rep for Immunext, a small but very important pharmaceutical start-up. Immunext manufactures Respira."

Daniel shook Thomas's hand, noting his sharp features, expensive suit, and spicy cologne.

Thomas powered on an iPad. "I know you guys are pressed for time, so let's get started. I promise it won't take me more than a couple of minutes to fill you in on everything you need to know so you can start prescribing."

"Aren't the others coming?" Daniel asked, referring to the practice's two other pediatricians and their nurse practitioner.

"Oh, they've already had the presentation and have been prescribing for the last several days," Teddy said. "This is just to get you up to speed, because you have patients on your schedule this afternoon who will be coming in asking for it."

Daniel nodded. He wasn't a fan of meetings like this cutting into his workday. But presentations from pharmaceutical corporations were important. All the doctors and nurse practitioners relied heavily on them for information on new drugs. With a visit from a drug manufacturer, they could learn everything they needed to know about a pharmaceutical in as little as five to ten minutes and start writing prescriptions immediately, especially if Teddy was already on board with the drug, and clearly he was in this case.

The sales representatives also left plenty of sound bites that he and the others often used to support the sales of their products. Sound bites that, to be honest, he sometimes felt a little disingenuous using, but he usually ended up doing so, anyway, because time was always limited, and it was easy.

A few months back, Teddy had made it clear he was interested in grooming Daniel as a partner, so now he was including him not only in drug meetings like this but also in some of the practice's business meetings. The possibility of becoming Teddy's partner would be a major game-changer in terms of Daniel's career. Not only would he practically double his salary overnight, he'd earn much more respect from his colleagues. It would also be a big step toward owning his own practice one day. He wasn't quite sure if that was what he wanted to do career-wise, but he was a big believer in keeping his options open.

Thomas handed Daniel a one-page information statement. "We at Immunext are so excited to roll out Respira to this region. It's the first pharmaceutical of its kind. A new class of pharmaceuticals called immunoceuticals," Thomas said, smiling widely. "Respira is exciting because it both protects against rhinovirus *and* provides a child's immune system a powerful boost."

As Thomas spoke, Daniel couldn't help but think about Mia again. He wondered what she was up to this afternoon and wished he'd been able to spend one more day with her before returning to work. Their two-week honeymoon had gone by way too quickly.

"As we all know," Thomas was saying, "rhinovirus has been proven to be a gateway to serious upper respiratory infections, like bronchitis and pneumonia. It also depresses the immune system, which could make children more susceptible to an influenza infection. And we all know how deadly influenza can be—especially for children."

Daniel felt the pharmaceutical rep was laying it on a bit thick. It was just the common cold they were talking about. Even though Teddy seemed very excited about Respira, Daniel was doubtful many of his patients would be interested in it. Much of their practice, especially the parents of their most affluent patients, were already hesitant about vaccines, often cherry-picking or flatly refusing them. Daniel was pretty sure if they were worried about vaccines, they'd be worried about this drug, too, especially since it was another injection.

At the end of the presentation, Teddy cut in, "It's important to be very careful with semantics with this one. The way we've been framing Respira here at the clinic is that it's not a vaccine—at least, not in the traditional sense. So, we never use the word, okay? And the risk of serious side effects? One in a million. A kid is more likely to be struck by lightning. A parent couldn't ask for better odds."

Daniel nodded.

"What's more," Teddy continued, "parents need to be told that protecting their child from rhinovirus helps protect all the children their child comes in contact with, including those who have underlying health conditions. So, protecting their child could save other lives, too. It's very important to include this, especially if a parent seems hesitant."

Thomas smiled at Teddy. "Great job, Teddy. You should come and work for us at Immunext."

Teddy and Thomas laughed.

Thomas's eyes snapped back to Daniel. "All joking aside, Dr. Winters," he said, "if you present Respira to parents the way Teddy just did, few parents will feel comfortable refusing."

"What do you think, Danny?" Teddy asked. "Eradicating the common cold?"

"Sounds exciting," Daniel said, but he wasn't so sure he meant it.

"It is." Teddy smiled. "Respira is going to change everything."

CHAPTER 3

RACHEL

GRAY CLOUDS HUNG low and ominous in the sky as Rachel Jacobs, twenty-six, hurried up the sidewalk and rang the doorbell at 323B Jamestown Street—one of many modest duplexes off Topanga Canyon Road.

As she waited, she pulled from her coat pocket the postcard she'd received in the mail from her daughter's pediatrician and read it for a second time. It advertised a new drug that could be important for Suzie's health. She refolded the postcard and stuffed it in her pocket. Pushing a wisp of blonde hair behind her ear, she listened to the muffled chaos ensuing from the other side of the door.

A raindrop plopped on her forehead.

Then another one.

As she wiped the raindrops away, she heard the distant rumble of thunder.

Just when she was about to knock again, the door flew open, and her babysitter, Martha, appeared. She was holding a little boy and looked as exhausted as ever—just like Rachel imagined someone might look after spending a day in hell.

"I'm so sorry I'm late," Rachel said. Her boss, Jeff, had kept her working late again for the third evening in a row, and she worried that Martha might decide to stop watching Suzie because of it.

Martha flashed her a weary smile. "No problem. Come on in."

She pushed open the screen door and motioned for Rachel to follow her, then disappeared down the hallway, a small white dog yapping at her feet.

Rachel stepped inside and grimaced. The place reeked like a dirty diaper. It was also messier than usual. She stepped over a one-eyed Dora the Explorer doll and followed Martha deeper into the home. When she reached the playroom, a bare-bottomed toddler suddenly streaked past, squealing in delight. Martha quickly turned on her heel and chased after him.

Rachel scanned the room and saw her eighteen-month-old daughter sitting in a playpen in the back corner of the room. When Suzie's eyes met hers, she squealed and pulled herself to her feet. With Fluff Fluff the bunny, her favorite stuffed animal, clutched in one of her pudgy hands, she held out her arms. "Mama! Up! Mama up!"

Rachel's heart filled the way it always did when she finally saw her daughter after a long day of work. "Hi, princess," she cooed and scooped the little girl into her arms. She buried her nose in Suzie's butter-blonde ringlets and soaked up her sweet baby smell. She was wearing a pink princess dress, and it had what looked like ketchup stains on the front. Rachel said goodbye to Martha, then headed back out of the disaster of a home, hoping that someday soon she'd be able to afford something nicer for Suzie.

Ten minutes later, Rachel swung open the door to her small one-bedroom apartment at Chatsworth Commons. She set Suzie down, peeled off her damp cardigan, and began preparing dinner. After they'd eaten, and Suzie had been bathed and read to, Rachel rocked her to sleep, then settled her down in her crib and placed the raggedy stuffed bunny at her side. Finally having a moment to herself, Rachel stepped out of her work clothes and grabbed the baby monitor so that she could take a long bath.

As the water ran, she stared at herself in the mirror, realizing she looked almost as exhausted as she felt. Being a single mother was hard. Really hard. She was always rushing to get somewhere and was often late.

She picked up the baby monitor to check on Suzie. Assured her daughter was sleeping peacefully, she stepped into the hot water and sat down. She sighed, enjoying the heat, and willed her muscles to relax.

Since having Suzie, she'd become a chronic worrier. She worried she wasn't spending enough time with her, that she wasn't present enough when she was, that she wasn't feeding her the right foods, using the right diapers, that leaving her in the hands of someone like Martha instead of a real day care was going to ruin her somehow. But she was doing her best. She really was.

She was one semester away from earning a computer science degree online from Old Dominion University. Entry-level jobs paid $10,000 more than what she was making at her crap job at the law firm, and most offered a full package of benefits. Once she graduated and landed a job in the field, she'd be able to put Suzie in a real day care and maybe even get a new apartment in a safer area.

Things will get better. They have to, she assured herself.

After her bath, she slipped her pajamas on and went to Suzie's crib. "Good night, sweetie," she whispered. She leaned over the railing and pressed her lips to her daughter's soft forehead, then went to her bed and sat down.

As she did every night, she reached into the nightstand and pulled out a small metal box. She worked the dial on the combination lock with her thumb and forefinger as quickly as she could, then yanked down hard on it.

The lock released, and she opened the box. Inside was a loaded .38-caliber Smith & Wesson her aunt had given her before she'd made the move to LA. She'd gotten into the routine of unlocking the box every night to ensure she didn't forget the combination in the event she and Suzie ever needed it. She closed the box, locked it, and secreted it away again in her nightstand.

Listening to the wet whisper of cars passing on the street outside her bedroom window, she picked up the postcard from Suzie's pediatrician's office. Healing Hands Pediatrics was one of the most sought-after pediatric clinics in Los Angeles, and many famous people took their kids there. Although Pacific Palisades was a thirty-mile drive from Chatsworth, the trek was worth it because she knew that Suzie would receive the very best care. If Martha hadn't known the clinic's office manager and pulled some strings, it would have been next to impossible to get Suzie seen as a patient, even though she had fairly good health insurance. They had a waiting list for new patients that was more than a year long.

She read over the postcard again and wondered if she could get Suzie an appointment tomorrow since she had the morning off, a rarity with her hectic schedule. She'd call right away when they opened and see. She didn't want to miss out on an important new drug that might help her daughter.

She flipped off her bedside lamp, and the room went black. Curling up beneath the covers, she listened to the wind outside push against her window until sleep finally stole her away.

CHAPTER 4

DANIEL

WHEN DANIEL GOT home, the house smelled like a mixture of lemon-scented cleaning products and a home-cooked meal. Bruce darted ahead of him as Daniel set his umbrella in the foyer. He shrugged out of his coat and hung it on the coatrack, then followed the dog's lead deeper into the house. He found his new wife waiting for him in the kitchen.

Dressed in nothing more than one of his white dress shirts, she knelt and handed Bruce a treat. "Here you go, good boy," she said and massaged the scruff around the dog's neck.

"Um, *I* was a good boy, too," Daniel said, strolling up to her. "Don't I get a treat?"

Her smile grew wider, and she walked into his arms. He kissed her and tasted wine and cinnamon on her lips.

"You get *two* treats, Doc."

"Yeah? And what would those be?"

"Dinner. And me." She winked.

Daniel glanced at his dog, who was now lying next to the couch, crunching on his dog biscuit. "You hear that? I get her. Not you. Me."

Mia grabbed his hand and led him to the double French doors that opened to an expansive partially screened-in deck. The table was set, and string lights illuminated the homey space with soft, warm light. She guided him to a seat and motioned for him to sit.

"You relax. I'll be just a minute with the food," she said, then disappeared inside. As he waited, he sipped iced jasmine tea and watched swollen clouds float in packs above the choppy Pacific. He sat thinking about how far he'd come from the cluttered double-wide trailer he'd lived in with his twin sister and father most of his childhood.

His father had been addicted to both alcohol and women—and ended up throwing everything away chasing both. When his dad committed suicide, Daniel didn't go to the funeral. He had attended too many of them already. He'd buried his mother when he was six. And a brother just a few years later. Now the only family he had was Mia and his twin sister, Claire.

He'd been stunned when, during his medical residency, he'd received a certified letter from the lawyer of a wealthy uncle he'd met only once. He'd willed his Malibu home to Daniel. Daniel had moved into the house right after his residency and started working at Healing Hands Pediatrics less than a month later.

Mia walked out onto the deck and set his plate in front of him: New York strip steak, potato salad with bacon drippings, and roasted asparagus. All his favorites.

A few minutes later, Mia was sitting across from him, and he was filling her in on his day.

"What exactly is rhinovirus?" she asked, stabbing at her roasted asparagus.

"It's just a fancy name for the common cold."

Mia raised an eyebrow. "Interesting. I didn't realize catching a cold was so dangerous. I thought we built up our immune systems by getting sick. So, this drug is basically for convenience? So that kids don't miss school and parents don't miss work?"

"I guess that would be true for some families. But many of today's kids have compromised immune systems, and getting the common cold can be dangerous for them," he said, repeating the pharma rep's words without any forethought.

She still looked doubtful.

He was doubtful, too. He thought Thomas's pitch had been weak. The whole aspect of rhinovirus being a gateway to more dangerous illnesses had seemed to be a stretch. But then again, there was no denying that Teddy was excited about it—and Teddy had almost three decades of experience as a pediatrician, which more than trumped the two years that Daniel had under his belt. Maybe he was missing something.

"Why do so many kids have compromised immune systems now?" Mia asked.

"Plastics, pollution, all the chemicals they add to our food." He shrugged. "No one really knows."

He realized he didn't want to think about work anymore. He was at home with his new wife, his dog. He wanted his brain to be here now, too.

"How about you? What'd you do today? Other than ignore my texts?" he asked, feeling a little ridiculous about being concerned earlier in the day when she hadn't replied to his texts as quickly as she usually did. She'd replied midafternoon and had apologized for taking so long to get back to him. She said she'd left her phone on the deck and hadn't seen his texts until later.

She wiped her mouth with her napkin. "Um, I believe I paid you back handsomely for that."

"That you did," he agreed. She'd sent a sexy photo along with her apology.

"I stayed pretty busy."

"Doing—?"

"Let's see. Well, I walked the beach this morning, then went to the market. I finished unpacking our luggage and did some laundry. I cooked dinner . . ."

Daniel studied Mia as she talked. Her presence in his life made him realize that there had been a part of him that had been lying dormant all these years. A part that was only now being fed by having someone warm to come home to. Not just any someone, but a woman whom he truly connected with. There was still so much to learn about her. So much that he didn't know yet. But that only lent to the mystery, the excitement.

"Oh, wait. I almost forgot," Mia said, her eyes widening. "You never told me about the panic room."

He knitted his eyebrows. "The what?"

"Panic room!" She stared at him. "You know, a room they build in some houses to store valuables. Or in case there's a break-in. I've read about them in books but had never seen one before today. You didn't know about it?"

"I had no idea. Where is it?"

"In the bedroom closet behind the full-length mirror," she said. "I was placing a bin on one of the top shelves earlier and bumped the mirror with my shoulder. The thing just popped open."

Interesting.

They were still talking about the panic room when Daniel's cell phone rang. He checked the name on the screen. It was Andy, a young medical student who was interning at the free clinic in Tarzana where Daniel volunteered. Daniel had taken Andy on as a sort of mentee, and Andy still called every now and then for advice. Andy was also his racquetball buddy, although the sport was one of many things that had fallen by the wayside since he'd met Mia.

Daniel excused himself and went into the living room to take the call. "Ready for another ass whooping, big guy?" he asked.

Andy laughed. "Seriously? You're an old married man now. You don't stand a chance."

Daniel chuckled. "Sorry I haven't returned your calls. I just got back into town yesterday."

"No worries. Have a good honeymoon?"

"Yes. It was pretty amazing," he said, snippets of memories flashing into his head. "So," he said, "what's up?"

"I was wondering if you guys are prescribing Respira at your clinic yet," Andy said.

"Yeah, the clinic started about two weeks ago. I just started prescribing it myself today. Why?"

There was silence on the other end of the line. Then: "Have any of your patients experienced bad reactions to it?"

"With the Respira?"

"Yeah."

"Not that I know of. But, like I said, today was my first day back. Why do you ask?"

"We've just had some . . . problems."

"How do you mean?"

"A handful of toddlers have had seizures within hours of administration," he said. "A few kids have complained of migraine headaches. But you know the type of volume we get here. I didn't think much of it at first, because it's certainly not unheard of for kids to get seizures after vaccines, but we also had a kid, a four-year-old, go into cardiac arrest today. Right here in the clinic," Andy said.

Daniel rubbed his chin. "Due to the Respira?"

"Yeah, man. It freaked me out. Respira was all the boy got, and it happened ten minutes after the injection. No history of cardiac issues."

"That's awful. Is he okay?"

"We were able to get him back into rhythm fairly quickly, but he's in the hospital, having tests run. I was wondering if you guys were experiencing the same kind of thing, because it just seems like a shitload of reactions in a month's time."

"And you're positive the other episodes were due to the Respira?"

"Well, not a hundred percent. How can you be? That's why I was calling. I wanted to see if other clinics were having the same kinds of issues."

"I'd imagine we're not, but I'll check. What does management there say?" Daniel asked.

The other end of the line was quiet for a moment. Then: "They don't seem very concerned. They just keep saying they don't think the two are connected."

After finishing his conversation with Andy, Daniel found Mia sitting out on the deck again. Her head was bowed, and her thumbs were flying across the keyboard of her phone.

When he stepped onto the deck, she jumped.

"Sorry. I didn't mean to startle you."

She turned toward him and smiled. But her smile was odd. "Everything okay?" she asked.

He sat down across from her. "Yeah. Just work."

Mia's cell phone buzzed, alerting her that she had an incoming text. She ignored it.

"You need to get that?" he asked, watching her closely.

"It's probably just my boss again. He wants me to work the late shift tomorrow night." She smiled. The same strange smile. He'd never seen this particular expression on her face before tonight.

A lump of anxiety filled his stomach.

"Would you mind pouring me another glass of wine?" she asked.

"Of course not." He picked up her glass and slipped back in the house.

He grabbed a new bottle from the kitchen. As he uncorked it, he watched Mia from the kitchen window. She was texting again.

She's just replying to her boss, he assured himself.

But then, what was up with the peculiar smile, Daniel?

That damn voice again. The last thing he wanted was to be suspicious of his wife after all the effort it had taken to learn to trust her. He was probably just in a weird headspace, a little unsettled because of what Andy had just told him.

He tore his eyes away from Mia and poured wine into her glass. Then he peered down at Bruce, who was staring up at him with naked adoration, his tail thumping on the hardwood floor.

He grabbed a treat from the cookie jar, tossed it to the dog, then joined his wife back on the deck.

❖❖❖

Later that night, Daniel made love to his wife under the spray of a hot shower. After they were done, they crawled into bed.

Flipping through channels with the remote, he stopped on Jimmy Kimmel. Mia was naked, nestled next to him, her head on his outstretched arm, her nose buried in her Kindle. Her warm, bare skin against his felt luxurious.

He studied her as she read. Her face was a mask of concentration, her dark blue eyes serious as they moved across the screen of the device. Her skin looked as smooth as porcelain. She had a thin one-inch scar above her left eyebrow, the only blemish in an otherwise perfect, unspoiled face. *Her good looks are just the icing on the cake,* he reminded himself, knowing that it would be dangerous to get wrapped up in her beauty. He had fallen in love with her for her personality, for what was inside.

Not her looks.

His thoughts returned to her texting on the deck earlier.

She's a liar. She lied to you tonight.

"Dammit. Stop."

"Hmm?" Mia looked up at him.

Shit. He must have said that out loud.

"Nothing." He smiled tiredly at her.

She went back to reading, and he felt his body relax. He flipped off the TV and shut his eyes. The long day at work, the lovemaking, and the sound of Bruce snoring at the end of the bed were lulling him, and he was fading quickly. Any suspicions about Mia would have to wait for another day. That is, if he allowed himself to entertain them at all.

As he dozed off, something jarred him. A light flashing from Mia's phone on the nightstand on her side of the bed. Her phone was receiving another silent text, and he wondered for a moment if the voice might have been right.

CHAPTER 5

DANIEL

AT THE OFFICE the next morning, Daniel found the information statement for Respira that Immunext had given him. He reread it, then went online and navigated to the medical trade journal website, UptoDate.com, and read more about the drug. Nothing jumped out at him as worrisome. Just to be sure, he checked his other go-to, Medscape—and again, nothing concerning.

He went to talk to Teddy.

He found the big man sitting behind his desk, sipping coffee and flipping through a trade journal.

"Hey, got a minute?" Daniel asked.

Teddy smiled. "For my favorite doctor? Always. What's up, Danny?"

Daniel told Teddy about Andy's experience at the free clinic. "On top of the seizures and migraine headaches, Andy said that yesterday one child went into cardiac arrest."

The smile faded from Teddy's lips. He grabbed a fidget spinner and sat back in his chair.

"Cardiac arrest, huh? That's not good," he said. "But the million-dollar question is: Can they say for sure it was the Respira that caused it?"

"Andy said the cardiac arrest happened ten minutes after the injection was administered. It was all he was given, and the kid has no history of cardiac issues."

"Poor kid. But if you're asking if I think Respira is safe, my answer is yes. It's as safe as they come. Have you looked at the information Thomas left?"

Daniel held up the information sheet. "I was just doing that."

Teddy nodded. "Also, we've already administered close to six hundred doses and have had no reports of any serious adverse reactions."

At those words, the seed of concern Daniel was feeling vanished, and his shoulders relaxed. That's all he needed to hear. As he'd suspected, Andy's experience at the free clinic had been an anomaly.

"Thanks, Teddy. Just playing it safe."

He left the office and walked into examination room six to find his first patient of the day, Suzie Jacobs, marching a rolling office chair across the room. She was a petite little thing with blonde ringlets and huge blue eyes and bore an uncanny resemblance to her mother.

"Goooood morning," he said in a singsong voice he reserved for his youngest patients. At the sight of him, the little girl squealed loudly, then darted to her mother and buried her head in her lap. She cautiously lifted her head and gave him side-eye. When she saw that he was looking at her, she sunk her face into her mother's lap again.

Daniel laughed. "What? Not happy to see me today?"

The girl continued to hide.

"How's she been?" he asked her mother.

"Great. She had a little cold a couple of weeks ago. It was better within a few days, though."

"Good."

Daniel pulled up Suzie's record on his laptop. "Still no medications?"

Rachel picked Suzie up and sat her on her lap. "Nope. None."

Daniel entered the note, then set down the laptop. He rolled his chair over to the little girl and listened to her heart and lung sounds. When he was done, he handed Suzie his stethoscope to play with.

"Eating well?" he asked, feeling her lymph nodes.

"More than me," Rachel said and smiled.

He finished his examination, then sat back in his chair. "So, I see you're here for Respira?"

"I'm not sure. I got this in the mail," she said, holding the postcard out to him. "It says there's a drug available that might be important."

Daniel gave her the spiel on Respira. "Not only will it protect against rhinovirus, it's full of vitamins that will boost her immune system."

"Is it a liquid?"

"No, it's a series of three injections."

She seemed to consider it. "And if she gets this, you're saying she won't catch any colds?"

"Well, I can't say that for certain. No drug is one hundred percent effective. But I can tell you she'll be less likely to get colds. She'll also be less likely to catch things like pneumonia and bronchitis. Conditions that could land her in the hospital."

"What's it called again?"

"Respira."

"Respira," she repeated. "And it's safe?"

"Absolutely." He reached over to the counter and picked up one of the colorful information statements they were required to give to parents. "Drugs like Respira are tested rigorously before they get FDA approval."

"So, there's no chance of bad side effects?" Rachel asked.

"The odds of a bad side effect are one in a million," he assured her. "Look at it this way: she's more likely to get struck by lightning." Sound bites from Immunext.

The woman shifted her daughter to her other knee. The little girl was clutching a raggedy stuffed rabbit and cooing at it.

"What do you say?" Daniel asked.

"Okay. If you think it'll be good for her to have."

Daniel smiled and stood up. "I'll call the nurse in to give it to her. Like I said, it's a three-series treatment, and the doses have to be administered two days apart. We're opening at 7:00 a.m. for the rest of the year to accommodate our parents' schedules, so if you need a couple of early slots for the remaining injections, let them know at the front desk."

Rachel nodded.

Daniel smiled. "Sounds good. I'll send the nurse in. I'll see you guys in a couple of days."

As Daniel walked out of the examination room, he heard Rachel talking to her daughter.

"Dr. Winters is going to give you something to make you even healthier, sweet girl. Isn't that great?"

Daniel frowned, feeling a pang of uneasiness. Logical or not, Andy's phone call still haunted him.

CHAPTER 6

RACHEL

RACHEL PULLED OUT of the parking lot at Healing Hands Pediatrics and headed back to Chatsworth.

She was glad she'd decided to bring Suzie in. The medication sounded like it would be a great thing for her daughter.

And for her.

She thought about how irritated her boss, Jeff, had been a couple of weeks ago when she had asked to take two days off because Suzie had come down with a cold. How afraid she'd been ever since that Suzie might get sick again, and she'd be fired.

She thought about Dr. Winters. How he'd smiled at her. Not only was he good with Suzie, he was also easy on the eyes. He wasn't very old. Maybe ten years her senior. Somewhere in his thirties. Every time she brought Suzie in for a well-baby appointment, she tried to wear something nice. Not that she thought he'd be interested in someone like her, but stranger things had happened, right? Over the past few months, she'd wondered what it would be like to hook up with a man like him.

How different her life would be if she married someone like a doctor. Someone who had the means to provide for her and Suzie.

Not only did Rachel not have a husband, the aspiring actor who'd knocked her up had never even wanted to meet Suzie. *His loss,* she thought bitterly. The last thing she wanted to do was force her daughter on the guy. He'd proven he wasn't deserving of either of them.

Suzie began to whimper in the back seat.

"Suzie? What's wrong, honey?"

"Mama! Up!" Suzie screamed.

Rachel glanced into the rearview mirror but couldn't see her daughter's face because her car seat was rear-facing.

"I can't pick you up, sweet girl. Not right now. We have to hurry and get to Miss Martha's. Mommy will hold you for a couple of minutes when we get there, okay?"

As Rachel pulled onto Highway 405 North, the whimpering became louder, and Suzie's cries to be held became almost nonstop. She pressed the gas pedal harder, hoping to get back to Chatsworth a little quicker. She stared out at the highway in front of her through her cracked windshield and tried to soothe her daughter by talking to her, then by playing each of her favorite songs from the *Frozen* soundtrack.

When the cries grew into flat-out screams, panic bloomed in her chest. She swung onto the next off-ramp and parked at a Chevron gas station. She jumped out of the car and went to the rear passenger side door and yanked it open. Suzie's back was arched, and her big blue eyes were wide with pain. Her face was beet-red, and her cheeks were soaked with tears. "Mama! Up!" she cried and opened her arms wide to be held.

Rachel unfastened the car seat straps, then picked her up and held her tightly against her chest. "It's okay, sweet girl," she cooed. "It's okay."

With Suzie in her arms, Rachel returned to the driver's seat and fumbled for her phone. With her free hand, she called Dr. Winters's office. She told the receptionist what was going on, and the receptionist placed her on hold. A minute later, a nurse named Deepali was on the line. Rachel explained what was going on.

The nurse spoke calmly and confidently. "It's completely normal, Ms. Jacobs. Sometimes the injection site gets tender. Does she have a fever?"

Rachel felt her daughter's forehead. "I'm not sure. I mean, I guess she feels a little warm. But she's been crying so much, it's hard to tell."

"Once you get home, check her temperature. If she has a fever, just alternate Children's Tylenol and Motrin. Don't worry. I'm sure she'll be fine."

Rachel got off the phone feeling a little better. She tried to soothe a crying Suzie for a few minutes, then strapped her back into her car seat. As soon as she set her down, though, the pleas and screaming started again.

"It's okay, Suzie. It's going to be all right, okay?" she called behind her as she pulled out of the gas station's parking lot and headed back to the highway. But Suzie's screams only got louder and shriller. She drove as fast and as safely as she could, but every time Suzie screamed, Rachel felt like her heart was being ripped in two.

When Rachel finally pulled up to Martha's duplex thirty minutes later, Suzie suddenly went quiet. A chill tiptoed up Rachel's spine, and she jumped out of the car and rushed to her little girl to make sure she was okay. When she pulled open Suzie's door, her little face was pink and tear-stained, but she was breathing. She'd just fallen asleep. Probably worn out from all the screaming.

Rachel looked at the clock on the dashboard. She was expected at work in twenty minutes. She wrung her hands, knowing she couldn't just drop Suzie off at Martha's house when she'd been so upset. What if she woke up in pain again? Disoriented, wondering where Mommy was?

"Dammit," she whispered to herself. She gently shut the car door, walked around the vehicle, and slid behind the wheel. Exhaling hard, she called her boss's cell phone, hoping she'd be sent directly to voice mail. Jeff wasn't going to be happy, especially after she'd taken those two days off last month. But she didn't have a choice.

Suzie came first.

No matter what.

While she waited for the call to connect, she couldn't help but find it both ironic and troubling that she'd said yes to a medicine that promised Suzie would get fewer colds, then had to take off work because of it.

"Good morning, Rachel," Jeff answered curtly, as if he already knew what she was going to say. And he probably did. After all, why else would she be calling?

Rachel flinched. "I'm sorry, Jeff, but I'm not going to be able to make it in today. My daughter's sick."

"Really. Again?"

She bit into her lower lip hard enough to taste blood. "I mean, she might be okay in a little while. I don't know. If she is, I'll be in later. I promise."

"Don't bother," he said. "Can I expect you tomorrow?"

Oh, God. I hope so. "Yes. Definitely."

"Fantastic."

The call disconnected.

Prick, she thought. She imagined how good it would feel to be able to tell him where he could stick his crap job. But she couldn't afford to lose it. Not now. Not only did she have just $7.03 in her checking account until her next paycheck and a nearly empty pantry, she had a young child who needed the health insurance the job provided. She shot Martha a quick text, telling her she wouldn't be dropping Suzie off, then drove to her apartment.

When she scooped Suzie out of her car seat, the little girl whimpered but didn't wake up. Inside the apartment, Rachel grabbed the thermometer from the medicine cabinet in the bathroom and went back to the bedroom and set down Suzie on the bed. She placed the thermometer under her daughter's arm.

Ninety-nine point one. Nothing to be worried about.

She pressed softly on Suzie's thigh where she'd gotten her injection, but Suzie didn't react.

That's weird, she thought. *If she was screaming because of pain at the injection site, wouldn't she have at least flinched?*

Rachel settled Suzie into her crib, grabbed the baby monitor, and closed the bedroom door. Being home during the day like this without having a million things to do was unusual. She wasn't sure what to do with herself.

She went to the kitchen table and stared at the stack of mail—mostly bills—and her belly twisted in knots. She was in an awful financial hole and had no clue how she was going to get out of it. She thought about sitting down and calling a few of her creditors to make payment arrangements. It would be easier to do it now instead of trying to do it on work time with Jeff breathing down her neck. But the sheer thought of it exhausted her.

She walked back to the bedroom and changed into pajamas, then picked up her daughter and lay her in bed with her. She held Suzie close and just a few minutes later escaped into the comforting arms of sleep.

❀❀❀

At 2:00 p.m., Suzie's high-pitched cries shattered the silence of the small apartment. Rachel jerked awake and gathered her baby into her arms.

"Shhh," she cooed, standing and bouncing Suzie. The little girl's back felt like it was on fire. Taking her temperature confirmed that her fever had crept up to 101.0 degrees.

Rachel went to the kitchen and found the liquid Children's Tylenol, then drew a lukewarm bath and set Suzie in the tub. She pressed cool washcloths to the back of her little girl's neck and forehead, hoping to make her more comfortable. But Suzie's cries quickly morphed into screams.

"It's okay, honey," Rachel kept saying, tears running down her own cheeks. "It's okay, sweetie. It's going to be okay."

Fifteen minutes later, Suzie finally calmed down. Rachel dried her off and dressed her in pajamas, and the little girl fell back to sleep. "Mommy loves you, Suzie. Mommy loves you so much," she whispered. She took deep breaths of her own to try to fight off her anxiety. The mental static in her head was earsplitting.

She's going to be okay, she told herself. *She's going to be okay.*

But talking to herself wasn't working. She needed someone else to talk to. She found her phone and called her sister, Laura. She hated talking to Laura, because most of their conversations ended badly. She suspected Laura still resented that she had gotten the hell out of Minnesota before their sixty-year-old mother was diagnosed with full-blown dementia.

Since Laura was the one still living in Minnesota, their mother had become Laura's sole responsibility. But it wasn't as though Rachel had planned it that way. When she'd left Minnesota, her mother had seemed completely fine, so it wasn't fair to be angry with her. She had simply been following her dreams. What was so wrong with that?

Rachel's and Laura's lives couldn't have turned out more different, and over the years, they'd only grown further apart. But she didn't have anyone else to turn to. No one else with children, at least. Besides, Laura's kids were always dealing with different health issues. Every time they talked, it seemed she was always shuttling her kids to a different specialist, so Rachel knew she had a lot of experience with doctors and medications.

She was relieved when Laura answered.

"How's Mom?" Rachel asked.

"Ugh," Laura said. "She managed to sneak out yesterday. Took the damn minivan to the supermarket and bought about twenty pounds worth of candy."

"Yikes. Is she okay?"

"Yeah. She's watching *The Price Is Right* and shoveling M&M's into her mouth."

"I thought *The Price Is Right* only came on in the morning?"

"The kids record it for her."

At the age of nineteen, Rachel had moved from Nowhere, Minnesota, to Los Angeles with a guy she'd been dating with dreams of becoming an actress. But after years of auditions, she'd landed only three small roles—each with fewer than five lines—two of which perished on the cutting-room floor. Then when she got pregnant, she was forced to exchange days running between auditions to late nights of waiting tables for a practical office job. She told herself that one day, when Suzie was older, she might try her hand at acting again, but for now she needed a more reliable paycheck and health insurance.

Rachel never would have thought for a moment that she'd ever envy her sister's boring suburban life in Minnesota, but she was envying it now. Laura's big house, her loving husband, kids in a nice, private Montessori school, and still enough money left to go on vacations every year. And here Rachel was in the big city, a failure as an actress, barely making it as a mother, and hardly a dime to her name.

"What's up?" Laura asked.

Rachel told her about the doctor's visit and Suzie's screaming fits.

"My kids have temperatures higher than that all the time," Laura said. "And sometimes they cry like banshees for hours. It's just what some kids do after getting their shots."

Rachel was stunned to hear her sound completely calm about it.

"But why?" Rachel asked.

"Hell if I know."

"The nurse said it was due to tenderness at the injection site," Rachel said.

"Yeah. That's probably it."

"But see, here's the thing. When I press on the injection site, she doesn't even react."

Silence. Then: "Yeah. I don't know."

"Did your girls get Respira?" Rachel asked.

"They've had their first two doses. We go in tomorrow for the third."

"And they were fine after theirs?"

"Sophia cried a little bit. But that was the extent of it."

That made Rachel feel a little better.

"Being a mom is scary, Rachel. But I'm sure she'll be just fine."

"Yeah, I guess so. But what could possibly be hurting her so bad that she'd scream like that? It bothers me that I don't know. That she can't tell me."

"You're overthinking it, Rachel."

Wanting to know what was hurting her daughter was *overthinking it?*

"I'm not sure I'm going to get her the other two doses. Not after how she reacted to this one," she said, more thinking aloud than anything.

"Don't say that," Laura snapped. "You have to. And if you don't, don't even think about bringing her around my kids. I'm just saying. Rhinovirus is the gateway to some nasty stuff. Illnesses I don't want my girls to get."

Rachel knitted her eyebrows, wondering what the hell her sister was talking about.

She knew she shouldn't have called her.

"Plus, I heard they're talking about adding Respira to the shot schedule soon," Laura said, referring to the schedule of immunizations recommended by the Centers for Disease Control and Prevention. "So, if she doesn't complete the series, she won't be able to go to day care or school."

Right now, Rachel couldn't give a crap about day care or school. At the moment, her daughter's pain and well-being were all she could handle thinking about.

"Don't be one of those crazy mothers who makes the mistake of thinking they know more than their doctor," Laura said.

Talking to Laura was only making her feel worse. But she knew that Laura had a good point. Who was she to question Dr. Winters? After all, if she was as smart as he was, she wouldn't be working for a jackass she hated for slightly over minimum wage.

"Seriously, just think about it, Rachel. You really think they would tell us Respira was safe if it wasn't?"

CHAPTER 7

DANIEL

AFTER WORK, DANIEL drove to a florist on Sunset Boulevard to buy Mia flowers. He was feeling guilty about the suspicious thoughts he'd had the night before.

So what if Mia had smiled oddly?

Also, how much did it really matter if the person texting her hadn't been her boss? It's not like they had to tell each other everything. Maybe she'd been in the middle of a personal text conversation with someone and just hadn't wanted to share it with him? So the hell what? For their relationship to stay as healthy as it was, they needed to remain individuals. Checking up on each other at every moment and expecting 100 percent sharing was immature—and they were hardly kids anymore.

It pissed him off that he'd listened to the meddling little voice last night and had actually questioned Mia after all the effort it had taken this past year to let down his guard with her. After watching couples implode beneath the pressures of coupledom his entire life, it was important to him to give her a wide berth. Plenty of room to be herself, to preserve her independence. That was another thing he'd noticed the most with unhealthy couples. How one, or sometimes both partners, began to take a sense of ownership of the other. At that point, things quickly went downhill. That was the last thing he wanted for him and his wife. They had a great relationship. They treated each other with respect. He wanted to make sure those things didn't change.

Besides, he'd also promised himself before they got married that he would perform random acts of romance as often as he could. Just because they were married shouldn't mean that he should stop trying to sweep her off her feet.

After picking up a dozen orchids—her favorite—he drove up the coast to Jiminy's to hand deliver the flowers. Jiminy's was an upscale seafood restaurant nestled a couple of miles from Malibu, just off the Pacific Coast Highway. It was popular with tourists and always packed.

He pulled into the crowded parking lot, grabbed the orchids, and climbed out of the SUV. As he walked to the doors of the restaurant, a cool wind blew in from the ocean, tousling his hair, and a chill swept through his body.

The parking lot and entrance to the restaurant were decked out with colorful Christmas decor. He smiled as he walked past wreaths, twinkling trees, and mistletoe, embracing the whimsical feeling of the season. Most of his Christmases as a child had been miserable, but he was living a new chapter now. A brand-new life. Christmases with Mia were bound to be magical.

As soon as he walked inside the warmth of the restaurant, the aroma of grilled fish wafted into his nostrils, and a young, bubbly blonde, whom he pegged to be in her early twenties, stood smiling behind the hostess station and wearing reindeer antlers. A large red circle was painted on the tip of her nose. Her name tag read Julie.

"You shouldn't have." She grinned.

He returned her smile. "They're for Mia Winters. I was hoping I could see her for a moment."

Julie crinkled her red nose.

Daniel realized the hostess might not recognize Mia's new last name. "Formerly Mia O'Brien," he said, using her maiden name. "We were married recently."

A spark of recognition lit up Julie's face, followed by another nose crinkle. "Sorry. Mia's not here. She's off tonight."

An icy sensation raced through Daniel's body. Mia had told him that she was going to be pulling the late shift tonight. That that's what her boss had been texting her about.

I told you she was lying to you.

Daniel scratched the outside of his elbow with his free hand. "Are you sure?"

"Yep. Positive," Julie said. "But maybe she's coming in later. You want me to check?" she asked, glancing nervously past him. A line was forming. He was holding it up.

"I bet that's what it is," Daniel said. "No worries. You don't need to check." He looked down at the orchids. "But could you do me a favor?"

Two minutes later, Daniel was back in his car. He had left the flowers with Julie, so she could make sure Mia got them when she came in later. He thought about Mia's texts again last night. Feeling an undercurrent of uneasiness, he reached for his phone to text her, to ask her where she was.

But then he froze.

He trusted her, so checking up on her was unnecessary. No matter what the voice in his head wanted him to think. He had probably just misunderstood her last night. Got her hours wrong. Hell, she might even still be at the house when he got home.

No. You're not mistaken, Daniel. She lied—

He hurled the voice into a room in the back of his head, slammed the door, locked it, then headed for home.

His phone buzzed a few minutes later. He glanced at the display on his dashboard. It was Dr. Josh Thornton, the doctor on call.

"Hey, Dan. It's Josh. I wanted to let you know I got a call from the mother of one of your patients. Suzie Jacobs?"

Daniel frowned. "Yeah?"

"Her mother said she's had a temperature of 102.5 for a few hours. I told her to alternate Children's Tylenol and Motrin and to go to the emergency room if it reached 104. Just wanted to let you know."

"Thanks, Josh. She received her first dose of Respira today, so her immune system's probably just kicking in."

"Makes sense," Dr. Thornton said. "I wouldn't have even called you, but Ms. Jacobs sounded pretty upset, so I wanted you to know."

"Thanks," Daniel said. "Let me know if she calls back."

"You got it."

When Daniel pulled up to the house, his heart dropped like an anvil in his chest. The driveway was empty.

❖ ❖ ❖

Ten minutes later, as he stood in the kitchen filling Bruce's food bowl, Daniel realized he still felt a curl of dread in his stomach.

Why did trusting someone have to be so hard for him? He stared at the liquor cabinet that he'd inherited along with the house, knowing a drink would help him relax a little. Over the last few years, after a long and difficult battle with alcohol, the liquor in the kitchen cabinet had strangely offered little temptation. In fact, he'd prided himself on the fact that he could be in such close proximity to it and not be seduced. But it was tempting him now.

Just one glass.

That's all he'd allow himself. He needed it to dull his agitation, his worry.

No, Daniel. There's a reason you don't drink at home.

He continued to stare at the colorful bottles, the contents of which promised relief.

Just one glass, he reasoned.

NO, the voice hissed.

The voice hated alcohol. It usually took only two drinks to make it go away.

Running a hand over his mouth, he turned away. "Yeah, probably a bad idea."

Bruce whined at his feet. Daniel looked down and saw the animal staring at him. "Okay, *definitely* a bad idea." But damn, it was hard.

Daniel yanked open the refrigerator and grabbed the pitcher of iced jasmine tea instead. He poured a glass, then went out to the deck. As he sipped his tea, he inhaled the chilly air and watched the last of the day's colors fade into pastels across the sky.

"It's lonely without her, isn't it, boy?" he asked Bruce.

Bruce stared up at him and responded with a throaty growl.

He looked at his phone again and thought about texting Mia. Not to check up on her this time, just to make sure she was okay.

Hi, beautiful. Just checking in. Everything okay?

She replied less than a minute later: Very busy tonight! Be home after 2. Miss you. xx

He felt a surge of relief. Yes, they must have just missed each other. He was glad he'd decided to text her. Now he could relax. He was heading upstairs with plans to shower and then crawl into bed when his phone rang. It was the doctor on call again.

"Dr. Winters here," he answered.

"It's Josh. Sorry to bother you again, Daniel, but I thought you'd want to know that the patient I called about earlier . . . Suzie Jacobs? She's in the emergency room at Northridge Hospital. She's having seizures."

❖❖❖

Daniel was lying in the dark with his eyes open when Mia walked in the front door. It was 2:30 a.m. The news about Suzie's seizures had made it impossible for him to sleep. Not because he hadn't experienced a patient having seizures before, but the seizures coupled with the call from Andy disturbed him. Since speaking with Dr. Thornton, he hadn't been able to get Rachel Jacobs's face out of his mind.

He lay there, listening as Mia quietly entered the room, undressed, and switched on the shower.

What is she washing off? the voice asked.

He flinched in the dark. It had a good point. Mia didn't usually shower at night unless they had just had—or were having—sex. Before he could stop himself, his mind filled with images he didn't want to entertain.

A few minutes later, the shower faucet squeaked as it was turned off.

When he felt the bed shift beneath Mia's weight, he murmured, "Hi, beautiful."

Silence. Then: "Did I wake you? I'm sorry. I tried to be quiet."

"It's okay. How was work?"

"Good. But I'm wiped out."

"Long shift?"

"Yeah. Nine hours. My feet are aching."

He did the math in his head. Then did it a second and a third time, just to be sure. According to what she'd told him last night, she'd been one of the closing staff at the restaurant tonight, which meant she'd gotten off at 2:00 a.m. So, nine hours meant she'd been there since 4:00 p.m.

But when he had stopped by Jiminy's, she hadn't shown up yet. And that was at 5:30 p.m.

The skin on his arms prickled.

Why was she lying to him?

❁❁❁

When Daniel awoke next, it was 4:45 a.m. He turned to find Mia's side of the bed empty.

Why was she already up? She couldn't have gotten more than a couple of hours of sleep. He replayed her coming home earlier, taking a shower.

Lying to him.

He pulled on his robe and walked downstairs, inhaling the aromas of freshly brewed coffee and fried bacon. Through the floor-to-ceiling windows at the back of the house, he saw Mia sitting outside on the deck, bundled up in a pink heavy cotton robe. Her dark hair was pulled back in a high ponytail, and she was staring out at the ocean with a scowl on her face.

He walked to the kitchen and poured a cup of coffee. Taking a long sip, he continued to study his wife from a distance. She looked so serious. Worried, even. He wondered what she could possibly be worried about?

Why didn't she say anything about the orchids last night, Daniel?

That's right. She hadn't.

He searched the kitchen, then the living room for the flowers, but there was no sign of them.

Did she even go to Jiminy's?

And if she didn't, where did she go?

He took another long sip of his coffee and went to the French doors that led out to the deck. He saw that she'd made him breakfast. He clung to the gesture. After all, if she'd gone to the trouble of waking after fewer than two hours of sleep to make him breakfast, she must love him, right?

And if she loves me, she wouldn't lie to me.

You're being naive, and you know it, Daniel.

Glowering, he stepped outside.

This was all new territory for him. Being this crazy about a woman. He was finding it difficult not to overthink everything. It was possible she'd simply forgotten the orchids. She'd probably been exhausted at the end of her shift, so that made perfect sense. Probably more sense than any of the distressing things he'd been entertaining.

He was being ridiculous.

Overly cautious.

You didn't leave a card. Maybe she thought the orchids were from someone else.

No. After all, who else would be sending her flowers? The voice was screwing with him. Sending him false signals. Making him worry unnecessarily. Maybe he'd run his course with it, and it was time to part ways.

He'd join her on the deck, and she'd thank him for the orchids. Then he'd ask her about Jiminy's, the time discrepancies, and she'd explain his worries away.

He opened the door and watched her straighten in her seat. When she turned to him, he saw that her face had rearranged itself into one of her old smiles. A sincere one. The type that had always comforted him.

"Good morning, handsome."

"Good morning." He bent down to kiss her, searching for anything different in her kiss, her touch. There was nothing.

The morning air was chilly. The temperature had dropped again overnight, and it was finally feeling more like winter. He made a mental note to take the extra standing heater out of storage and set it up on the deck.

She pointed to his covered plate. "Surprise." She smiled and removed the silver cover. He saw eggs Benedict and bacon, extra crispy, the way he loved it. A glass of orange juice sat beside it.

"Well, aren't you the perfect wife," he said, forcing a smile of his own and watching for her reaction.

She simply continued to smile.

He walked around the table and took a seat.

"Is it too cold out for you?" she asked, pulling her robe closer. "Would you prefer to eat inside? I wasn't sure."

"I'm fine. Unless you want to."

"No. I'm comfy," she said, tucking her legs more snugly beneath her body. "I love this weather."

They talked for several minutes as he ate his breakfast. He waited for her to mention the orchids, but she never did. Instead, she talked about a carrot cake recipe she wanted to try, a new yoga class in town that she wanted to check out. A new book she was reading. She was a voracious reader and often had three books going at one time. The new book was her third on numerology in the last few months. He ate and listened, studying her as she talked.

As he chewed his last bite of toast, she propped her elbow on the table and rested her chin in the palm of her hand. Her blue eyes contrasted sharply against the dull gray morning, and he thought she looked especially beautiful.

She yawned. "I'm going to take a long nap after you leave. I'm freaking exhausted," she said, smiling wearily, flashing perfect teeth.

It was all those hours on her feet, Daniel.

All nine *of them.*

He watched her gaze into his eyes, pretending nothing had happened. That everything was status quo. Like she hadn't just lied right to his face. He felt something break inside of him. Something gravely important. Something that he was almost certain was irreparable.

He wanted to stop this in its tracks. Say something to her. Tell her he had stopped at the restaurant and had left the orchids. Give her a chance to explain herself. To possibly clear everything up. But as he opened his mouth to do so, the little voice stopped him.

Shh. Not just yet. Let's see where this goes.

And this time, he listened.

CHAPTER 8

DANIEL

THE SKY WAS gunmetal gray as Daniel drove to work, the thick cloud cover making everything appear dull and colorless.

Before marrying, Daniel had talked to Mia at length about honesty, how critical it was to him, and he'd thought they'd been on the same page. Yet she'd lied, anyway. Had this been the first time she'd lied? Or had she been lying all along? And if so, why?

And perhaps more important, about what?

As he pulled into the parking lot at the practice, he realized he needed to shake it all off. At least for now. He was at work and needed to focus on his patients. It was time to compartmentalize. Thankfully, this was something he'd become skilled at over the years.

The first task on his list was telling Teddy about Suzie's seizures. The physician he'd spoken to at Northridge Hospital's emergency room last night said that Suzie's CT scan and other test results had looked fine. After speaking with the doctor, Daniel had made a courtesy call to Rachel to reassure her that seizures, as scary as they were, weren't uncommon in young children these days.

Some kids experienced them with even lower fevers than what Suzie had run. Some without a fever at all. Still, he told her to bring Suzie in first thing this morning for a quick examination. It was more to reassure Rachel than anything. But he wanted to talk with Teddy before he saw the Jacobses this morning to make sure his boss supported his analysis.

When he stepped into Teddy's doorway, his boss glanced up from his paperwork.

"Danny!" He smiled. "Still married?"

Daniel tried to smile—if only to be polite—but the joke hit too close to home this morning.

Teddy's smile melted from his lips. "You look like shit. Are you feeling okay?"

Daniel rubbed the back of his neck. "I didn't get much sleep."

The smile was back. "Oh. Still on your honeymoon, I see."

Ignoring the comment, Daniel told Teddy about Suzie's seizures last night. "After what I heard has been happening at the clinic in Tarzana, I—"

Teddy's top lip curled a little; then the man held out a thick hand to stop him. "What was that medical student's name again? The one who told you they were having problems with Respira in the valley?"

"Andy Cameron," Daniel said.

Teddy scribbled something down; then his chair squeaked as he leaned back into it. "Look, Dan, all drugs present a risk. It's a numbers game; you know that," he said. "As long as the benefits outweigh the risks, a drug is a winner in my book. Plus, we have no way of knowing that Respira caused your patient's seizures. The seizures could have been caused by anything. Maybe she had crackers that had GMO ingredients in them. Or used fluoride toothpaste. Lord knows enough parents are carrying on about those things, too, these days."

Teddy laced his fingers together and leaned forward. "But let's say, *hypothetically*, that Respira did cause the girl's seizures. The CDC and FDA both monitor that type of thing. If there's a problem, they'll let us know. And until then and only then, our jobs are to administer it. Having said that," Teddy said, sitting back in his chair and twirling his fidget spinner again, "this practice's official position is that the girl's seizures and Respira are not related. Understood?" Teddy stared at him, his lips now a tight line. The trademark mirth on his face nowhere to be found.

Daniel nodded. "Understood."

Daniel heard movement behind him. He turned to see Thomas from Immunext. The man was wearing a black designer suit and a red tie and had sprayed on too much cologne again.

"Good morning, Dr. Winters." Thomas smiled, his oversize teeth sparkling like diamonds.

Daniel greeted him, wondering why he'd be at the office so early. Also, twice in the same week. Thomas's eyes seemed to linger on Daniel for a moment; then he filed past him, into Teddy's office.

Teddy greeted him cheerfully and told him to take a seat. Daniel watched Thomas lower himself into a chair.

"Is that all, Danny?" Teddy asked.

"Yeah. Thanks."

Teddy nodded. "Great. Then please shut the door behind you."

CHAPTER 9

RACHEL

"SHE WAS INCONSOLABLE yesterday after we left here," Rachel told Dr. Winters, speaking rapidly as she followed him down the examination hallway. She was trying to relay to him every detail she could remember about Suzie's seizure. Also, everything that had led up to it and everything since.

Rachel couldn't get the memory of her daughter's seizure out of her mind. Seeing Suzie in her crib, grunting, her little body convulsing, her back arching, and her eyes rolling back in her head, had been horrifying. There had been nothing she could do but hold her. She'd felt so helpless, so useless.

"She must have been in a lot of pain to have been screaming like that, right?" she asked as they entered the examination room.

Dr. Winters had her set Suzie on her lap, and he began examining her. "Are you feeling crummy, Suzie?" he asked.

Rachel watched Suzie stare at Fluff Fluff as though Dr. Winters hadn't said anything. Rachel pointed out how pale she looked. The black circles beneath her eyes.

"You just spent most of the night in an emergency room. I'm sure she's just exhausted." He looked up at Rachel and smiled warmly. "I'm sure you both are."

Rachel was beyond exhausted. She was also worried that she'd failed her daughter. She was going to ruin Suzie if she didn't do better. She racked her brain, trying to think of anything else that had happened after the shot that she could tell Dr. Winters. The more he knew, the more likely he could help her.

Rachel looked down at her daughter, who was curled against her, her thumb in her mouth. "She also started sucking her thumb again today. She hasn't done that for months."

"Just a little regression. Not surprising at her age with the scare she had yesterday," Dr. Winters reassured her.

Rachel pointed out that Suzie's eyes looked different. They looked distant, empty.

"Exhaustion will do that." Dr. Winters smiled.

She remembered Suzie's diapers. "And her diapers since yesterday have been foul. I've never smelled anything like it. I know you said on the phone that the shot didn't do this, but—"

"What I said was that *anything* could have caused her seizure. The fever was probably the culprit. Seizures can happen if a child's temperature rises too quickly, but, frankly, there are a lot of reasons why kids have seizures. We really don't know what all the variables are yet. There's a good chance she's even had seizures before, and you didn't notice."

Rachel felt her mouth tighten. "No. That's not possible."

"Please don't get me wrong," Dr. Winters said, looking up at her. "I'm not questioning your parenting skills. It's just that seizures can be hard to catch, even by professionals. Sometimes it just looks like the child is daydreaming."

Dr. Winters shined a penlight into each of Suzie's eyes. "Has she been out of the country lately?" he asked.

"No," Rachel said. "Never."

Dr. Winters nodded.

"But the seizure *could* have been caused by the shot, right? I mean, it's only logical, since she got the shot yesterday."

Dr. Winters powered on his laptop. "It's a possibility, but a very small one. Like I said yesterday, one in a million." He hit a few keys on his laptop. "The good news is, I've read the discharge summary from Northridge Hospital, and like I told you, her CT scan looks good. As did her blood and urine."

He pushed the laptop away. "Suzie's going to be just fine. Kids' brains are extremely resilient."

Rachel watched Suzie's eyes drift slowly around the room. Usually, her daughter would be clutching her tightly and hiding from Dr. Winters, but today she seemed barely aware that he was even in the room. This was not normal for her. But then again, maybe Dr. Winters was right, and she was simply exhausted.

"I'll examine her again tomorrow morning before her second dose. In the meantime, you should both try to get some sleep."

Get some sleep? Easy for him to say. She had a job she needed to show up to, or else she and her daughter would be out on the streets soon.

Dr. Winters grabbed one of his business cards from a plastic card holder, turned it over, and jotted something down. He handed her the card. "Here's my personal cell number. If you have any worries or questions, call me directly. Okay?"

"Okay."

Rachel was hesitant to leave. Just looking at Suzie like this for five minutes didn't seem nearly enough time for him to see what was going on with her. To know that she was really, truly okay.

But what else could she do?

She took the card and thanked him.

CHAPTER 10

MIA

MIA STOOD IN the brisk cold, watching waves break on boulders, sending up explosions of saltwater and foam.

Surfers were out in droves, wearing dark-colored wet suits and bobbing on the choppy water. She closed her eyes, letting the salty wind whip her long hair into her face until her cheeks stung. Then she gathered her long mane into one hand and walked from the deck to the French doors to retreat into the warmth of the house.

Her house, well, at least partially hers.

For now.

She gazed at the opulence laid out in front of her for a long moment, then moved slowly through the spacious living room, her bare feet sinking into the plush cornflower-blue rug. She moved through the room, running a palm over the soft buttery leather of the overstuffed couch, the rough river rock of the grand fireplace, then walked to the kitchen and studied the professional-grade gas stove, the many top-of-the-line appliances, and marble countertops. She was surrounded by luxury and living in one of the most expensive zip codes in the world.

She'd won the husband lottery.

The trick now was to keep the husband for a while.

But doing so might be even more difficult than she'd expected.

She reached for the bloodstained cloth in her shirt pocket and pressed it against her nose. Her left nostril had been bleeding off and on since she'd received the unexpected call—a call that had left her feeling threatened, unsafe. Her nose always bled when she was stressed. But it had finally clotted, and now the cloth came away clean.

She wasn't sure yet if the news she'd gotten was legitimate or if someone was playing a sick joke on her. She'd had a lot of sick jokes played on her over the years.

Knowing Daniel would be home soon to pick her up for dinner, she went upstairs to finish getting ready. It was important to be *on* tonight. She was meeting Daniel's twin sister, Claire, for the first time and would have to bring her A game, even though she'd barely had any sleep. She'd been having difficulty sleeping for years now. Her past had a tendency to visit her, unbidden, when she closed her eyes at night. She usually tried to catch up on her sleep in the daytime. But today she hadn't had that luxury.

Upstairs, she went to the bathroom mirror and smoothed her hair. Then she blotted more concealer over the scar above her left brow, swiped on a little more powder, and repainted her lips. She stepped away from the mirror to inspect her handiwork.

It was critical to keep up the facade that had helped her catch this new husband, this unbelievable new life, neither of which she deserved, and both of which she could lose at a moment's notice for half a dozen reasons. And things were starting to get much more complicated.

Speaking of complicated, a text came in: I was hoping we could talk again tonight.

Her mood darkened. Yes, they would talk, but it would have to wait. She couldn't have him texting her. She'd already told him as much. Why couldn't he follow simple instructions?

She pursed her lips and wrote: Do not text or call me. I will call you tomorrow.

He replied instantly: OK. Sorry.

She heard the hum of a car's engine. Daniel was pulling into the driveway. She flicked her phone to vibrate mode, tossed it into her purse, and took one last look in the mirror.

Gently pressing her lips together, she smoothed her cashmere top with the palms of her hands. It was time to become Mia again. The Mia her new husband knew and loved.

❁❁❁

The scents of garlic, oregano, and thyme wafted through the air as Mia and Daniel waited for Daniel's sister and brother-in-law to arrive.

They were sitting at a table for four at an Italian restaurant in Calabasas, an upscale neighborhood in the San Fernando Valley. Daniel had warned her about his sister on the drive to the restaurant. That Claire wasn't exactly thrilled about their relationship. Apparently, she was upset that they'd married so quickly and was likely to be pretty vocal about it during dinner. Daniel said that Claire lacked a few social graces, one of them being a filter, and as a result, she often came across as harsh.

Mia already knew how Claire felt about her because she'd secretly read the texts and emails the two had exchanged over the months—and she knew tonight was going to be a challenge.

Mia already harbored a healthy disdain for other women. Not just ones like Claire, who tried to steal away hard-won prizes like Daniel, but most women. Yes, there had been an exception or two in the past, but not many. Women had always hated her. Some even seemed to have a sixth sense about her and didn't trust her.

One morning in sixth grade PE class, Mia had been stepping into her gym shorts when a girl had thrown a large cockroach at her. The insect had landed on her head. In its anxiousness to flee, and hers to remove it from her head, the bug had become hopelessly tangled in her long hair. She'd screamed and torn hair from her scalp as she'd tried to get rid of the insect. Now even after all these years, she could still hear the roar of her classmates' laughter and see the girls' savage smiles.

After managing to get the cockroach out of her hair, she'd beaten the shit out of the pretty but vicious little blonde who had masterminded the prank, but the damage had already been done. She was now deathly afraid of insects and loathed other women even more.

That was just the first of several incidents she'd go on to have with other women, so she avoided them when she could. But since avoidance hadn't always been a possibility, she'd spent years learning how to handle them, and now she was rather skilled at it. But Claire was a different class of person than she was used to and might require new tactics.

"There they are," Daniel said, scratching at his elbow. It was apparent he wasn't looking forward to the dinner, either. He stood up and glued a smile on his face. She followed suit and watched the couple as they approached with the hostess, quickly recognizing both from the photos she'd seen of them online.

Claire and Daniel were twins, but they didn't look very much alike. They had the same dark hair and olive skin, but that's where the resemblance ended. Daniel was six feet two and athletically built with strong features and a sturdy chin. Claire stood at barely five feet and was round with soft features. The kind of looks that would easily blend into a room.

When Claire's gaze landed on Mia, her eyes grew steely. She gave Mia a long once-over, then threw Daniel a frosty look, as though she were displeased.

"We're lucky we weren't late," Ben said, his face flushed by the cold weather. "The new puppy got out, and I must have chased him at least ten blocks."

"You're fine," Daniel said. "Is he okay?"

"Yeah. But one more block, and he would've been a goner."

"I'm glad you managed to catch him," Daniel said. He made the introductions. "Mia, this is my sister, Claire."

Mia forced a smile and held out her hand. Claire stared at it for a moment. When she finally accepted it, her hand was moist, and her handshake was limp and quick.

"This is Ben," Daniel said. "Ben, Mia."

Unlike Claire's, Ben's greeting was warm. He walked around the table and threw his arms out by his sides, inviting Mia into a hug. Daniel had said Ben was a good guy. That he was a great provider and dad to his nephews. He also considered him a saint for putting up with his sister.

Mia accepted Ben's warm embrace and hugged him back.

"Welcome to the family, Mia," Ben said with a wide smile. "It's so great to finally meet you. Daniel here has been selfish, keeping you to himself all this time."

Mia watched Claire shoot her husband a dirty look, but Ben didn't seem to notice. In Mia's experience, men didn't catch half the things women noticed or did.

"It's great to finally meet you, too," Mia said. She glanced at Claire. "*Both* of you."

Claire eyed her suspiciously as they took their seats.

Mia felt Daniel's hand on her thigh. He squeezed it as though trying to reassure her.

The waitress appeared and took their drink orders. Claire and Ben ordered Perrier. Mia noticed that when Daniel ordered a whiskey on the rocks, Claire looked peeved.

"Dan says you're from Phoenix," Ben said when the waitress walked off.

Mia nodded. "That's right. Born and raised."

"What brought you out to LA?"

"I needed a change," she said, repeating the lie she always told. "And I'd always dreamed about living here, so I figured it was now or never."

"Been here long?" Ben asked.

"About two years now."

"Like it?"

"Love it."

"I'm sure you do," Claire interjected, her voice sharp as glass.

Mia looked curiously at the woman, taking care to keep her own expression pleasant.

"And what is it you do again?" Claire asked.

Mia knew well from the correspondence she'd read that Claire already knew what she did and didn't approve of it. She seemed to think that because Mia was a waitress and had married a doctor, she was automatically a gold digger.

Mia told her again what she did.

"A waitress," Claire said slowly, as though she was amused. "That's pretty . . . what's the word I'm looking for? *Ambitious?*" Her smile was obnoxious.

Mia bit into the inside of her cheek, then quickly relaxed her jaw. "Yes, I suppose it is. Kind of like working in retail sales," she said with a smile of her own. "That's what you did before you married Ben, right? Worked at Sephora?"

The corners of Claire's mouth pulled down.

Yes, I did my homework on you, too, sweetie. Mia tried to keep the expression on her face pleasing, to appear completely at ease, in control, but her body wasn't cooperating. Something dark had risen up inside of her, and now adrenaline was coursing through her bloodstream.

Calm down, she told herself.

Claire had no clue what she was capable of.

Mia picked up her wineglass and took a long sip of her merlot. She stared back at Claire, whose eyes were now angry little marbles.

"Okay, now you ladies are even," Daniel said. "Can we try to play nice now? We're family, after all. Whether we all like it or not."

It was obvious that playing nice was the last thing Claire wanted to do. She scowled at Mia and picked up a knife and a roll. The rounded blade of the butter knife glinted beneath the candlelight, sending old laughter echoing through Mia's head. Of the girls in middle school. The blonde who had thrown the cockroach in her hair was named Audrey. She'd been the leader of a small gang of popular girls. After Mia had beaten the shit out of her, Audrey had avoided her and gone after other girls. Mia wondered what a girl like Audrey was up to now. If her crimes had gotten any worse over the years.

She thought about all the female bullies who had come after her. Much older ones, later in life. Three had been wearing orange jumpsuits. Mia had retaliated with a meat cleaver and spent two days in the hole.

"Mia?"

It was Daniel's voice.

Mia blinked herself back to the present and realized she'd been staring hard at Claire.

Claire was watching her, a startled expression on her face.

Shit. She'd lost it for a moment.

"You okay?" Daniel asked.

"I'm fine," Mia said, forcing herself to smile. She glanced at Claire. "Sorry, I didn't sleep well last night. I must have checked out just now." As she spoke, she could feel the weight of Daniel's stare. She knew she'd screwed up.

"Look, I'm going to come right out and say it," Claire said. "Some things have really been bothering me. So, it's not enough that you guys just up and get married within months of meeting each other, but it bothers me that you didn't sign a prenup." Her eyes locked on Mia's. "No offense, but my brother has had a rough life, and he worked very, *very* hard to get to where he is now—"

"Claire!" Daniel barked.

"What?" Claire snapped. "I mean, prenups are so common nowadays. It's actually strange *not* to have one, especially when one of the spouses is obviously so much more successful than the other one."

"Your brother didn't ask for one," she said, forming her words carefully.

"Well, he should have," Claire hissed.

"And he's not capable of making that decision for himself?" Mia asked.

Claire glowered at her.

"Look, Claire," Daniel said, "you're my sister, and I will always love you. But frankly . . . my marriage is none of your damn business."

Claire turned crimson.

"He's right, Claire," Ben said.

Claire jerked her head toward her husband, and her eyes flashed. Clearly, she wasn't used to being spoken to the way she was being spoken to tonight. Mia couldn't help but wonder why.

The table went quiet. Mia felt the weight of Daniel's stare again. She turned to look at him and saw his eyes were no longer on Claire. They were on her, and a worried expression marred his face. *What now?* she wondered.

"Mia, are you okay?" he asked. "Your nose is bleeding."

She brought her hand to her nose and came away with blood. She grabbed the napkin from her lap and pressed it against her nose. "Excuse me," she said, as she stood up, and headed for the ladies' room.

CHAPTER 11

DANIEL

AS SOON AS Mia was out of earshot, Daniel turned on Claire. "For the love of God, Claire! You are way out of line tonight. Even for you!"

His sister stared at him, her nostrils flaring. "*Now* I know why you waited so long to introduce us. Come on, Dan, seriously? She looks like a freaking Victoria's Secret model. I *know* you know better."

Daniel was opening his mouth to respond when her lips started moving again.

"Not just that, but did you *see* how she just looked at me? She looked like a freaking psychopath. Where the hell did you find this woman?"

Claire was right. The way Mia had been staring at his sister *had* been strange. It reminded him of a similar incident on their honeymoon. But the first time it happened was so fast, like a blip, and he hadn't really thought anything of it. Now he wondered if maybe it was a medical issue. Something he should have her look into.

Daniel always tried to have the utmost patience with his sister because they were blood, they had a long history together, and he loved her. Neither he nor Claire had been very social children or even adults for that matter . . . perhaps because people had always let them down. Other than their now-deceased brother, his relationship with Claire had been the only real bond he'd had for the first couple of decades of his life outside of his high school friend, Billy Hayes. Also, Daniel knew that Claire's heart was in the right place. She was just being protective of him. She'd grown up with the same father and had seen the long line of beautiful but parasitic women he'd spent his free time with. She had formed the same prejudice against them that he had.

Claire had seen firsthand what those women had driven their father to ultimately do. They'd all taken advantage of him, each new woman worse than the one before her. Because of those women, their father was hardly there for them and was always broke.

As children, Daniel and Claire learned to quickly distrust women who looked like the ones their father dated. One night years ago, their father had just had a breakup with yet another one of them and, drunk out of his gourd, left the living room where he, Daniel, and Claire were all watching television. It had been one of those rare times when they'd spent an evening together as a family. Their father's eyes had been glazed over that night, and he'd been especially quiet. Usually when they were together, he told corny jokes and a lot of them. But not that night.

That night he'd slowly but steadily emptied more and more beer cans, enough of them to create a sizable tower on the TV tray he kept next to his moth-bitten La-Z-Boy recliner. During a break while watching *Star Search*, he'd disappeared into his bedroom. A minute later, a gun fired. Daniel knew what had happened the instant he'd heard the gunshot. He told Claire to run to a neighboring trailer and have someone call 911. Then he'd gone to his father's bedroom and opened the door. The gore he'd seen on the other side had been permanently etched into his brain.

Daniel waved down their waitress and ordered another drink. When she walked off, Claire spoke again. "How the hell old is she, anyway?"

"She's thirty-seven. Our age. She just looks younger."

"And how well do you know her?"

"I know her very well."

That's a lie, and you know it.

Be quiet!

Claire shook her head. "*Very* well? Seriously? How could you? It hasn't even been a year. A year is *nothing*, Daniel."

"Claire," Ben interjected.

"What?" Claire snapped.

"I know everything I need to know," Daniel answered, his tone matter-of-fact. He was beginning to wonder if it was true, but it wasn't any of his sister's business. "Anyway, when did it become a crime to marry a beautiful woman?"

"Don't pretend you don't know what I'm talking about. They're all the same, and you know that. Seriously. You really want to follow in Dad's footsteps?"

Daniel bristled. That would be the worst thing he could do.

"She's nothing like any of Dad's women," he said.

Claire snorted. "She looks exactly like all—"

He slammed a palm down on the table. "That's enough, Claire!"

Claire jumped a little in her chair and blinked at him. But at least she shut her mouth.

"Look, I'm not sure what you're trying to accomplish here except for making everyone miserable. In case you missed it, Mia and I are already married. And I've already decided not to sign a prenup. It's done. So, live with it."

"You're right, Dan," Ben said. "She seems very nice."

"Yeah, *nice*," Claire said, glaring at her husband. "I'm sure *that's* the word that comes to mind when you look at her."

"Get to know her before you judge her," Daniel said. "She's going to be part of your life for a very long time."

Claire crossed her arms. "We'll see about that."

"You don't understand. She won't even let me hire a housekeeper. She insists on doing all the cleaning herself. And she didn't quit her job. So that kind of throws your little theory out the window, doesn't it? She's a good woman. You'll see. And she treats me like a king."

Claire's arms were folded tightly across her chest, but she was listening.

Silence stretched between them. "I hope to God you're right," Claire finally said.

"I am."

No, you're not.

Daniel watched Mia make her way back to the table. He cleared his throat, alerting Claire to cool it.

He smiled at Mia as she sat down. "You okay?"

"Yeah. Sorry about that. My nose always bleeds this time of year. It's just the change in the weather."

"Happens to our oldest son, too," Ben said.

Daniel watched his sister stare at his wife, concern creasing her face. Then her eyes swung to his and softened a little. "The boys have an appointment with you tomorrow."

"Which ones?" Daniel asked, glad to finally shift the conversation.

"All four of them."

Daniel rubbed his chin. "Is everything okay?"

"We received a postcard. About that new medicine."

Daniel's stomach tightened.

"Seriously, Dan, when did you guys become such salespeople? First, I get an email, then a postcard, and then someone from your office calls this morning, asking if I want to make an appointment. What does this miracle drug do? Babysit?"

The last thing he wanted to talk about, much less think about, tonight was Respira. He filled in his sister with as few details as possible.

Her eyebrows knitted together. "Seriously? The last I heard, people just got a cold, and they were okay."

Jesus. Is this dinner almost over?

"Well, you're the doctor," Claire said. "The boys and I will be there in the morning."

The waitress finally appeared and set his drink in front of him. Daniel thanked her and took a long swig of his whiskey. He set his glass down. "Look, why don't you cancel their appointments for now?"

Claire's brow furrowed. "Cancel? Why?"

"Let's give it a few more months."

"You were just talking about it like it was the best thing since sliced bread, and now you're saying to wait?" Claire's eyes narrowed. "What aren't you telling me?"

Christ. Why can't she just take my damn word for something sometimes?

"What's your concern, Daniel?" Ben asked. His eyes narrowed. "Is it not safe?"

"Of course it's safe. It's just that it's very new, and I'd rather my nephews wait until it's been on the market for a little while. That's all."

He realized all three of them were staring at him. Waiting for him to go on.

But he wasn't going to. He was done talking about Respira for the evening.

❀ ❀ ❀

"Well, that was lovely," Mia said with a little laugh as they pulled out of the restaurant's parking lot and headed home.

"I am so sorry for my sister," Daniel said tiredly. Between the things on his mind and Claire's rudeness toward Mia and their marriage, his nerves were fried. He was ready to be home, in bed with his wife lying naked beside him and his dog at his feet. "It's not you, I promise. She's been this way for as long as I can remember, especially when it comes to women I'm involved with. But she got out of hand tonight—even for her."

He reached for Mia's hand and squeezed it.

"She's just protective of her brother," Mia murmured. "I think it's sweet."

"Sweet?" Despite his lousy mood, he felt a smile tiptoe across his face. "You're being charitable. I don't think that's a word anyone has ever used to describe Claire. Not even as a kid."

At least he'd gotten the dinner with Claire out of the way, and she'd had a chance to meet Mia. Maybe she'd quit blowing up his phone and email now.

As he guided the vehicle onto the entrance ramp to the highway, he circled back to Mia's behavior earlier. It was the first time he'd seen her angry. But then again, maybe anger wasn't the best word to describe what he'd seen. Her behavior had been strange—as though she'd been having an episode of some kind. Maybe even a seizure.

He thought again about his lie to Claire. There was still a lot he didn't know about Mia. Specifically, about her past. Of course, he'd realized this before, but he hadn't much cared. What he cared about most was how she made him feel and what she contributed to his life. What they could contribute to each other's lives going forward. Their pasts were now beyond their control. She'd mentioned her childhood had been bad, troubled. His past had been troubled, too. The last thing he wanted to do was relive those terrible years again by talking about them. But now that he'd caught her in a lie, he wondered if he had been naive.

"How are you feeling?" he asked.

"Fine. Why?"

"You checked out a little. Right before your nose started bleeding."

"Oh, that. Sorry. I'm just exhausted. I haven't been sleeping well."

She looked as though she wanted to slit your sister's throat, Daniel.

Daniel had to agree. She had.

"Are you sure?" he asked. "Maybe it's something you should have checked out."

"It's really nothing to worry about. I just need to get more sleep." She angled her body toward him. "That new drug your sister asked you about? Isn't it the same one you were talking to Andy about the other night?"

He exhaled loudly. "Yeah. They've been having some problems with it in Tarzana." The car was quiet while he tried to decide if he wanted to say more. "And on top of what Andy told me, I have a patient. This eighteen-month-old. Really cute little girl. She wound up having a seizure hours after getting it and—"

"Oh, no. Seriously?"

He shook his head. "It's probably nothing. Young kids get seizures. It's not uncommon these days."

The car was quiet for a little while. Just the sound of tires on pavement.

As the Tahoe hugged the mountain, he glanced out the window and stared at the black water of the Pacific glistening beneath the moonlight.

"But if you don't think it was the drug that caused the seizure, why tell Claire and Ben to wait?"

Because my gut told me to. He rarely went with his gut when making decisions, especially medical ones—and he kind of hated that he had this time. Decisions, most of them, anyway, should be based on logic. On facts, *not* feelings.

"I guess there's a small part of me that isn't convinced they aren't connected. But the last thing I want to do is make a big deal out of nothing."

As Daniel silently navigated the twists and turns of the Pacific Coast Highway, rain began dotting the windshield.

"So, what are you going to do?" Mia asked.

"I'm sorry?" he asked, flipping on the wipers.

"I take it you're not going to give it to any more kids until you know for sure it's safe?"

The liar is judging you. She of all people.

Daniel's face grew hot. He was tired of talking . . . even *thinking* about Respira. "It's safe," he said, watching the wipers swipe across the windshield.

"It's just that you said—"

"*All* medications come with risks, Mia!" he snapped, his voice so loud, it filled every inch of the car.

He froze, realizing the words had just burst out of him without his consent. His sister and Ben had whittled away at his patience until he had none left.

The alcohol. It makes you angry, too.

Mia's hand slid off his shoulder. In his peripheral vision, he could see her shift her body toward the passenger door, away from him.

A jagged streak of lightning shot across the dark sky, and the rain began falling in sheets. He tightened his grip on the steering wheel and eased off the accelerator. "I'm sorry. I shouldn't have spoken to you that way," he said. "I didn't mean to."

She didn't say anything.

He glanced at his wife. She was gazing out the passenger window into the darkness.

You're also stressed because she lied to you. And we're going to find out why.

❋❋❋

As soon as they got home, Mia excused herself, claiming she was tired and going to bed. When Daniel tried to hug her good night, she stiffened beneath his touch.

She obviously had not gotten over his snapping at her. Nor should she have. He knew he'd been wrong. Yes, her words had hit a tender spot, and yes, dinner tonight had required all his patience and quite a bit more, but the voice had been right. Had he not been drinking, he never would have spoken to her that way.

He walked into the kitchen to get some tea, but when he pulled open the refrigerator and saw an opened bottle of chardonnay, he lingered. He deserved a glass after such a shitty dinner.

And he'd only have one.

One would barely affect him. It would calm him down.

Don't do it, Daniel. You've already had enough tonight.

"One more won't hurt," he whispered.

Remember . . . never, ever at home. You don't want to turn out like your father, do you?

"I'm *nothing* like him," he snapped, his words slicing through the stillness of the large kitchen.

He hated breaking rules. In fact, he'd always had a powerful need to do the right thing. Maybe because all his life he'd seen his father do so many things wrong.

Three maximum while out and never at home were his rules. But those rules suddenly seemed too strict. Maybe it was time for new rules. That way he wouldn't have to break them. Hell, he worked hard, he was an adult, he knew his own limits. Maybe he didn't years ago, but he'd matured a lot since then. One at home would be fine. Something to chase away the jagged thoughts circling in his head.

He grabbed the bottle, filled a glass, then returned the wine bottle to the refrigerator. He sipped the chardonnay and checked his phone. Andy from the free clinic had tried calling him while they were at dinner. He'd also sent him a text: Hey, call me. It's important.

Daniel stared at the message, debating whether to call him. But it had been a long, stressful night, and he had a hunch Andy would want to talk about Respira again, which was the last thing he wanted to think about right now. Just thinking about the drug was starting to piss him off again. Yeah . . . he'd wait and call Andy tomorrow.

He opened the refrigerator again and grabbed the wine bottle.

Daniel. No . . .

"Two. Two at home, and that'll be it. Scout's honor," he whispered.

He drank the wine, rinsed out his glass and set it in the drying rack, then trudged up the stairs to bed. Tomorrow would be a better day. He'd apologize again to Mia for raising his voice. He'd make things right.

And maybe send more orchids to Jiminy's . . . again without a card.

CHAPTER 12

ANDY

ANDY CAMERON FELT the familiar burn start just above his knees and slowly flood his quadriceps.

It was a welcome pain to which he had all but become accustomed during his ritual five-mile run through the hills of Hollywood just before daybreak. He didn't take the smooth, even roads of Brush Canyon Trail but the rougher terrain just past where the trail dead-ended. It was a hiking trail made of packed dirt and full of potholes and razor-sharp rock. It made the ascent to the peak of Mount Lee a brutal but highly satisfying trek.

Up here, above the Los Angeles basin, the air was cleaner, crisper, and extremely cold. The daily struggle cleared his head and afforded him a bit of solitude in which he could think, plus there was a fantastic view of the Hollywood sign.

Thinking was something he had been doing a lot of these days. Since the clinic started administering Respira, his stress level had sky-rocketed. Mothers had been calling wondering if their child's adverse reactions and trips to the emergency room were due to the drug. Andy had gone to management twice about his concerns. First to his assistant manager, who said the kids' ailments weren't connected to the Respira and had given him orders to tell parents as much. Not feeling right about his assistant manager's direction, he had decided to go to the department manager. But he was told the same thing. The last few days he'd been calling other doctors to get their experiences, but everyone seemed hesitant to talk much about it. He'd reached out to Dr. Winters again because he knew Winters would be straight with him, but Daniel hadn't gotten back to him yet.

The burn from the lactic acid was now ripping through his calves. But he craved the pain. It was the only thing that cleared his head. He quickened his pace yet again and focused his mind on the repetitive sounds of his footfalls hitting the gravel.

Thud. Crunch!

Thud. Crunch!

He was entering the final stretch. He could almost see the city's emergency communications center up ahead at the peak of Mount Lee. A moment later, he saw the familiar green sign that read **PROPERTY OF THE CITY OF LOS ANGELES**.

A man was standing next to it, wearing a jogging suit and smoking a cigarette. Just before Andy passed him, the man tossed the cigarette and stamped it out. Andy nodded as he passed him, but the guy didn't acknowledge him.

Thud. Crunch!

Thud. Crunch!

Suddenly, there was a new sound. More thuds, more crunches. Someone was behind him. Probably the jogger he'd just passed. He found it strange that a smoker was running up here. This hill wasn't for novices.

His diaphragm felt like it was on fire as he approached the chain-link fence. The remaining few yards seemed like an eternity. But finally, he reached the metal fence. He collided with it, and the sound of the metal clanking was music to his ears.

He bent at the waist and drew several deep breaths. Then he coughed up phlegm, his lungs irritated from the physical exertion and the frigid mountain air.

But he'd made it. Again.

Feeling a sense of accomplishment, he straightened, then raised his arms above his head to get a deeper inhalation.

About ten yards away, the man in the jogging suit slowed his pace to a leisurely walk. Andy watched him, warning bells flashing in his head. Something about this guy was wrong. Was he about to be mugged?

As the guy drew closer, Andy could see more of his features. He was of medium build. Dark hair with weird bangs. Andy was working up a composite of the guy, trying to store his features in the hard drive of his brain, when a pair of arms grabbed him from behind. They pinned his own arms to his side, and as he struggled to free himself, something was thrown over his face. Something that smelled grotesquely sweet.

He went down hard, crumpling to the cold ground. Disoriented, he looked up and saw two men hovering above him. One had a towel in his hand. Andy tried to twist away from him, but the guy was fast. He pressed the towel to Andy's face again, and Andy inhaled the sweet odor a second time.

As he drifted in and out of consciousness, he could feel hands gripping each of his wrists and holding his ankles. Two men grunted as they carried him.

Who are these guys? he wondered dimly.

And where are they taking me?

Everything was blurry and distorted. He knew he needed to do something. To fight back. Try to get away. But his body felt as limp as a dishrag.

Then he felt a new sensation.

He was tumbling backward.

Falling.

The men must have let him go, and he was rolling. As he watched the blur of dead grass, rocks, and blue sky rush past, he realized where he was. The men had tossed him off the trail, and he was rolling, headed for a cliff. He tried to grab something to hold on to, but his arms wouldn't respond.

Then suddenly everything felt and sounded different. He wasn't tumbling anymore. He was falling. His eyes at half-mast, he stared up at the bright white welcoming letters of the Hollywood sign as he plummeted toward the unforgiving ground below.

CHAPTER 13

RACHEL

THE MORNING SKY was streaked with shades of pink and gold as Rachel pulled onto the on-ramp of Highway 80 West, heading back to Chatsworth.

She and Suzie had just left Dr. Winters's office, where Suzie had gotten her second injection of Respira. Rachel had been nervous about letting Suzie get the second shot, but Dr. Winters had reassured her once again that Respira was safe. Plus, Rachel couldn't afford for Suzie to get as much as a sniffle right now. Jeff had been surprisingly understanding about Suzie's seizure. He said he had two young nephews with epilepsy, so he could empathize, but she knew his patience had about run its course, and she wouldn't have any more wiggle room with taking off work. If he fired her, then what would they do? It wouldn't take long for her landlord to evict them if she had no way to pay the rent.

This morning, Dr. Winters had asked them to stay in the waiting room for twenty minutes after the injection. During those minutes, Suzie had behaved normally. In fact, Rachel had barely been able to keep up with her daughter as she'd darted from the little playroom to the aquarium by the registration desk, up to other little kids, back to the playroom, then back to the aquarium. One would never guess she'd been racked with a seizure just two days ago or had been so lethargic and listless.

After the twenty minutes were up, Rachel grabbed her daughter, and they hit the road. Staring out at the highway before her, Rachel forced herself to get out of her head for once and to focus on the world around her. Cars were flying past her ancient Honda, many of them luxury vehicles: BMWs, Lexuses, Range Rovers, Teslas. To her left, a teenage girl drove a sleek white Mercedes sports coupe. *Damn, that must be nice,* she thought, and wondered—as she had many times since moving to LA—what it must feel like to live such a cushy life.

Hell, if she had the kind of money it took to afford a car like that, she wouldn't have any problems. Or at least not as many. She'd be able to breathe easier and would be able to make different choices, one being not working for an asshat like Jeff.

Where did I go so wrong? she wondered. Stuck working at a job she was miserable at for a paycheck that barely stretched to the next one. Living in constant fear that she'd lose everything if her daughter got so much as a cold. Tears of frustration slipped down her cheeks, and she wiped them with the back of her hand. *You're just exhausted,* she told herself. *And it's making you sad and moody. Everything's going to be fine.*

She was still trying to calm herself down when, about ten miles from Martha's place, the car once more filled with Suzie's high-pitched screams.

CHAPTER 14

DANIEL

AFTER SEEING SUZIE Jacobs, Daniel walked to Teddy's office. He and Teddy had an appointment with Lisa Stockton, a sales representative with the insurance company Santa Monica Mutual. When Daniel walked into his boss's office, Teddy was watching the news on the seventy-two-inch plasma screen that hung on the wall in his office. The sound was muted, and images of emergency vehicles and a gurney with a body bag being wheeled to an ambulance filled the screen. The caption on the screen read: *Man, 30, Found Dead Near Hollywood Sign.*

"Jeez, what some people will do in this town to get their fifteen minutes of fame," Teddy said with a chuckle. Daniel stared unseeingly at the coverage, a lot on his mind.

Lisa arrived, and Teddy flipped the television off. Daniel tried to give the woman his undivided attention as she spoke, but his mind kept creeping back to his personal life.

To Mia's lie.

To her behavior at dinner.

To how he'd yelled at her in the car. As if the voice had taken over for a few seconds. He shook the thought from his head. It was ludicrous to even think that. He considered shooting Mia a quick text. To check up on her. See what she was doing today.

"Danny?" Teddy said, jarring him back to the present moment. "Did we lose you already?"

"Sorry," Daniel said, raking his hand over his mouth. "I didn't get much sleep last night."

"Newlywed," Teddy muttered to Lisa.

Lisa laughed, then cleared her throat. "I was saying that Santa Monica Mutual couldn't be more excited about Respira. Reducing rhinovirus in children. Possibly even eradicating it. That's just incredible."

"Our words exactly," Teddy chimed in.

"But, while it's great for the kids, their families, and businesses," Lisa said, grabbing an iPad, then looking directly at Daniel, "let's be honest: healthier kids mean fewer doctor visits. Your practice is going to take a major hit. Plus, there are the costs of administering and storing Respira. We know it doesn't come cheap. But we're all in this together, which is why we've put this incentive program in place for you. I know you guys are busy, so I'll make this short and sweet."

She held up her iPad for everyone to see. "Based on the size of your practice, if you get sixty-three percent of your patient base to complete the three-stage series of Respira by the end of the year, you'll receive . . ." She started talking figures.

Significant ones.

Daniel frowned as he listened.

"Those numbers are approximate, of course, depending on how your patient base shakes out throughout the year, but it'll be pretty close to what I mentioned."

Teddy elbowed him. "And this is just from *one* insurance company."

"I don't understand. Why would an insurance company give us a bonus like that?" Daniel asked.

Teddy turned to Lisa and smiled. "He's new to the business side of things."

Lisa smiled back, then addressed Daniel. "That's okay. That's what I'm here for. Try not to get too hung up on semantics, Dr. Winters. It's more of a reimbursement than a bonus. We develop these programs to help physicians offset their losses. You're running a business, and what's best for the patient isn't always what's best for your bottom line." She paused, as though giving him a moment for her words to sink in. "For us, it's the opposite. The more patients who get this treatment, the fewer illnesses we'll have to pay out for. We've done the actuary studies and predict that Respira will be saving us . . . well, let's just say *a lot* of money. And we're sharing that windfall with you. It's a win-win for everyone."

Teddy smiled at Daniel and winked. "Do your part with the prescribing, and you'll get a nice cut. I see another trip to the Caymans in your future."

❧❧❧

Daniel sat out on the covered deck of Margot's in Malibu and breathed in the intoxicating aroma of steak being grilled on an open flame. For the second time today, he tried calling Andy, but his call went directly to voice mail.

He set his phone on the table and stared out the window of the restaurant, but instead of marveling at the beauty of the ocean, he was replaying his workday. It had practically flown by. Suzie had come in for her second dose early that morning. He had been relieved to see the little girl back to her usual self. Her color had looked great, and she'd been as energetic as ever, chattering away and playing with the stuffed bunny she was carrying. Rachel had reported that she had been doing well. No additional seizures, GI issues, or fevers. Her listlessness was gone, and her appetite and mood were back to normal. Still, despite himself, Daniel had felt a little queasy when he'd sent Deepali to administer the girl's second injection. He'd also been glad when he'd seen that his sister had canceled his nephews' appointments.

Taking a sip of his drink, he surveyed the restaurant. He was waiting for Billy Hayes, a high school friend he'd met back in Tyler, Texas, who was late as usual. Billy was the only person from his childhood he'd kept in touch with over the years. He was also the one who'd introduced Daniel to drinking way back when they were just sixteen. Usually, they'd coordinate their dinners for when Daniel volunteered at the free clinic in the valley because Billy lived out that way, but since Daniel was taking a hiatus from volunteering, they were meeting in Malibu.

He glanced at his phone. Mia was working at Jiminy's again tonight. He'd sent more orchids as an apology for snapping at her and had received a notification an hour ago that the orchids had been delivered to the restaurant. But Mia hadn't texted him yet.

He decided to text her. Maybe she'd mention the flowers, and he could give his mind a rest.

Hey. How's work going?

A few minutes later, Mia responded: Very busy here.

He typed: Thinking about you.

Her reply was short: Got to go.

Daniel reread the messages. They were very impersonal for Mia. Short. Maybe even a little cold.

She also didn't mention the orchids again.

Daniel dragged his hand down his cheek, wondering why she wouldn't. Was it because she was still angry with him? Or was it because she wasn't sure it was Daniel who had sent them? After all, he again hadn't included a card. She should know they were from him, right? Who else would be sending her flowers?

He was thinking about how quickly his perfect life had become complicated when Billy finally walked up.

"Hey, bro!" Billy stretched his arms out, and Daniel stood to hug him. Billy smelled like spicy aftershave, an improvement over his usual signature scent of sweat and motor oil. "Sorry I'm late."

"That's okay." Daniel grinned. "I'm used to it."

Daniel sat back down and watched Billy survey the place. He whistled through his teeth and nodded approvingly. "Not bad. Not bad at all."

At six foot four, Billy stood two inches taller than Daniel. He was also leaner. His short, blond hair was slicked back, and he had what appeared to be a fresh cut across his nose. "Damn, it's good to see you." Billy smiled. "It's been, what? Three months now? What's a brother got to do to see his best friend every once in a while, huh?"

They usually met like clockwork every month. But since Mia, a lot of things had been relegated to the back burner. A waitress stopped by the table. Billy ordered a Heineken, and Daniel ordered his second whiskey.

As the waitress walked away, Billy leaned back in his chair and chuckled. "Shit, man. I still can't believe you went and got married. Married! You've been swearing since high school you'd never get hitched."

"I never thought I would. But Mia changed everything for me."

Billy stared at Daniel. "I don't know, man. Better you than me."

"What do you mean?"

"Women, dude," Billy said. "You had it right the first time. You can't trust them. All that estrogen and shit. Makes them unstable. And sneaky as hell."

Daniel's thoughts trailed back to his problem with Mia.

"I've been doing some freelance work lately that only confirms it," Billy said.

"Freelance work? Wait. You left Tiremart?"

"Yeah, man. Months ago. Those dudes were crooks."

Billy's beer arrived. "Thanks, hon," he said to the waitress with an East Texas drawl that a lot of women seemed to find charming. "Why don't you go ahead and bring me a second? This one ain't gonna last very long."

As she walked off, Billy chugged back some of his beer and gazed out the window at the blue waters of the Pacific. "Damn, I could get used to this," he said and set the bottle down. He sat up straighter in his chair. "Anyway, I'm doing something that pays ten times better now."

"Yeah? What are you doing?"

"I get paid to tail wives."

Daniel frowned. "I'm sorry. Tail wives?"

"I know, right? Just did a job in the Hollywood Hills. Followed around this rich-ass stay-at-home mom to see where she was going when the kids were at school. Followed her for a week. Turns out she was meeting with some married studio exec. Sometimes at this fancy hotel off La Cienega. Sometimes right in their own house. This morning I gave Mikey—that's the guy I work for—a flash drive of pictures confirming what the husband had pretty much already known. Mikey said the dude cried like a baby when he saw the proof. And the sad thing is that this chick? She's pretty typical. At least in this town."

A sick sensation bloomed in the pit of Daniel's stomach. He finished drink number two in three long swallows. He felt the voice opening its big mouth again, but he mentally cast it to the back of his skull.

"You okay, dude?" Billy asked.

"I'm fine."

"That nervous tic of yours," Billy said, motioning to his own face. "Seems to have gotten way worse." Billy watched him for a moment, then went on. "Anyway, Mikey's getting more business than he can handle because this town is just swarming with wives looking to cash in on their clueless husbands. They come here looking for fame and fortune, and when that doesn't work out, they forget the fame and go for the fortune. And they'll do just about anything to get it.

"They look for actors, producers, doctors, lawyers, any dude with money. Fat dude, thin dude, thick hair, no hair, white skin, black skin. As long as they have money, they don't care." Billy continued, "You wouldn't believe the elaborate schemes they go through to meet these guys. How they manufacture chance meetings and shit. Pretend to run into them. Then they either take them for half of what they got, or string them along for the lifestyle and the title of being a so-and-so's wife—all the while keeping a little someone extra on the side."

Daniel thought about the night he'd met Mia at the hotel bar. How she had asked to sit next to him. Had known he was a doctor.

"Seriously, bro. You ever have any suspicions about your old lady, I could look into her for you. For real, though, you should've let me do it *before* you tied the knot."

Daniel shook his head. "That's not Mia."

"Huh?"

"The type of woman you're talking about. I'm saying that my wife is nothing like that. She'd never cheat on me."

Billy snickered and shook his head. "Never say never, man. Seriously, after all the shit I've seen, *nothing* people do surprises me anymore." He took a long pull of his beer and sat back in his chair. "So, how did you guys meet, anyway? Online or something? Company party? You saw her from across the room, and it was love at first sight or some shit like that?"

"A hotel bar."

"No shit." Billy studied him. "You approach her, or she come up to you?"

Daniel said softly, "She came up to me."

Billy stared at him. Daniel didn't like the look in his eyes.

Daniel's phone rang. He looked at the screen, hoping it was Mia. But it was a number he didn't recognize. One with an 818 area code.

The valley.

"This is Dr. Winters," he answered.

The female voice on the other end sounded frantic, out of breath. "It's Rachel Jacobs. Suzie's mother."

"Rachel? Is everything okay?"

"No, everything is *not* okay!"

CHAPTER 15

RACHEL

IT WAS ALMOST 1:00 a.m. Rachel sat next to Suzie's gurney in the emergency room and watched her daughter sleep. Her nerves were raw and ragged—and she was running on pure adrenaline. She was also on her third cup of stale coffee and was fighting the stomach acid that kept inching its way up her throat.

The room was separated from several other similar spaces by a thick green curtain. Even though it smelled of antiseptic, the area looked as if it hadn't been cleaned in a while. At least not properly. There was a cobweb in a corner with what looked like a Doritos chip caught up in it.

Above the rhythmic beeps of Suzie's cardiac monitor, Rachel could hear the muffled sounds of the ER: doctors barking commands, the moans and complaints from sick or injured patients, a man yelling for more pain medicine, nurses laughing about something at the nurse's station. The small space was bare except for the gurney, a locked medicine cabinet, and a poster on the wall that showed the smiling face of a young boy with his mother as they played in a park. The words underneath the image read:

Because You Want The Best For Your Kids. Ask Your Pediatrician About Respira Today.

A ball of fire rose in Rachel's belly, and she felt an almost uncontrollable urge to rip the poster from the wall and tear it into tiny pieces. She peered down at her sleeping daughter with the IV in her arm. Reaching for her purse, she dug inside and found the postcard for Respira. She stared at it, then began ripping it up. When the pieces were so small she couldn't rip them anymore, she stood up and went to the wastebasket. She let the tiny scraps flutter into the dark abyss, wishing she'd never even heard of the damn drug.

Suzie had been inconsolable again on the way home from Dr. Winters's office. She'd arched her back, screamed, and cried for an hour straight. Then that evening, Rachel had been simultaneously cooking spaghetti and studying for an exam for her computer science class when she heard strange noises on the baby monitor. She'd dropped everything and rushed to the bedroom and saw that Suzie was having another seizure. She had called 911, then called Dr. Winters from the back of the ambulance.

She leaned forward, took her little girl's warm hand in hers, and visualized Suzie getting better. As she sat with her chin resting on the cool metal railing of the gurney, the visualization quickly morphed into a daydream of her having the life her sister, Laura, had. No more rushing around every day. Getting to stay home with her daughter and be the mom she really wanted to be. Not always worrying about losing the roof over their heads, knowing that she'd always be able to put food on the table.

Suzie stirred in the bed and opened her eyes. Rachel's heart sped up. She leaned in closer. "Why, hello, sweet girl," she cooed.

The green curtain screeched back, and a doctor and nurse stepped into the exam cubicle. The doctor squinted tiredly at the chart in his hand. "She see her pediatrician today?"

"Yes. This morning."

"Any vaccines?"

"No."

"What about Respira?"

Rachel was surprised by the question. She nodded. "Yes. She got her second dose."

The doctor traded a quick look with the nurse.

"What?" Rachel asked.

He moved to Suzie's bed. "We've just seen similar reactions in other kids," he said, pulling a penlight from his lab coat.

"From Respira?" Rachel asked.

"Mm-hmm," the doctor said, leaning over the gurney and checking Suzie's eyes.

Rachel's gaze flitted to the nurse. The small, petite woman offered her a thin smile, then looked away.

"She had a seizure after her first dose, too," Rachel told the doctor. "But her pediatrician said he didn't think Respira caused it."

The doctor was silent as he continued to examine Suzie. Rachel figured he hadn't heard her and was about to tell him again when he turned toward her.

He snapped off his gloves and chuckled darkly. "Your pediatrician should spend a little time in the emergency room."

CHAPTER 16

MIA

A LITTLE BEFORE 2:00 a.m., Mia hurried out of a small ranch house into the chilly early morning air, jumped in her cherry-red Volkswagen Jetta, and slammed the door. She slipped her key into the ignition but paused before turning it.

Images of her car exploding had plagued her for years. Monte, the only other man in her life whom she'd been seriously romantic with, had continuously teased her, saying that if she ever left him, that's the way she would go out.

She'd be blown to pieces.

Nothing left of her but a mixture of bloody body parts and metal.

She knew her fear was illogical. After all, Monte was safely behind bars right now on drug charges and would continue to be for years. But the knowledge didn't make her any less afraid. Monte had always been resourceful. And she knew firsthand that plans—even elaborate ones—could be arranged from the inside. Her insides jittery, she held her breath, turned the key, and the engine roared to life. She sighed, feeling like she always did, as though she'd dodged a bullet.

She shifted into drive and pressed hard on the accelerator, the car's tires crunching on loose gravel. She'd left the heater on, and now freezing air poured from the vents. Shivering, she turned the heat off until the car had a chance to warm up.

Several minutes later, her twin beams were slicing through the darkness as she navigated the tight twists and turns of the Pacific Coast Highway. Every once in a while, she was taken by surprise by oncoming headlights appearing from around a corner. Many of the cars had their brights on; their headlights illuminated her car's interior, momentarily blinding her. For long stretches afterward, the night would become still again. Just hers.

Despite the late hour, she was far from tired. Thoughts were swarming like angry bees in her head. Daniel had been watching her like a hawk lately. She knew this because she'd been watching him, too.

Did he suspect something?

Or was his behavior the result of her slip with Claire at dinner?

When she thought back to the way she'd behaved that night, she still got angry with herself. She could only imagine what the episode had looked like to Daniel and the others. It was just one of the many parts of her that she couldn't allow others to see. Not anymore.

She was going to have to do better.

As she navigated the winding turns of the highway, she carefully revisited the lies she'd told Daniel, looking for anything contradictory. But she couldn't think of anything. She wished she hadn't needed to lie so much already, but they'd been necessary. There was a good reason humans were capable of deceit. Some things needed to be tucked in the darkest corners and kept there. But lies didn't come without risk. She knew from experience that untruths built a delicate web that could easily unravel at any moment. So the fewer she had to tell, the better.

A truck rounded a bend, its lights beaming into the Jetta's interior and momentarily blinding her. She tightened her grip on the steering wheel and navigated the vehicle carefully. When her eyes again adjusted to the darkness, she flipped the heat back on. Now that the engine had heated up, warm air blasted her neck and her feet. Comforted by the heat, she let herself think back on tonight.

Visiting him had been a mistake. She hadn't expected to feel something for him, and the last thing she needed was more complications. She would consign him to the background, at least for the present. She couldn't let herself get sidetracked. Her most important job right now was to make Daniel happy and to keep his trust.

That was her priority.

Besides, she didn't know yet if she could trust the guy.

As of now, her plan was in a holding pattern. She was forced to wait on news that would determine her next move. She hated waiting. Hated feeling as though things, especially such important ones, were beyond her control.

When she pulled into the driveway, she glanced at the digital display on her dashboard: 2:40 a.m.

Perfect timing.

Once inside the house, she slipped off her shoes and tiptoed across the hardwood floor and up the stairs, Bruce hobbling at her feet. She pushed open the bedroom door and saw that the room was dark except for the icy blue light of the television and a slender beam of moonlight creeping in through the curtains.

As soon as she stepped into the room, she smelled liquor. Daniel was lying in bed on top of the covers, fully dressed in a white button-down shirt, tan pants, and black socks. He was snoring loudly.

Had he gotten drunk tonight?

She recalled the look Claire had given him when he'd ordered a drink at the restaurant Wednesday night. As though she'd disapproved.

She also recalled how he'd overdone it with drinking one night while they'd been honeymooning in the Caymans, and she wondered if maybe she wasn't the only one with secrets.

She hurried into the shower, then when she was done, walked quietly back into the room. Daniel was still snoring. Even louder now. She went to his nightstand and curled her fingers around his phone, then turned so her back was facing the bed. There were several unread texts from Claire.

Claire worrying about Mia's strange behavior at dinner . . .

Claire claiming she was concerned about him . . .

Claire pleading for him to reply to her texts.

"Mia?" Daniel said, his voice hoarse.

Startled, Mia jumped a little. In one fluid motion, she tucked the phone into the waistband of her cotton pajama pants and turned toward him.

"Yeah, handsome," she said softly. "I just got home from work. I was trying not to wake you."

He was silent for a moment; then he grunted and turned over. He mumbled something mostly unintelligible—the only word she could make out was *Teddy*—then he began snoring again.

She carefully set his phone back on his nightstand exactly how he'd left it, then went to the closet to grab a heavy blanket. She draped it over him, then powered off the television.

She slid into bed and let herself remember. She thought of her mother. The nicotine-yellow ceilings of her childhood. The perpetually empty cupboards, Diet Coke cans filled with stained cigarette butts. Her mother was an ex-beauty queen turned shut-in who had survived on disability, pain pills, and meeting random men on Craigslist. Men who didn't give a shit about her. But she hadn't cared, either, because she hadn't given a shit about herself.

For years, her mother had rarely left her armchair. She'd hated the world. Hated her own daughter. Probably also hated herself since her beauty had faded. Unfortunately, it had seemed to be the only thing she had going for her. It was certainly the only thing Mia had ever seen her nurture.

Moonlight streamed in through her bedroom window, bathing the side of Daniel's face in a bluish hue. She studied him for a long moment, then turned her attention to the sound of the waves gently lapping the shore outside and the shadows dancing across the walls.

CHAPTER 17

DANIEL

IT WAS STILL dark outside when Daniel awoke. He turned toward the nightstand, his head feeling as though it was filled with cement. He fumbled for his phone and silenced the alarm. He felt awful. What the hell had happened to him?

What do you think *happened?*

The call from Rachel flashed into his head. Suzie having seizures again.

Jesus . . . no . . .

Was Mia still in bed? He turned his head, and the room slanted a little.

Yes. She was in bed. For once.

He tried to remember her coming home last night, but he couldn't remember anything. He must have already fallen asleep. He rubbed his eyes, and last night slowly started trickling back to him. He'd pulled a bottle of Jameson whiskey out of the liquor cabinet once he got home after talking with Rachel.

Shit.

He must have drunk enough to black out.

I thought for sure you would turn out different, Daniel.

What? "Different from what?" he whispered.

From your father . . .

Bristling, he shook the voice from his head. He looked down and realized he was still wearing his clothes from yesterday. *Dammit!* He struggled out of bed, trying not to wake Mia. Every inch of his body ached as he shuffled carefully toward the toilet.

When he reached the bathroom, he noticed the shower floor was wet.

He frowned, realizing Mia must have taken another shower after getting home.

What's she washing off, Daniel?

He squeezed his eyes shut and stood silently for a moment before opening them again and turning the shower on. After dressing, he walked down the hallway to his home office and saw that his desktop computer was still on and the bottle of Jameson sat uncapped and empty next to the monitor.

The bottle had been almost full.

Shit. Not only had he broken his own rules, he could have killed himself. He turned his attention to the computer. He could vaguely remember being online, but he couldn't remember why or what he'd done.

He sat down and saw several browsers were still open. Apparently, he'd found a site called GetTheFactsAboutRespira.com and had opened several articles. He pulled up last night's search history. All the rest of his searches had been Respira-related . . . except for one.

He had also apparently searched *Mia O'Brien.*

The conversation with Billy must have gotten to him last night. He was clicking on the search to see what results had come up when he felt warm breath on his ear. "Why are you up so early?"

Daniel jumped. He quickly clicked off the browser window, hoping Mia hadn't seen his search.

"Jesus, Mia," he said, turning to face her. "You scared the shit out of me."

❀ ❀ ❀

Daniel arrived at the office earlier than usual. Still nursing a throbbing headache, he felt his way through the darkness and across the wall until his fingers made contact with the light switch. He flipped it on, and with a few flickers, the fluorescent lights came to life, casting a flat brightness over the large waiting room.

The alcohol from last night was still circulating in his bloodstream. He needed some coffee. A lot of it. He walked into the clinic's small kitchen and brewed a pot. He'd spoken to Mia as little as possible this morning, not wanting to let her in on the fact that he'd blacked out last night. He was ashamed of his lack of control.

He wondered if they'd talked last night. What he might have said, especially with everything that had been troubling him lately. After pouring a cup of coffee, he went to his office and started up his computer. Once it booted, he froze, his fingers hovering above the keyboard. He debated whether he should continue his search for Mia O'Brien. Or if he should continue researching Respira instead. Teddy would be arriving in a couple of hours, and Daniel wanted to talk to him about Suzie Jacobs. He couldn't in good conscience simply write off the second instance of the girl's seizures.

The child would have to be a priority.

His personal life would have to wait.

He vaguely remembered reading information about Respira last night that had concerned him. Information that Medscape, UptoDate. com, and Immunext's information statement hadn't contained. He brought up Google and did a search for *Complaints about Respira*. He scrolled past the CDC's and Immunext's websites, knowing they'd mirror the information his other go-to sites had contained. He wanted to dig deeper this time. Look at a wider variety of sources than usual.

One of the results on the page was an article titled "Parents Concerned about Respira." It had been posted to the website he'd visited last night at home: GetTheFactsAboutRespira.com. He clicked on it and read it, bile burning his throat. Apparently, there were many—even hundreds—of parents concerned about the drug.

Frowning, he clicked over to an article titled "Pediatrician Speaks Out about Respira Dangers" and read that Dr. Sean Hemsworth, a pediatrician in Sherman Oaks, had discontinued the administration of Respira less than two weeks ago due to safety concerns. He also read about an adverse event reporting system and database that the CDC and FDA managed that he'd never even heard of.

Sirens blared in his head. *This is crazy,* he thought, wondering why Teddy didn't have them reporting to the database here at the practice. His situation was a little more unique than most pediatricians, because most of his office visits involved the treatment of acute illnesses or referrals to specialists and not the standard well-baby or well-child appointments that often included the administration of vaccinations. But even so, if he'd known about the database, there would have been at least a handful of adverse reactions he would have reported.

He followed a link to the drug's package insert. He clicked on it and scrolled through to the Adverse Reactions section. He carefully read through the long list, noting that among the possible reactions reported by parents and practitioners after administration of the drug were cyanosis, depressed level of consciousness, anaphylactic shock, paralysis, pneumonia, arthritis, diabetes mellitus, afebrile convulsions, seizures, and death.

He rubbed his chin.

First, this list looked very little like the information he'd read about Respira on UptoDate.com or Medscape, and it was completely dissimilar to the information printed on the colorful vaccine information statement the clinic was handing out to parents. In fact, the two documents looked like they belonged to two very different pharmaceutical products. Second, seizures were listed as an adverse reaction. So, why was the practice's official position that the girl's seizures and Respira weren't related? He was pretty sure he knew the answer, and he didn't like it.

You're just opening a can of worms. Listen to Teddy, and do your job. Stop messing around with this.

He ignored the voice and reread the list more slowly, heartened only by the fact that the reactions listed were rare. But for the first time in his career, he wondered what the word *rare* really meant.

Daniel printed the manufacturer's package insert and then clicked on another link labeled "Stories from Parents" where he found more than a hundred testimonials submitted by parents around the world who claimed their children had been damaged by Respira. He also found links to a message board and a Facebook group populated with parents talking about the drug. The post threads were charged with infighting and name-calling. Some of the parents were standing up for the drug, saying they were happy that their children received it and that their kids hadn't had any issues with it. Other parents were furious, saying if they'd known their kids would have reacted to it as badly as they had, they never would have approved it for their children.

He printed some of the comments, then tried to navigate back to the first page of the story, but he received a 404 error message.

The article was gone.

In fact, the entire website was suddenly down.

Weird, he thought, frowning.

He returned to the kitchen and poured another cup of coffee. When he was back at his desk, he leaned forward in his chair and rubbed the back of his neck. Although he understood some of the stories from parents were probably not 100 percent accurate, that some of their children's health issues might have in fact been caused by other things, there were too many to discount. All these parents couldn't be wrong, and they certainly deserved to be heard. He looked at his watch and realized Teddy would be in soon. They definitely needed to talk.

Don't, Daniel. He won't like it.

"I know he won't, but he needs to know," he said softly.

You'll only be asking for trouble.

"We're talking about children's lives here," he hissed.

Daniel was slumped in his office chair, thinking, when he heard movement coming from the front of the office, then footsteps in the examination hallway. He glanced at the clock. More time had passed than he'd realized.

Teddy's voice rang out. "Danny? Is that you?"

The big man poked his head into Daniel's office and grinned. "Oh, shit. Don't tell me the missus kicked you out already."

Daniel didn't even bother to smile. "Can we talk?"

The grin slid off Teddy's face, and he stepped into the office. "Everything okay?"

Daniel shook his head. "I think we may have a problem."

"What is it?"

"My patient Suzie Jacobs. She was taken to the ER again last night. She had two seizures. One that was at least seven minutes long."

"Is she okay?"

"From my understanding, yes. The seizures were contained fairly quickly, but she was admitted for a lumbar puncture and an infectious disease consult."

"I see. So, what's the problem?"

"Teddy, we administered her second dose of Respira yesterday morning."

Teddy's eyes narrowed to crinkled slits, but he didn't say anything.

"It's clearly the Respira, Teddy. Both times her seizures happened just hours after she received a dose."

"What hospital did you say she's at?" Teddy asked.

"Northridge," Daniel said.

"So, let me get this straight. You're saying that Northridge Hospital was able to *link* the girl's seizures to Respira? They determined that Respira *caused* the girl's seizures?"

Daniel could see what Teddy was doing. "Teddy, we can't write this off as coincidence again. That's just not right."

Teddy exhaled loudly. "Listen, Daniel, not to be insensitive, but shit happens. The drug is an easy scapegoat, but there's no way to know it caused the girl's seizures. I mean, what is she? A year old?"

"Eighteen months."

"Eighteen months. So, it's very possible that she's had seizures all along. Maybe her parents are just starting to notice them."

Daniel grabbed the printout of the drug's sixteen-page package insert and held it up. "Teddy, it's right here. Seizures are one of the possible adverse reactions. And from my research, they appear to be a fairly common one."

Teddy waved the printout away without looking at it. "Just because it's been reported as an adverse reaction doesn't mean you can reliably establish a causal relationship between the event and the drug."

"I understand that, but it's definitely something worth looking into. Teddy, there are hundreds of—"

Teddy held up a hand to silence him. "The last thing this clinic needs is to go on the record saying Respira is unsafe just because a patient may or may not have had a bad reaction to it. That's just irresponsible. This drug is going to help a lot of people."

"But at what cost?" Daniel countered, thrusting a printout of the parents' comments from a Facebook feed toward the other doctor.

Teddy snatched the printout from his hand and skimmed it.

"There are more than five thousand concerned parents in this one group alone," Daniel said. "Look at these posts and the comments."

Teddy looked up. "Where did you get these?"

"A parent support group on Facebook."

Teddy's face filled with disgust. "Facebook, Daniel? Is that where you're getting your science these days?" He tossed the printout back on Daniel's desk.

"No. Of course not. I checked several sources, including VAERS," Daniel said, referring to the Vaccine Adverse Event Reporting System used by the FDA and the CDC to monitor vaccine side effects. "I have some important questions. For one, I wasn't even aware this reporting system even *existed*. They never mentioned it in medical school and we're not using it here. Why?"

"Because we're busy, that's why," Teddy snapped. "Plus, I've never had a parent be able to prove to me that a health issue was caused by a drug I administered."

"But the way I understand it is that we shouldn't be making that determination ourselves. If a parent even thinks the drug might have caused a health issue, we should be reporting it so that the FDA and CDC can get an accurate picture of how children are tolerating these drugs."

Teddy waved his hand. "You're wasting your time, Danny. Hardly anyone uses the damn thing."

He's getting angry, Daniel. Just shut up about this, and do your job.

"But, Teddy, aren't you the least bit concerned that—"

"Yes, I am very concerned. But what concerns *me*," Teddy said, pushing his bulk out of the chair, "is that you want to deny a lifesaving drug to our patients."

Lifesaving?

Teddy had obviously bought Immunext's propaganda hook, line, and sinker. This was the common cold they were talking about. The freaking common cold. Not the big bad wolf Immunext was making it out to be. Like Mia had suggested, this drug was more for convenience than anything for most kids.

"I didn't say that I wanted to deny it, Teddy. I'm just saying that we should look into it. And maybe we should hold off on administering it until we can get some answers. Maybe Thomas from Immunext can come by the office and explain all of this away. I might just be missing something here. Isn't it worth at least that? There's already been more than six hundred of adverse events for this drug and it's only been out for a few months."

Sweat was glistening on Teddy's forehead. "Look, Daniel, six hundred reports of adverse events is peanuts considering how many kids are receiving this drug."

"But if as physicians we're underreporting events to the database, then the FDA and CDC aren't getting an accurate picture of what is happening. Can't you see the problem here?"

Teddy either didn't hear his question or decided to ignore it. "Danny, this is *my* practice. And at my practice, we go by what I say, not the rantings of some parents looking for a scapegoat for their children's unfortunate health issues." He paused to catch his breath. "Again, this practice's official position is that the girl's seizures and Respira are not related. Got it? *But,* if you really feel this girl is having problems with the drug, you may discontinue it for her care. But *only* hers."

Teddy charged to Daniel's office door and spun around once he reached the hallway. "Don't think for one goddamned minute that you'll get a penny of that bonus if you're not willing to pull your weight around here. If you don't help us meet that quota, you can kiss your bonus goodbye. Along with any partnership."

CHAPTER 18

Mia

MIA WATCHED INTENTLY as blood swirled down the drain. She'd been so distracted by her thoughts, the glass she'd been holding had slipped from her hand. She'd still been distracted when she bent to pick up the pieces, and she'd sliced the inside of her hand on an errant shard.

She switched off the faucet and watched the blood ooze from the wound for a few seconds, then reached for a clean dish towel. Earlier, she thought she'd caught Daniel doing a search on her name online, but she'd been too exhausted to be sure. What she did know for certain was that he'd deleted his search history before leaving for work. In all the months they'd been together, he'd never cleared his history, so why now?

Probably for the same reason why he'd been doing a search on her.

Her hand throbbed as she watched the blood soak into the white dish towel, and she wondered if the wound would need stitches.

If Daniel had been searching her name, he wouldn't have found anything of substance on her. Only a photo that had been posted on social media by a coworker at Jiminy's. He'd find no social media, no home listings, no schools attended, or anything else of real consequence—which she realized could be a problem. There'd be questions, but she had crafted a response to those types of questions months ago.

What she was far more concerned about was the reason *why* he would have been looking her up. Was it because of her little slip, or had he learned something? Every time she tried to think of possibilities, her thoughts slogged through quicksand. She was trying to function on less than an hour of sleep. Her mind was mush.

She went back up to the bedroom, grabbed her purse, and dug inside for a vial of sleeping pills. She tossed two on the back of her tongue and swallowed them. She'd get some rest; then she'd try to figure things out. Sleep was critical. She had to be sharp enough to piece things like this together. Just one little misstep . . . just one . . . was all it would take for her perfectly crafted world to come tumbling down.

The only thing she was completely sure of right now was that the energy between her and Daniel had shifted. It seemed to have begun the night of their dinner with Claire and Ben. The way Daniel had snapped at her in the car on the way home that night had her worried. It was the first time that he'd ever raised his voice to her. She'd been treated much worse by others, of course, but Daniel had never come close to speaking to her like that before. He was more considerate of her feelings. Maybe the spell that she'd so carefully constructed was starting to wear off.

She grabbed the first aid kit, then went downstairs. As she wrapped her hand, a cold, icy rain beat against the house and thrummed steadily against the tall windows that faced the ocean. It had been raining all morning. The type of weather you weren't supposed to get much of in Southern California.

After she was done bandaging her wound, she stepped closer to the window and peered out at the sea and watched it angrily toss water against the shore. She wasn't sure what was gloomier, the morning outside or the thoughts that were fermenting inside her head.

The chill in the air reminded her again that Christmas was only a few weeks away. Just days ago, she was excited about decorating, but now she couldn't be farther from the mood. She turned to face the lamplit living room. Grabbing an afghan and her Kindle, she curled up on the couch.

Bruce sprung up and lay his big head on her hip. She massaged the dog's ears, and he closed his eyes and sighed loudly. She stared at his nub, remembering Daniel telling her that Bruce has been hit by a car as a puppy and left on the side of the road. Daniel had discovered him at the animal shelter and adopted him just hours before he'd been scheduled to be euthanized.

She turned her thoughts to her Kindle. She powered it up and checked Facebook. She had opened several social media accounts under two aliases over the years and used them to keep track of a few people from her past. She scrolled her news feed, and a headline caught her attention: "Questions Remain after Suspected Murder-Suicide of Pediatrician's Family."

Curious, she clicked on the story and read that a local pediatrician was thought to have killed his family and then himself a few nights ago. But the doctor's father was challenging the story, saying that his son wasn't behind the killings, and he had proof. Her interest piqued, she kept reading.

CHAPTER 19

RACHEL

RACHEL PUSHED THE door open to her apartment and carried her sleeping daughter inside. It was almost 1:00 p.m., and she was exhausted. They'd just stayed overnight at the hospital where the doctors had run a battery of tests, including a lumbar puncture. The good news was that everything had tested negative, and they had ruled out a brain tumor and other more serious things. The bad news was that Suzie was still behaving strangely. They had a consultation next week with a neurologist to have even more testing done.

Give it time. She'll get better, Rachel tried to tell herself. *She did last time.*

Rachel thought again of what the emergency room doctor had said about other kids having bad reactions to Respira. She'd also mentioned her suspicions about the drug to the doctor who had overseen Suzie's care in the pediatric ward. But he had quickly dismissed the possibility of Respira's role in the seizures in pursuit of other causes. She couldn't help but think that he was overlooking the most obvious cause. Then again, he'd gone to medical school and she hadn't.

Rachel dragged the Pack 'n Play to the kitchen and lay Suzie down inside. There was no way she was going to let her daughter out of her sight. The hospital pediatrician who had discharged her said that seizures took a great toll on a body, both physically and mentally, so to not worry if she slept most of the day.

On the stove was the pot of half-cooked spaghetti she'd been boiling last night when she'd discovered Suzie was having a seizure. The noodles had hardened and clumped together. She dumped them in the garbage, scrubbed the pot, then set a teakettle on the burner to boil.

Something felt wrong. How could the emergency room doctor allude to the fact that Respira could be the reason for Suzie's seizures while Dr. Winters and the other pediatrician were adamant it wasn't? Why weren't they all in agreement? Shouldn't doctors be in agreement about things like this? It disturbed her that they weren't.

From the corner of her eye, she saw Suzie move. Rachel turned to her and saw that her eyes were open. She grabbed a towel to dry her hands. "Hi, sweetie." She smiled. "We're home!" she sang. "Aren't you happy, honey?"

Suzie blinked, then she stared quietly at something behind Rachel. Rachel turned to see what had caught her attention but saw nothing but the refrigerator.

"Are you hungry, sweet girl?"

Suzie hadn't eaten anything for over twenty-four hours, so Rachel knew she had to be starving. But Suzie didn't respond. She wished Suzie had a way of telling her exactly what she'd been feeling. What was hurting. Not knowing what she was experiencing was the most terrifying part.

Rachel switched off the burner. "Well, let's get you in the bath."

As Rachel washed Suzie with warm soapy water, she forced herself to sing their usual bath time songs, the silly ones that Suzie usually loved so much. But Suzie didn't as much as smile. Didn't reach for her rubber duckies. Didn't splash around. She just stared quietly at the water pouring from the faucet, as though she was in her own little world.

She did this after the first injection but eventually snapped out of it. She'll snap out of it this time, too.

Suzie was limp as Rachel dressed her in a pair of Disney Princess pajamas. By the time Rachel laid her back down, she was fast asleep again. Rachel pulled the Pack 'n Play next to the couch and grabbed a pillow and blanket off the bed for herself.

She was exhausted. All she wanted to do was curl up and cry herself to sleep. But she needed to find out more about the drug they had been injecting into her daughter. She opened a browser on her phone and started searching.

❖ ❖ ❖

Two hours later, Rachel Jacobs stood at the clinic's front desk, demanding to see Dr. Winters. She was so angry, she could barely see straight. Even though she was holding Suzie, she couldn't stop herself from raising her voice at the receptionist.

Dr. Winters appeared, a confused look on his face. He glanced at her, then Suzie. "It's fine, Margy," he said to the receptionist. "I'll take her back."

Rachel followed him down the examination hallway to an empty room. As soon as they were inside the exam room, she started firing off questions.

"Why the hell did you tell me Respira was safe?"

Dr. Winters stared at her.

"And don't give me this 'because the FDA approved it' shit. Obviously, they were wrong to approve it!" she shouted. "How the hell can you tell a parent that a medicine is *safe*, when even the package insert says that over seventy *horrible* things might go wrong? That she could even die!"

Dr. Winters threw up his hands. "Rachel, let's try to calm down."

"Calm down? Really? Respira gave my daughter seizures again! She could have died!"

"Ms. Jacobs, please, I know this is stressful for you. It is for all of us."

Tears welled in her eyes. "You weren't there. You didn't see her," she said, wiping her nose with her forearm.

Dr. Winters reached out to place his hand on her shoulder, but she recoiled from his touch. She glared at him. "Have you ever *seen* a baby have seizures?"

Dr. Winters nodded. "Yes, I have. It's terrible."

"I want to know why you would tell me Respira didn't cause her seizures when the manufacturer's insert clearly says that it could," she said. She plunged her hand in her purse and plucked out a folded piece of paper. She slammed it on the examination table and banged her hand down on it. "It says it right here. Seizures!"

"Rachel, please calm—"

"Stop *saying* that to me!"

Dr. Winters shut his eyes and pinched the bridge of his nose.

"You *lied* to me! Right to my face! You said that the odds of something bad happening to her were one in a million! That there was a greater chance she could get struck by lightning! Where does it say any of that on this insert?" she asked, slamming her hand down again on the sheet of paper. "Do you have any idea how many parents say the same thing happened to their kids? Seizures and other horrible things? Do you even care?" Rachel asked. "If I'd known there was even a *chance* any of those things could have happened to her, I *never* would have let you give her that poison once, much less twice!"

"The package insert lists *possible* reactions, not *likely* reactions," Dr. Winters said. "But you're right. In Suzie's case, I think we should discontinue the treatment."

Rachel's mouth fell open. "You think?" she said, mocking him.

Rachel saw the door open. Dr. Reynolds, the older doctor with the large gut, was standing in the doorway.

"I'm not saying Respira caused Suzie's seizures," Dr. Winters was saying, "but it's best we eliminate it as a variable so we can get a better idea as to what's going on with her, okay?"

"Are you kidding me?" Rachel snapped, her eyes flitting from Dr. Winters to the big doctor, back to Dr. Winters. "How much more obvious does it have to be for you guys? She gets the damn shot, then a few hours later has seizures. She gets another shot, and the exact same thing happens. Only worse! You don't have to be a damn doctor to see a pattern here!"

"Correlation doesn't equal causation, Ms. Jacobs," the big doctor said.

"It also doesn't equal coincidence! Seriously? Are you really going to stand here and tell me the drug had nothing to do with this?"

The silence in the room was earsplitting.

"The important thing is that she's okay," Dr. Winters said.

"That she's *okay*? Look at her. She hasn't talked or even tried to walk since the seizures yesterday. She won't even smile. NONE of this is okay!"

Rachel looked at Suzie. She was staring into the middle distance as though in some sort of daze, just as she had for hours now.

The big doctor interjected. "Ms. Jacobs, please. Raising your voice isn't helping anyone. For your child's sake, let's be calm here."

"For her sake? Or for yours? Do you not want other parents to hear me? To know what you both did to my daughter?"

"If you're implying we harmed your daughter—"

"Oh, no. I'm not implying. I'm flat-out *telling* you that you did it. Dr. Winters assured me Respira was safe. Twice! And *twice* he lied right to my face."

"Enough, Ms. Jacobs," the big doctor said angrily. "Seizures like Suzie's are common in young children." A vein in the man's neck throbbed. "Look, if you aren't satisfied with the care your daughter is getting here, you are free to leave and not come back."

An icicle of panic shot through Rachel's heart. They wouldn't dare leave Suzie like this. They had to fix her. It was their *job*. She shook her head. "You can't be serious."

"Oh, but I am," he said. "In fact, I'm done arguing with you. I'd like for you to leave now. And please, find another doctor for your daughter. Apparently, this practice isn't a good fit."

Rachel's jaw dropped. "What?"

"Teddy, can I speak to you in the hall—" Dr. Winters started.

Dr. Reynolds threw his arm out in front of him, gesturing for Dr. Winters to be quiet. Then he crossed his arms and stared at her, the corners of his mouth pulled down.

"I can't believe this," Rachel said.

"Goodbye, Ms. Jacobs," the doctor said, his words even, firm.

Hatred flooded Rachel's veins. When she spoke, her voice was laced with venom. "You're both going to regret this."

CHAPTER 20

DANIEL

DANIEL FOUND IT disturbing that a patient's mother had read a package insert, yet the first time he ever had was just this week. All this time he'd simply gone by Teddy's recommendations, a quick search on Medscape and UptoDate.com, and the sound bites the pharmaceutical representatives had given him. Maybe sometimes a quick article in a throwaway journal or newsletter or mentions at the medical conferences he attended. He'd been taught that the information he was getting from these sources was sufficient, but he'd obviously been missing important information.

As he drove home, his brain felt like it had been through a meat grinder. The fact that there hadn't been one thing he could say to help Rachel or Suzie Jacobs made him feel impotent. Rachel had made good points. Simply assuring a parent that Respira was safe when it clearly carried the risk of causing serious injury or even death wasn't—or shouldn't be—enough. As a doctor, he felt he had a responsibility to possess a better understanding of Respira so that he could give parents sufficient information to make informed decisions. He had to supply his patients with all the truth, regardless of how Teddy insisted medicine be practiced at his clinic.

When he walked in the front door, the house again smelled like scented candles and a hot dinner. He was tossing his keys in the bowl by the door when Mia appeared in the foyer, looking especially sexy in a midriff-baring T-shirt and skinny jeans. She was also barefoot, the beautiful arches of her feet on full display, her perfect toes painted with lavender-colored polish. He noticed her hand was wrapped in a bandage.

"What happened to your hand?" he asked.

"It's nothing. Just a little cut. I wasn't paying attention and dropped a glass."

"Want me to look at it?"

"It's fine." She studied his face. "Are *you* okay?" she asked. "You look exhausted."

"I'm fine." But it wasn't true. He wasn't even close to being fine.

She stood on her tiptoes and kissed him on the mouth, then wrapped her arms around him. He breathed in her familiar coconut and lime scent. She hugged him tightly, then pulled away a little so she could see him. There was still concern in her eyes. "Want to talk about it?"

No, Daniel. She can't be trusted.

He stared at her, debating.

"You look like you could use a drink," she said.

He nodded. He needed something to help him calm down, relax.

"I just poured some wine. Chardonnay sound good?"

"Chardonnay sounds great." He wondered again if she knew he'd been drunk last night. Probably so, considering he'd fallen asleep in his clothes. Was there anything else from last night that he should be remembering? Anything he should be embarrassed for? If there was, she wasn't letting on. She seemed to be in as good a mood as always. And concerned.

His thoughts were interrupted by a buzzing sound.

Her phone. It was coming from the back pocket of her jeans. But she didn't check it.

"I made you dinner," she said, her voice soft, sweet.

"It smells fantastic." He tried to smile, but it was beyond him.

Why isn't she checking her phone, Daniel?

Maybe she doesn't want to be rude. Maybe she wants to give me her undivided attention.

You're being naive again.

Shut up.

You still didn't finish that search on her name. Are you afraid of what you'll find?

He'd do it later. He needed to keep his focus on Respira at the moment. If he added anything more to his plate, he might snap.

He really needed that drink.

A couple of them.

He was glad he'd come to his senses and amended his rules so that he wouldn't have to feel guilty for breaking them again.

Three drinks maximum while out.

Three drinks at home.

He probably wouldn't drink to his maximum. It would just give him a bit of cushion.

Mia peeled away from him and walked toward the kitchen, still ignoring her buzzing phone.

They ate at the dining table: chicken kebobs, roasted sweet potatoes and onions, and a homemade carrot cake. They both drank chardonnay with the meal (her, one glass; him, three), enough to put the voice to bed for a little while. The candles in the middle of the table threw shadows over the walls of the room and illuminated her gorgeous face.

"So . . . tell me what's on your mind," she said.

He considered telling her but realized he still distrusted her. Although he'd vowed to himself at least half a dozen times he was going to let go of her lie, it was much easier said than done.

Tonight was different, though. He wanted to forget about it, even if just for a little while. He needed to talk to someone about what was going on at work. Someone whose opinion he respected. He *needed* a confidante. Someone to bounce everything off of. Christ, he wanted so badly to talk to her about it all. He needed her companionship, her softness, her warmth. Besides, he was hardly perfect himself. He'd screwed up just last night, drinking himself into oblivion. He wanted to call it even, but he didn't know if he'd be able to.

Quit making excuses for her. You trusted her, and she lied to you.

"You first," he said. "Tell me about your day."

Mia told him that she'd finally met one of their next-door neighbors, apparently a former child star from an old television show Daniel used to watch when he was in high school. She said they'd talked for a while, and he had been nice and seemed very down-to-earth. But Daniel barely heard her. His mind was already back at the office. In the examination room with Rachel and Suzie Jacobs. Teddy was standing in front of the frightened woman like a big ogre and was telling Rachel that she and her daughter were no longer welcome at the practice. Teddy's behavior had been shocking. Daniel had never known him to act that way with a patient before.

Mia planted an elbow on the table and rested her chin on the palm of her bandaged hand. He noticed again that her nails were just nubs. She'd stopped biting her nails for a while. He couldn't help but wonder why she'd picked up the habit again.

What is she so stressed about, Daniel?

"Okay, your turn," she said. "Something is definitely on your mind. Tell me about it."

She looked legitimately concerned, genuinely loving.

It's an act, Daniel. Don't fall for it.

"I'm here for you. You know that, don't you?" she asked.

He raked his hand over his mouth. Gave her a tight smile, then exhaled loudly. "There's a lot going on at work," he said.

She nodded and narrowed her eyes. "It's that new drug again, isn't it?"

He opened his mouth again, and before he knew it, the words just started spilling out. He told her about his patient, Suzie, having seizures again. About the research he'd done. Research about Respira that had blown his mind. About his argument with Teddy. About how angry Teddy had gotten. About Rachel barging into the office this afternoon, and how Teddy had kicked both her and her daughter out of the practice.

Mia sat patiently the entire time and listened. After he finished, she was quiet. He wondered if she was having cold feet about speaking freely with him, about asking questions after being snapped at the other night on the way home from dinner.

"I wanted to say more to Rachel," he confessed. "But I couldn't. My hands were tied. I've never felt like such a coward in my life. I didn't say anything because I didn't want to put my job in jeopardy. My damn *job*. Christ, who makes a decision based on that?"

"I'd imagine a lot of people do," she said, reaching for his hand.

He shook his head. "Not me. I'm not built that way. I took an oath to do no harm," he said, tears of frustration burning his eyes. The last time he'd cried was at his brother's funeral, decades ago. "I don't believe in this damn immunoceutical. I never did. What you said the other night was spot-on. It seems to be more of a convenience drug than anything. And it might be coming at an awfully high cost to some kids. Just the mere possibility that I could be hurting children makes me feel sick."

He cleared his throat and straightened a little in his seat. "I mean, I could be jumping to conclusions. I have more research to do and people to talk to."

They lapsed into silence, both looking out at the water. Finally Mia spoke. "I found something today I think you'll find interesting."

He waited for her to go on.

"Do you know a Dr. Hemsworth? He's a pediatrician from Sherman Oaks."

He remembered the article he'd read. Hemsworth was the pediatrician who had discontinued Respira due to safety concerns. But how did Mia know about him? He frowned. "Yes, why?"

"So, you know that he supposedly killed himself and his family a couple of nights ago, right?"

Hold on. Yes. He'd heard about that on the radio on his way to work on Monday, but he hadn't connected the dots . . . that the man had been the same doctor who had spoken out about Respira.

"Did you know him?" Mia asked.

Daniel shook his head, thoughts swirling around in his brain. "No, I didn't."

Mia told him about an article she'd read this afternoon about Hemsworth. About the doctor's father saying the murder-suicide had to have been a set-up. Hemsworth Senior said his son loved his family. That they were all very close. He also said he'd ordered a private autopsy just before his son's body had been sent for cremation, and the private pathologist he'd hired had reported that Hemsworth had been shot twice in the chest.

"What?" Daniel said. "How do you shoot yourself twice in the chest?"

"I know, right?" Mia said. "Hemsworth Senior said his son called him the day prior to the murders, saying that he'd received a death threat and had asked for advice on what he should do. When Hemsworth Senior asked his son who was threatening him, he said it was someone who was angry that he'd been talking publicly about the harm Respira had caused his patients."

Daniel raked his hand over his mouth, trying to comprehend what Mia was saying.

"There's also a witness. A teenage boy who was dating Hemsworth's daughter claims he received text messages from her the night the family was killed. She wrote that someone had broken into their home, and she was hiding. She begged him to call 911."

"That makes no sense. How could they call it a suicide with all that information?" Daniel said.

Mia shrugged. "I have no idea."

"Where'd you see this story?"

"Online. It was buried in the *Los Angeles Times*'s website. I was going to send it to you, but now I can't find it."

❀❀❀

An hour later, Mia grabbed Daniel's hand and led him upstairs to the bedroom.

In bed, they kissed, and he buried his head in her hair, lulled by the connection they'd made. He realized he'd been starving to reconnect with her. And now that he had, he was feeling much less stressed. While his problems hadn't gone away, he was feeling much less alone now that he'd had the chance to vent. Mia pressed her body against his and kissed him hard on the mouth; then her lips moved to his neck, his chest, his stomach. As she began making her way down even lower, he realized something was very wrong. He wasn't responding sexually.

What the hell's going on? he wondered, trying to will himself to respond, but it wasn't working.

Mia looked up. "Is everything okay?" she whispered, her voice throaty and deep. "Am I doing something wrong?"

His face burning, he sat up. "God, no. You're perfect. I . . . I don't know what the problem is. This has never happened before."

It's because you're onto her, Daniel. You might think you've forgiven her, but you haven't.

Dammit, he wished the voice would just shut the hell up. Usually, the alcohol silenced it. Now all the negative emotions he'd brought home flooded back into his mind with a vengeance. On top of it all, he was also embarrassed.

She kissed him again. But knowing it would be no use, he gently extricated himself from her. "It's not you," he said, feeling his neck flush. "I guess I just have too much on my mind."

He wanted to change his rules yet again, go to the kitchen, grab another drink, self-medicate, calm down.

Don't. Do something that will help you think more clearly. Go for a run.

He hadn't run for months now. Before meeting Mia, he'd run several miles daily. So much had changed since meeting her. He crawled out of bed and went to his bureau. He grabbed a pair of sweats and yanked them on. "Sorry. I've just got so much on my mind. Maybe I'll go for a run."

Mia sat up in bed, pulling the sheets up over her naked body. "Really? This late?"

"Yeah. Maybe it'll help." He went to the closet for a sweatshirt.

"Want company?" she asked.

"No, thanks. I need to be alone. Then I've got more research to do." He grabbed his running shoes.

"Daniel?"

"What?" he asked, slipping on his shoes.

She folded her arms across her body. "I know this is probably a horrible time to ask for a favor, but I really need one."

He turned, curious. "Of course. What is it?"

"I need to borrow some money."

Money? The request had come out of left field. She'd never asked for money before. Besides, they had a joint account. "Is everything okay?" he asked.

"It's for a friend who's in a terrible bind." She looked uncomfortable, even squeamish.

A friend?

A scream sliced through his brain. "We're married," he said. "What's mine is yours. You don't have to borrow it."

She was silent. It was obvious she was uncomfortable asking. And he didn't want to make her more uncomfortable.

"How much do you need?"

"Five thousand dollars."

Billy's words flashed into his mind. *They only want guys like you for the money. They bide their time until they can ask for a divorce. Then they happily drive away with half of everything.*

He had no doubt that many women were capable of doing just that, but this was his wife they were talking about. Not some gold-digging con artist. And she was asking for the money, not stealing it.

"You know your name is on our joint account, right?" he asked. "And the checks are in the top drawer of my desk."

"I know. But I wouldn't feel right just taking that kind of money and not asking you."

"I appreciate that, but it's your money, too. It's fine."

Ask her who this friend of hers is. It's probably the person who keeps texting her. The one she doesn't want you to know about.

He lingered in the doorway, hoping she'd offer more information. But she didn't say a word.

Ask her, dammit.

"Thank you," was all she finally offered.

He nodded.

As he walked from the room, he realized that for the first time in days, he and the voice were in full agreement. Not only did he accept that she was hiding something, he wanted to know what.

❖❖❖

He was almost to the back door when he realized he'd forgotten his jacket.

As he lumbered back up the stairs to grab it, the pipes began rattling in the wall. Mia must be getting in the shower. Apparently, evening showers were becoming a thing for her. He reached the bedroom, and sure enough, Mia was nowhere in sight. The door to the shower was closed, and the water was running.

Find her phone, the voice blurted. *Find out who's been texting her.*
He hesitated.

Stop trying to be a saint, and do it.

He stared at the closed door again. Okay, fine, he decided. Just this one time.

Without giving himself a chance to second-guess the decision, he looked around for her phone. It wasn't on the bed or on either bedside table or on the bathroom counter. His heart beating in his throat, he found the skinny jeans she'd been wearing earlier on the floor. But it was no longer in the back pocket.

Her purse.

She usually kept it in the closet. He opened the closet door and saw it hanging in its usual place. He grabbed it, then dug his hand inside and pulled out her phone, a pen, and some coins. He threw the other items back in her purse and listened to see if the shower was still running.

It was.

He pressed the touch screen. A password request filled the phone's screen.

Dammit.

He tried her birthday. No. Their wedding anniversary. No. *Shit.* Their address. No.

Try 1111, the voice said.

She'd talked about those numbers a few times over the months. Apparently, the numerology books she'd read had an impact on her. He punched them in and was granted access.

He quickly found the Text app icon and pressed it. Her in-box popped up, and a list of text messages appeared. But the list was short. He frowned. There were only texts from him. Yet, in the last week, he'd heard several texts coming in. He'd seen her texting. There'd been a text tonight.

But those texts were gone.

There's only one reason she'd delete them, Daniel.

He checked her call log. Again, only calls from him and to him. That log had been freshly edited as well.

He squeezed his eyes shut. Then feeling more agitated and confused than he had when he'd arrived home from the office, he returned her phone to her purse and grabbed his own phone to text Billy.

CHAPTER 21

Rachel

GUILT CLAWED AT Rachel as she chastised herself for not researching Respira before agreeing to give it to Suzie. For simply trusting Dr. Winters. She usually researched everything—from what foods to feed her daughter to the safest cribs and toys—so why hadn't she researched this damn drug?

She remembered the first time she'd held Suzie. She promised herself that she'd do everything within her power to make sure her little girl had the best life possible. That she'd keep her safe and make sure her life turned out better than her own had. She'd let her down, hadn't she?

She paced the apartment, trying to figure out what to do. Suzie still wasn't herself. Although she hadn't had any repeat seizures, she still wasn't talking or walking, and she still had that faraway look in her eyes. Her diapers were still awful, and she was sleeping way more than normal. Instead of chattering away like she usually did, she just sat in the Pack 'n Play and stared off into space or at the walls.

This morning, Rachel had taken her to a pediatric clinic in the valley that accepted walk-ins. The female doctor had examined her for all of five minutes and declared she was fine. She said it wasn't uncommon for kids Suzie's age to regress a little. Just to make sure to offer her plenty of Pedialyte and other fluids while she had diarrhea so she wouldn't get dehydrated.

But Rachel knew that Suzie wasn't okay.

She wasn't okay at all.

Now that it was clear that the doctors weren't going to help her, Rachel decided to write a quick post on a support group she'd found on Facebook to see if she could get help from other parents.

She'd meant what she told Dr. Winters and the heavyset doctor. She wasn't going to let them get away with not telling the truth about the drug and hurting her daughter. Although she wasn't sure what she was going to do yet, she was going to do something.

Last night, she'd reached out to an old acting friend whose boyfriend was a reporter for a local NBC affiliate, and she'd asked him if he would cover Suzie's story. The journalist said that if Suzie had been hurt by her crib or some toy, he'd be all over it, but his network generally shied away from reporting negative stories about certain pharmaceutical drugs, particularly vaccines, because the manufacturers accounted for a large portion of their advertising dollars.

Rachel tried to figure out what to do about work. Although Jeff had told her to take Thursday and Friday off, he had been very clear that he expected to see her on Monday. It was a relief that he'd given her the days off because there was no way she could have left Suzie with Martha. Not so soon after the seizures. But now she had to make plans for next week.

She remembered her sister, Laura, had a small apartment above her garage in Minnesota, and as far as she knew, it was empty. Maybe she'd let them move in there for a little while. The cost of living was much cheaper in Minnesota. Plus, she could help Laura care for their mother, which would take some of the pressure off Laura and her family. It could be a win-win all around.

Taking a deep breath, she picked up her phone and called her sister. When she got Laura on the phone, she told her about the recent seizures. How the emergency room doctor and the new pediatrician said Suzie seemed fine now.

"Oh, good," Laura said.

"No, it's not good, because she's definitely not fine."

She could hear her sister sigh as if to say, *Here she goes again.*

"Seriously, Laura, she's acting really weird. If you saw her, you'd say the same thing."

"Weird how?"

Rachel told her about everything. "She's not even walking. This is not normal for her."

She also told her what she'd read on the internet. The things other parents were reporting. But when her sister went quiet, Rachel decided she'd better change the subject.

"Did you ever rent out your garage apartment?" she asked.

"Not yet. I don't know what the problem is. It's a great space."

"Would you consider letting me and Suzie stay there? Just for a while? Until I can get back on my feet? I'm thinking of moving back. At least for the time being. I could help you take care of Mom."

The other end of the line was silent. "Well, I don't know. Maybe. I don't . . ."

Rachel's face burned. Laura was searching for an excuse to say no, wasn't she? She could feel anger bubbling up inside her, and she was afraid of what either one of them would say next.

"Someone's at the door," Rachel lied. "I need to go."

Rachel ended the call quickly, before she said something she'd regret. She went to Suzie and gathered her into her arms. "I wish we had more family, sweet pea," she said, her voice cracking. She couldn't remember feeling so alone. So afraid. "I miss you talking to me. It's been so long since I've heard you say *Mama*. Can you say *Mama*, sweetie? Please? Just one time?"

Suzie didn't respond. She just stared at Rachel's chin.

Rachel sat on the couch and bounced Suzie on her lap. "Who's my sweet baby girl?" she asked, placing her face really close to Suzie's, hoping to get a smile out of her. She held Suzie's hands and lifted them up above her shoulders. "You are, Suzie! You are!" she sang.

But Suzie just grimaced and pulled away.

Tears burned Rachel's eyes. "Oh, honey. What's wrong?"

Suzie just blinked.

"I wish you could tell Mommy what you're feeling."

Rachel burst into tears. And once she started, she couldn't stop. She held her daughter against her chest and bawled.

Her phone dinged. A Facebook message was coming through. Wiping her face with the heel of her hand, she reached over and grabbed it. It was from someone named Sadie Carter, who was also part of the Respira support group. She accepted it.

> I read your post about your daughter. My 6-year-old son goes to Healing Hands, too. He sees Dr. Reynolds and has been having horrible migraines since his Respira injections, but the doctor said it was just a coincidence. But like you, I'm not buying it anymore. Anyway, a few of us are picketing in front of the clinic Monday morning in hopes of drumming up some media coverage. Would you be interested in joining us?

Rachel had just finished reading the message when she heard another message come in. This one from someone named Gail Whitman:

> I read what you posted about your daughter and
> would like to talk to you. I'm a journalist and run
> GetTheFactsAboutRespira.com. You're in the LA
> area, right?

❀❀❀

An hour later, Gail Whitman was on Rachel's doorstep. The journalist was an attractive woman with chin-length red hair and a kind face and seemed to be somewhere in her thirties.

Rachel invited her into the living room and took her coat. Then she lifted Suzie out of the Pack 'n Play. "This is my daughter, Suzie."

"Hi, Suzie," the woman said, smiling at her. Suzie didn't react.

"She's been doing this ever since the second shot. Looking so vacant. Like she's in a world of her own. She behaved this way after the first shot for about a day, but then she stopped and became her usual self again. The doctors say it's normal. Do you think she looks normal?"

Gail's eyes were warm. She shook her head. "I'm sorry, but no. It doesn't look normal at all."

Rachel nodded and offered to make Gail tea, then set Suzie back in the Pack 'n Play and went to the kitchen to prepare it. She poured water into the kettle and turned on the stove.

"So, like I told you on the phone," Gail said, pulling a laptop out of her bag and opening it, "I'm trying to get as many parents' stories out there as possible. There are an alarming number of you guys, especially considering this drug is so new. I want to do my part in making sure you are heard."

"How many parents have you spoken to?" Rachel asked, carrying a tray with two mismatched teacups and the teapot into the living room. She sat it on the coffee table in front of them and sat down across from Gail.

"You're number seventeen, and I have two more interviews scheduled for this week."

"All these kids are having seizures?"

"Some. Not all. Some families are reporting other symptoms."

"Like what?"

"Migraines, muscle weakness, transverse myelitis, speech impairment . . . all symptoms that could point to brain inflammation."

Rachel frowned. "So, you're saying Respira is inflaming their brains?"

"It appears as though it might be. The doctors and researchers who have been willing to talk to me about it think it's the amount of adjuvant in the drug. It's very high."

Gail explained that an adjuvant was a substance that was added to a drug to create an immune response. She said that in Respira's case, the adjuvant was aluminum phosphate. Each dose of Respira contained a very large amount of it.

"My sister says that any dangerous ingredients are in trace amounts. Amounts that aren't supposed to hurt children."

Gail studied her as though trying to figure out the best way to respond. "Let me put it to you this way," she said. "Say a child who is allergic to bees is stung by one. How much venom does it take for that child to develop an anaphylactic reaction and for his throat to close up? Not much, right?"

Rachel nodded.

"Besides, there are top aluminum scientists who say that there are no safe amounts when we're talking about injection because when injected straight into the bloodstream, the aluminum bypasses most of the body's filters and therefore can't be properly excreted," Gail said.

"If that's the case, why are they putting aluminum in drugs at all?" Rachel asked.

Gail shrugged. "Parents have been asking this question for decades. Now that there's more science available, a growing list of doctors and scientists are asking the same thing."

Rachel told Gail what the reporter for the local NBC affiliate had told her.

"Yes, isn't that maddening?" Gail said. "The drug industry has the media in their pocket, so no major network is going to report anything but positive messaging about Respira. Especially now that there's such a big push to get it on the vaccine schedule. It's sad, really. If Respira were a malfunctioning car seat, the media would be all over it. It would take just one severe injury, and a recall would be demanded. But when children die or are permanently disabled by pharmaceutical products like Respira, the media is as quiet as a mouse."

Rachel's leg was trembling. She pressed her heel to the ground to get it to stop.

"You wrote that Suzie screamed a lot after both doses?" Gail asked.

"Yes. Loud, constant, horrible screams. And she kept arching her back."

Gail nodded. "Many of the other parents I've spoken to have reported the same chain of events in their children. The constant, high-pitched screaming, then a reaction a few hours to even several days later. They call it an encephalitic cry. Many experts say it's caused by swelling of the brain."

Swelling of the brain? Rachel was horrified. "But her CT scan came back normal."

"Don't get me wrong. I'm not saying this was the case with your daughter. I'm a journalist, not a doctor. But having said that, while a CT scan can identify encephalitis, it can't rule it out. An MRI is more sensitive and reliable for identifying encephalitic changes."

"Well, if that's the case, then why didn't they do an MRI?"

"It's much more expensive. Also, not all emergency rooms have the machines."

Rachel shook her head. "Why would Dr. Winters lie to me and tell me it was safe?"

"He might not have been lying. He might honestly think it is. We as a culture seem to think that doctors know a lot about the drugs they prescribe, but that's not always the case."

"Can I sue him for hurting her? Or sue the clinic?"

"Unfortunately, no. With this class of drug, doctors and even the drug manufacturers can't be sued, even in cases when a child dies as a result of being administered the drug. They're completely protected." Gail went on, "Back in the 1980s, drug manufacturers threatened Congress saying they'd stop selling vaccines in the United States unless a law was passed giving them full immunity. Now the liability shield exists to protect the manufacturers and to ensure the continued development and sales of vaccines."

CHAPTER 22

DANIEL

DANIEL SAT AT one of the tables in the back of Jiminy's and pored over the information that he'd printed out on Respira while he waited for Billy to show up.

After spending several more hours reading and watching testimony from experts and reading parent testimonials and studies, he had more than enough information now to present to the small group of doctors at tomorrow's monthly brunch. He was going to show his colleagues what he'd discovered, and they could all figure out what to do about it together. Most of the others had more experience than he did and were well connected. They'd know what to do.

Certainly, the first step would be calling a meeting with Immunext. Also, discontinuing the administration of the drug at each of their clinics until they knew for sure it was safe. After tomorrow's brunch meeting, Teddy would finally understand his concerns, and he would no longer feel so alone.

Quit pushing Teddy. He's going to fire you.

Daniel didn't agree. Ignoring the voice, he looped back to what Mia had said about Dr. Hemsworth. He'd tried to find the article in the *Los Angeles Times* that she had said she'd read, but it was nowhere to be found. Daniel thought about the death threat she said the doctor had received. Mia said she didn't find it difficult to believe that a drug manufacturer or someone with strong financial ties to a drug would make a threat of that nature, but Daniel couldn't even begin to wrap his head around something like that being possible. It seemed more like a far-fetched conspiracy you'd find only in movies and books. Not real life. But maybe he was being naive.

Speaking of Mia, he looked around now, feeling a little intrusive for showing up unannounced to eat at the restaurant where she worked. It would probably look like he was spying on her. But, to be honest, he kind of was. He glanced at his watch. Mia's shift should be starting in five minutes. Billy was already twenty minutes late, and this time it annoyed him. If Billy couldn't be on time, would he be able to trust him to—

As if to answer his concern, he heard Billy's laughter from the front of the restaurant. A moment later, he appeared, swaggering to the booth and chatting with Julie, the blonde hostess with whom Daniel had left the first bouquet of orchids. The young woman wore an amused smile as she informed them that their server would be with them soon.

Billy plopped down in the chair opposite Daniel, his black shirt wrinkled and untucked. He gazed out at the ocean view from the restaurant's panoramic windows and let out a low whistle.

"Holy shit. This is even nicer than the other place. You are seriously living the life."

Yeah. I'm living the life, all right.

"Hey, I saw that ancient Tahoe of yours in the parking lot. When are you going to upgrade? Keep up with the Joneses a little better?"

"It runs fine. And I couldn't care less about the Joneses."

Billy laughed. "Whatever you say." He leaned forward, serious now. "So . . . you changed your mind and want me to follow your old lady, huh?"

Daniel nodded, feeling slightly nauseated.

Don't feel bad, Daniel. She asked for this.

The voice was right. Mia was obviously hiding something, and it was time to find out what. Who was she texting? Whose calls was she deleting? Where was she going if she wasn't going to work?

Find out, then kick her ass to the curb.

He forced the voice into its room. As he was shutting the door, it resisted. He pushed harder, and the door slammed shut.

Daniel saw Mia hurry into the restaurant and disappear behind a door that led to the kitchen. "She just showed up," he said, picking up his bourbon and taking a long pull.

"Where?"

Daniel watched Mia appear again and pointed toward the kitchen's swinging door. "She's the brunette."

Daniel studied his wife, not used to seeing her in this environment. She was wearing the Jiminy's employee uniform: a clingy white polo shirt and black jeans that hugged her amazing ass. Even though the waitresses all dressed the same, Mia definitely stood out.

"Her?" Billy asked.

"Yep," Daniel said, watching her walk to a computer.

"Damn, man."

"I told you."

Mia turned toward them to scan the restaurant, and her eyes met Daniel's. She froze, her face registering surprise. But then her features relaxed, and a smile spread across her face. She walked over, her gait confident, her hips swaying. "Well, this is a pleasant surprise. When you texted me that you were going out to dinner tonight, you didn't mention it would be here."

Daniel watched her closely. If she was uncomfortable about his being here, she didn't show it. He stood up and planted a kiss on her cheek. "I figured as long as I'm meeting a friend, I might as well get to see my beautiful wife."

He introduced Mia to Billy, and she stretched out her hand.

Billy took her hand in his and smiled. "Anything Dan's said about me is a complete lie."

"What if it was something nice?" Mia asked.

"Then he wasn't talking about me," Billy answered. He winked at Daniel.

Mia laughed, and her smile almost melted Daniel's heart.

Almost.

"Sorry, I got here a little late, so I need to get moving," she said. "I'll stop by in a few minutes to say hi, okay?"

They said their goodbyes, and Daniel watched her walk away. He noticed Billy was still staring at her.

"Stop drooling," Daniel murmured. His words came out harsher than he'd intended. He glanced at his drink. "Sorry. It's just . . ."

. . . that you've been drinking.

"No, man. I get it. You're stressed."

"Anyway, I told you she was gorgeous."

"Yeah, but everyone says that about their wives when they first get married. But shit, man. I can see why you're worried." Billy stared intently at Daniel. "I don't get it. You're a doctor . . . you're loaded . . . so, why is she still waitressing?"

"It's a long story," Daniel said, not wanting to get into it. "So . . . how does all this work?"

Billy leaned in closer and took on a more businesslike tone. "I've been getting $5k for this type of job, but since you're a friend, let's cut that in half. Twenty-five hundred, and we'll call it a day," he said.

"What does that include?"

"It includes following her for seven days, *if* I need that long. And so far, I haven't," Billy said. "I can start with day number one tonight, if you want me to."

Daniel nodded. "Okay, what else?"

"At the end of the seven days, you'll get a full report on where she went, people she talked to, how long she was with them. If there's anything worth photographing—and there always is—you'll get all the pictures. Sometimes video, too. Just depends on how close I can get without being seen."

Daniel scowled, his imagination running wild. But he needed to know the truth. At this point, anything would be better than worrying.

"Just so you know, though, I might have to duck out every once in a while to help Mikey because he's been really busy and depends on my help, but in cases when I can't watch her, I'll let you know, okay?"

Daniel nodded.

"Looks like I may be on the clock a little early," Billy grunted, yanking Daniel from the thoughts pinballing in his head.

He turned to see what Billy was referring to. A male server who looked like he could model for Calvin Klein was standing behind Mia as she gazed down at a clipboard. His hands were cupping her shoulders, and he was whispering something into her ear. Whatever he was saying was making her laugh.

They looked comfortable together.

Too comfortable.

That's probably where your five G's went.

Something primal flashed through Daniel. He considered getting up and walking up to the guy. Manually removing his hands from his wife's body. Mia pushed away from the guy and punched him playfully on the shoulder. Then she walked off and began tending to one of her tables.

Daniel tossed back the rest of his drink, an intense molten anger burning inside of him. He'd never considered himself a jealous man. But then again, he'd never felt as deeply and passionately for anyone as he did for Mia.

CHAPTER 23

DANIEL

THE NEXT MORNING, Daniel reminded himself to breathe as he removed his car key from his key ring and handed it to the valet outside of the Zephyr Grill, an upscale steak and seafood restaurant and popular weekend brunch spot in Brentwood.

The image of the young male server's hands on his wife's shoulders last night had been seared into his mind. The ease with which he'd seen the guy lay his hands on his wife had been disturbing. The guy had been young. Early to midtwenties. Is that what Mia liked? Younger guys? If so, he'd made a huge mistake.

I've been telling you this all along.

Shut up.

After returning from dinner with Billy last night, Daniel had changed his mind about waiting to look up Mia again online. But instead of finding anything unsettling about her, he'd found nothing. He wasn't sure what he'd expected to find. Maybe photos of her with an ex-boyfriend or two. Or something concerning that would raise suspicions, like maybe a secret social media account. But not only did he not find any of these things, he didn't find anything. Just one photograph of her with what appeared to be her coworkers at Jiminy's. Besides that one photograph, she didn't seem to have an internet footprint whatsoever.

That in and of itself raised suspicions. Who *didn't* have an internet footprint these days? Who didn't have at least one social media account? He knew she was private and didn't have a lot of friends. In fact, she'd mentioned only one friend to him, a guy named Sam who was in the military and stationed overseas. The guy was someone she'd known since childhood. But Daniel was the same way. Aside from dinners with Billy or Claire, and maybe playing racquetball every once in a while with Andy, he didn't really socialize, either.

He made another note to ask Billy if he knew someone who ran background checks. And once he was on the other side of this Respira stuff, maybe he'd hire someone to do one.

As the hostess led him through the maze of brunch-time patrons to the reserved table on the patio, the voice in his head wouldn't stop cautioning him. It had been warning him ever since he woke up early this morning.

Don't do this, Daniel. Teddy's going to be pissed.

He knew Teddy wasn't going to like what he was going to say. But he also knew that the man would have no choice but to consider examining Respira more closely once he saw all the information Daniel had compiled, how concerned all the other doctors would be.

In Teddy's defense, Daniel hadn't done the best job of presenting his suspicions so far. But this time, it would be different.

The hostess showed him to the table that had been reserved for his group, and Daniel found himself to be the first to have arrived.

Good. That gave him time to gather his thoughts.

He chose a place at the round table that provided him a good view of the rest of the seating area.

The patio was packed with people, and the air was dancing with lively conversation and laughter. He watched a group of heavily made-up women clink champagne flutes filled with what appeared to be mimosas. They made him think of Mia again.

About Billy following her.

He hoped to God that what Mia was hiding was innocent enough.

Daniel felt like a pigeon was trapped in his chest as he opened the folder in front of him and shuffled the packets of photocopied documents he'd put together.

Throw those away.

They'll want to know, he countered. *They'll thank me. After all, no one wants to hurt kids, especially doctors. Once they know what's going on, they'll want to examine the information, too.*

He glanced up and saw a famous actor and his wife waving to him from a few tables down. The wife's face looked shiny, pulled tight, and Daniel remembered hearing his nurse, Deepali, mention she'd recently had another round of plastic surgery. Their granddaughter was a patient of his. Daniel waved back, marveling at what his life had become. That he sometimes found himself sitting among people like this, some of Hollywood's most elite—it was a far cry from the crowded trailer back in Tyler, Texas.

You do understand you could lose all this by pushing Teddy too far, don't you?

He flinched as he pushed the voice back to where it belonged.

"You okay, sir?" the waitress asked, carrying a silver pitcher.

"I'm fine." He smiled. "If that's coffee, I'd love a cup."

She poured him coffee. After she left, he took a big gulp of the hot liquid, then closed his eyes and tried to center himself. He concentrated on the slight chill in the air. The ray of sun that was warming his shoulder. He was releasing a deep breath when he heard a voice boom, "Hey, guys, looks like there's a vagrant sleeping at our table!"

Teddy.

Daniel opened his eyes and watched his boss choose the seat next to him. He greeted Daniel with one of his trademark blows to the back. Teddy was flanked by Chet Wahler, an older and well-respected pediatrician from Beverly Hills. Both men were dressed in ugly plaid pants and bright shirts, likely heading for the golf course after brunch.

Chet was a big, formidable man with a receding hairline and leathery skin. He held out his hand to Daniel and grinned. "Dammit, kid. You look like you haven't slept since your wedding. Good for you."

Daniel smiled nervously. He'd always found Chet a little imposing. He was powerful. A pretty big deal in the medical community. All three of the senior physicians were.

In the next five minutes, another Beverly Hills pediatrician, Roy Alexander, arrived. Tall and athletically built with brilliant white hair, piercing blue eyes, and a strong jawline, he looked more like a movie star than a doctor. He was with Collin Sheers, a young pediatrician who had just started at Roy's practice. Collin's red hair blazed in the late morning sun as he took the only remaining seat at the table.

After placing their brunch orders, Roy announced that the younger doctor, Collin, was expecting his first child with his wife.

"I recommend hiring a couple of good nannies," Chet said. "Otherwise, once that baby comes, your weekends are going to be filled with nothing but diapers and screaming."

The doctors participated in more small talk. The mood was loose and friendly, but Daniel was only half-present. He was going over the facts in his head. The best way to present them.

I'm telling you, Daniel. Don't. Do. This.

"You okay there, Danny?" Teddy asked.

Daniel smiled. "Yeah, why?"

"You look like you just shit your pants."

Daniel forced a grin. "No, I'm fine."

When there was a break in the conversation, Daniel took a deep breath and seized the opportunity. "So, I'm guessing everyone here is prescribing Respira by now," he said.

Chet, Roy, and Collin nodded.

Next to him, Teddy cleared his throat. Daniel avoided his eyes.

"Why do you ask?" Roy asked, taking a long sip of his water.

"I was just wondering if you've received any complaints about it from parents."

He scanned all the faces, except for Teddy's. He heard his boss shift in his seat.

"Complaints?" Collin asked.

"Any severe adverse reactions," Daniel answered.

Chet chuckled, and his eyes darted in Teddy's direction. "What's this about?"

Daniel opened the folder and started passing out the sixty-three-page packets he had prepared. He placed a packet in front of each of the doctors. Everyone except Collin just stared at the cover without picking theirs up. Collin leafed through his.

"I think you're going to be troubled by what I've discovered," Daniel said. "Or hopefully, you know something that can put my fears to rest." Daniel glanced at everyone and went on. "A colleague told me he's been witnessing significant injuries in his clinic, including a cardiac arrest. Then a patient of mine, an eighteen-month-old female, experienced a seizure after her first dose. Then again after her second."

"Anomalies," Teddy muttered beside him, his tone cool.

"Like Teddy said, those are exceptions," said Roy. "You don't know if Respira caused her seizures. These children are in formative stages. Anything could have triggered these symptoms."

"Tell me," Chet interrupted. "Did the cardiac arrest happen instantly?"

"Within ten minutes of administration," Daniel said. "And hundreds of parents are reporting injuries after their child's treatments."

"Hundreds?" Roy asked, the crease between his manicured eyebrows deepening. "What do you mean? At your practice?"

Daniel turned to another page in his packet. "No. All over the country. There are groups of parents online who say—"

Roy chuckled.

Teddy joined him with laughter of his own. "Didn't I warn you about getting your medical information from Google? You need to spend more time in the journals, son."

Chet stared at Daniel, appearing amused.

Daniel's face grew hot. "There are over five thousand parents in one group alone on Facebook who are concerned—"

"Facebook? Social media is doing peer-reviewed studies now?" Teddy asked.

More laughter.

If they'd only let him finish a sentence, they'd see where he was going. He asked them if they were aware that a child had even died of respiratory arrest during the short study that preceded it going to market. That Respira hadn't been studied nearly long enough to demonstrate it could boost a child's immune system.

"Teddy, where'd you get this guy?" Chet asked.

"Look, Dan," Teddy said, completely ignoring the fact that he'd just said that a child had died during the drug's study. "The parents complaining about Respira probably mean well, but they don't know what the hell they're talking about. They're not doctors. And we've all seen rumors and untruths take hold on social media and spread like wildfire."

"You should at least read their stories," Daniel continued. "There are so many of them, and their stories are so similar."

"And anecdotal," Teddy said.

"Since when do we disregard evidence simply because it's anecdotal?" Daniel asked. "Anecdotal evidence is the basis for hypothesis. Hypothesis leads to research."

The table went quiet.

Now that he had their attention, he told him about two emergency room physicians he'd spoken to who claimed their teams had noted a marked increase in pediatric seizures over the last three months. "And the common denominator? Most of those patients had recently received Respira."

"And most of those patients probably recently ate peanut butter or vanilla ice cream," Teddy muttered.

I told you, Daniel. They don't give a damn. Just laugh it off like you were only joking, and change the subject.

"Did you know there's a lawsuit in Japan? And that they banned Respira due to safety concerns?"

Everyone was staring at him.

Good. They were still listening. He'd need to be quick and get into the studies before he was interrupted again.

"Do you know how much aluminum phosphate is in Respira?"

"If you're one of those people who has an irrational fear of chemicals, I'm afraid you're in the wrong profession, kid," Chet said. "Besides, the science has been settled about aluminum. It's perfectly safe in the amounts—"

Daniel shook his head. "That's what I thought, too, Chet. But it may not be true. Look on page ten."

Only Collin flipped to page ten. The other doctors just gazed at him. Daniel tried not to let it fluster him.

"Aluminum being safe might simply be old science. Not only old, but the studies that showed it was safe were not structured in accordance with established scientific principles and have been summarily debunked by scientists all around the world. On top of that, there's new science, and a lot of it, that says that injected aluminum can lead to many neurological issues, including brain damage. Not only are they finding high levels of aluminum in the brains of Alzheimer's patients but also brain-damaged children. And just one dose of Respira contains the upper limit of—"

Chet waved his hand. "That's absurd, Winters! Aluminum is everywhere. In food, water. If small amounts of aluminum were so damn deadly, we would all be dead right now."

"But there's a fundamental difference between ingesting aluminum and injecting it. Aluminum that's injected directly into the bloodstream bypasses most of our excretory channels," Daniel said, talking quickly. He shook the packet in his hand. "Twenty pages in this packet are abstracts from top aluminum scientists who have found that this form of aluminum can also cross the blood-brain barrier, which can cause a shitstorm of neurological issues and autoimmune conditions. Many cancers, even. The injected aluminum adjuvant that Respira contains has been shown to trigger immune activation events—"

"That's exactly what it's *supposed* to do!" Chet interjected. "Stimulate a stronger immune response."

"But the aluminum might be doing more than just stimulating an immune response. It appears it's also triggering an immune activation event in the brains of some children. The very neurological injuries that appear as adverse reactions on the insert are injuries that are caused by aluminum."

"One in a million," chimed Chet.

"Again, respectfully, I'm afraid that's not even close to being true. Look, flip to page fifty-three. There've been over six hundred safety reports filed. Not only that, but these are just the reported cases. The government estimates that only one percent of events like these are reported because a lot of practitioners and parents don't even know about this reporting system."

No one but Collin was flipping the pages.

Stop, Daniel.

Daniel stared at the doctors. "Aren't you guys seeing a big problem here?"

Silence.

"Guys, when parent after parent reports similar events with Respira as the common denominator, we have a responsibility to start paying attention. Don't we?"

"If it wasn't safe, then how did it pass the safety studies?" Roy asked.

Yes! He finally had someone's interest. "Well, here's the thing. In clinical trials, instead of using a saline solution placebo as a control, Immunext used a placebo that contained aluminum. Which I'm sure we all know can artificially increase the appearance of safety. Think about it, guys. There was no true placebo control. Isn't that insane?"

He noticed Roy was staring at Teddy—and he didn't look happy.

The waitress arrived with the food.

"I think I need another Bloody Mary, stat," Chet said to the waitress.

Roy and Teddy ordered second drinks as well. As the waitress left, Chet turned to Collin and pointed at his Apple Watch: "That thing worth the price tag?"

"Oh, absolutely," Collin said. He began to tell Chet about the watch's features. Daniel listened to the conversation in disbelief. The two doctors seemed more interested in a damn watch than the possibility that a drug they were giving kids could be dangerous!

"All right, enough business," Teddy said, clapping his hands. "My eggs Benedict require my undivided attention."

Daniel's pulse sped up even more.

Don't even think about opening your mouth again.

I have to! This isn't right. They're intentionally looking the other way.

Daniel stared incredulously at his colleagues. "Guys, I don't understand. How can you just sit here when—"

"Shut up, Daniel," Teddy growled. "You're ruining our brunch. You've said your piece. Now let it go."

Toe the damn line, Daniel.

Chet asked Collin to pass the buttered croissants that had been set in front of him. Roy groaned as he stuck a forkful of eggs into his mouth. He chewed a few times. "I have dreams about these eggs."

Daniel's heart was thumping so hard, he could see the front of his shirt moving.

Just shut up now, Daniel. You've worked so hard for this career.

But Daniel wasn't done. "Can someone tell me where I'm wrong? Look, I *want* to be wrong about this. But if I'm not, what do we do? We've got some important questions to ask. Of Immunext. Of the FDA or the CDC or the American Academy of Pediatrics. I honestly don't know where to start, but I knew you guys would."

Just the sounds of chewing.

Blood surged in his veins. "We're the ones on the front lines seeing these injuries in real time. As they happen. Isn't asking questions part of our job?"

"No. It is not," Teddy snapped. "That's the job of the research-ers and regulatory agencies. Our job is to take care of our patients. Diagnose them and administer FDA-approved medications."

"But what if the researchers are wrong? Or, God forbid, biased?"

Nothing.

"How about all the parents begging to be heard? Do we just ignore their concerns?"

"That's what therapists are for," Teddy said, a vein throbbing in his neck.

Chet regarded Daniel. "Thanks for entertaining us this morning, Winters, but I'm going to tell you what we're all going to do, okay?" He leaned forward in his seat and lowered his voice. "We're going to prescribe Respira as we've been doing until the FDA tells us to stop. And we're going to enjoy our big fat paychecks while we're doing it. And going forward, we're going to shut the hell up about what we read about on the internet in our spare time. If we were supposed to be privy to this information, it would be published in our journals.

Got it?" Chet fixed him with a hard stare. "Let me give you a piece of advice: In this business, the last thing you want to do is make waves. Make waves, and you'll destroy your career." His eyes flitted to Teddy. "*And* your practice."

Daniel stared incredulously at the man, then watched Teddy smile at everyone in apology. Teddy threw Daniel a cautionary look, leaned over, and hissed, "Not one more fucking word. Understand? Not one."

Teddy turned back to the other doctors and quickly shifted the conversation to golf.

Twenty minutes later, everyone except Teddy had left. Collin was the only one who even bothered to take his information packet, but Daniel noticed him throw something in the wastebasket on his way out.

Teddy stood up from the table. He quickly gathered the discarded packets and tossed them on the table in front of Daniel.

"Get rid of all this horseshit; then go home and pack a bag. I'm taking you to my hunting cabin. We need to talk."

CHAPTER 24

MIA

MIA WALKED INTO the bedroom and was surprised to see Daniel packing a duffel bag.

She frowned. "Where are you going?"

"Teddy asked me to join him at his cabin for the night." He went to his bureau and grabbed some jeans. Brought them back to the bed, rolled them up, and stuck them in the bag. "He'll be here any minute to pick me up."

Oh, no. "But I have the night off," she said. "I was hoping we could spend the evening together. I texted you, but—"

"He didn't give me any notice. *Or* any choice."

Well, you could have at least replied to my texts, she thought, remembering the texts she'd sent this morning. Picking at the bandage on her hand, she thought it best to just let it go.

She'd barely dodged a bullet last night with him showing up at Jiminy's. Any other night this past week, and she wouldn't have been at the restaurant. And she wouldn't have had an explanation for her whereabouts.

She'd gotten a bad feeling last night when he and his friend had been sitting at Jiminy's. Their eyes had been on her the entire time.

She sat on the bed next to Bruce. "Does it have to be tonight?" she asked. "I just picked up some Thai takeout. Your favorites are downstairs: pad Thai and mango sticky rice."

"Trust me. The last thing I want to do is spend the night with Teddy at his hunting cabin," Daniel said, stuffing toiletries in the bag.

"Did he tell you why he wants you there?"

"To talk about Respira. I brought up my concerns at the brunch today with all the doctors."

"Yeah? How did that go?"

He grunted. "He wasn't very happy about it, to say the least. None of them were."

Respira. She wondered if Daniel had thought any more about what she'd told him about Hemsworth. About the family possibly being murdered by someone connected to the drug. After all, if Hemsworth had been in danger, Daniel could be, too.

She'd found a Facebook page titled *Justice for the Hemsworths* this morning. Someone in the group had managed to make a digital copy of the piece in the *Los Angeles Times* before it had disappeared. She'd emailed the PDF to Daniel to read, but the last time she checked, he hadn't opened the email.

He zipped up his duffel bag, grabbed it, and headed out of the room without saying anything to her. She followed him down the stairs. "Did you get the email I sent you this morning?"

"No," he said, shoving his arms into a flannel jacket. "I haven't checked my email in hours."

"I found the piece that the *Los Angeles Times* published and sent it to you. The one with Hemsworth's father."

Daniel nodded. He was obviously distracted and upset, but it was unclear how much of his negative feelings were due to Teddy and the Respira situation and how much of it was directed at her.

She wrung her hands. "Do you think Teddy's going to fire you?"

The space between them suddenly felt chilly. "I honestly don't know. And if he did?"

She folded her arms across her body, her hands clutching her sweater. "I don't understand your question."

His eyes narrowed as though he didn't believe her. "Never mind."

As Daniel jammed his feet into a pair of hiking boots, Bruce's ears stood at attention. Then a horn bleated outside. Teddy had arrived. Bruce hobbled to the door and whined.

Mia went to Daniel and wrapped her arms around him. Then she stood on her tiptoes and kissed him on the mouth.

But the kiss wasn't returned.

She felt tears well up in her eyes. *Real* tears. "I'm going to miss you tonight," she said.

Daniel nodded. "I'll see you sometime tomorrow."

CHAPTER 25

DANIEL

DANIEL SLID INTO Teddy's silver Tesla Model S. The big man greeted him with a somber look on his face and a nod, then backed the car out of the driveway without saying a word.

Daniel fastened his seat belt, and when he looked up, he saw Mia was outside, waving goodbye.

"Is that the elusive Mrs. Winters?" Teddy asked.

"Yeah."

"Beautiful woman," he remarked, but not with half the heart he usually spoke with. Instead of offering some kind of joke, he was quiet. It reminded Daniel of how he had been acting just before he left for the honeymoon.

Teddy pulled onto the Pacific Coast Highway. "If you need to make any calls, you'll want to do it now," Teddy said. "Coverage in the mountains is iffy at best, and I don't have a land line at the cabin."

Billy. He'd need to call him and make sure he would be keeping tabs on Mia, especially now that he wouldn't be with her tonight.

He shot a quick text off to Billy and waited for an answer. But typical of Billy, one didn't come right away. He set his phone on his lap and sighed inwardly.

The tension in the vehicle was palpable, uncomfortable. He decided to address the elephant in the Tesla. "About this morning—"

"No," Teddy interrupted. "Let's save it for later. No work talk for the rest of the day. Tomorrow morning, you'll have my undivided attention."

Undivided attention.

After brunch today, he somehow doubted that.

Teddy flipped on some music. The Best of the Eighties.

Being in the car with such a subdued Teddy was awkward. He knew Teddy was angry. But dammit, he was angry, too. Angry at Teddy for demanding this trip. But even angrier with himself for not having the balls to say no.

Daniel cleared his throat. "So, where is this cabin of yours?"

"Los Padres National Forest."

"Hear it's beautiful up there."

"What you heard is true."

As they traveled down the Pacific Coast Highway, Daniel thought about Mia again. What would she end up doing tonight? Maybe the trip to the cabin wouldn't be so bad after all, because Billy might have a chance to find out something sooner rather than later. He checked his phone again, but no texts had come in.

They rode in silence. Just north of Ventura, Teddy turned onto Highway 33. Open vistas of sparkling blue ocean immediately gave way to concrete strip malls and rolling hills. They would soon be driving away from civilization and into the remote woods of Los Padres National Forest.

A long and subdued hour and a half after leaving Daniel's house, Teddy pulled off Highway 33 onto a dirt road that cut a swath through the tall Douglas firs. At the top of a hill, Daniel saw what had to be

Teddy's cabin. As he expected, the word *cabin* was a loose description for the gorgeous, rambling two-story structure.

"That's quite a cabin."

"A reward for not making waves."

Daniel felt stung. "Teddy—"

Teddy threw up his hand. "I *said* tomorrow."

They rolled up to a covered parking area, where a sleek red Jaguar and a shiny black Humvee were parked.

"Yours?"

"No. They belong to a couple of my buddies. Tonight's poker night. You play, right?"

It was well known that Teddy was a poker fanatic. Many weekends, he flew to Vegas and played around the clock.

"Just in that Christmas tournament you hosted a couple of years back."

"Oh, right. Wait. Weren't you the first one to bust out that night?" Teddy asked, grunting as he tried to climb from the vehicle.

"Yeah."

"Aw. Well, then, the boys are going to love you. Don't worry if you don't have the cash. I'll spot you."

The cabin was even more gorgeous inside. The main room was very masculine, wide and open, with a high-beamed ceiling and oak floors. The centerpiece was a massive stone fireplace on the far wall that spread ten feet wide and climbed up the cedar beams of the A-frame ceiling. A large elk head adorned the space above the mantel and seemed to stare right at Daniel.

To the left of the front door was a large kitchen separated from the living room by a red cedar bar and large farm table. To the right was a dark brown leather sectional sofa that could easily seat ten people. Behind it was a built-in fully stocked bar.

Sitting at the bar already were two men who looked about Teddy's age. They stood when they saw Daniel and Teddy walk in.

"Man, they'll let just about anyone in here these days," the taller of the two announced.

"That explains how you two mongrels got in," Teddy said.

The men approached Teddy, and they hugged, slapping each other's backs.

Teddy directed their attention to Daniel.

"Guys, I want you to meet our fourth. An associate of mine, Dr. Daniel Winters."

The tall man reached out his hand. "Cy Loughlin."

Daniel shook Cy's hand.

The shorter of the men whose face was hidden behind thick glasses extended his hand. "Jim Michner."

Teddy told him that Jim and Cy were with the FDA. They'd all been buddies for about thirty years. Daniel instantly wondered how they could afford the pricey vehicles he'd seen outside on government salaries.

"Thirsty?" Teddy asked, peering at Daniel. "Lord knows I could use a drink."

Daniel nodded.

Teddy walked to the other side of the bar. "What would you like?"

Ginger ale.

"Jameson. On the rocks."

Teddy smiled in approval. He grabbed a highball glass and two shot glasses. He poured shots of Jameson and set one in front of Daniel. "To our wives. And to our lovers. May the two never meet."

Cy and Jim cheered heartily. Daniel threw the shot back, enjoying the liquor's heat.

He set the shot glass down, hoping Billy was watching Mia.

He picked up his drink and went to the couch to discreetly check his phone for a connection. But he had none.

He heard a female's voice and looked up. A tall ebony-haired woman had entered the room. "You boys ready for me?"

160

The woman looked to be maybe in her midtwenties. She wore a tight black dress. Its scoop neckline barely contained her breasts, and it was clear she wasn't wearing a bra.

Had Teddy hired a stripper for poker night?

"Gentlemen, this is Candace," Teddy announced. "She's a professional poker dealer and will be dealing for us tonight. Because I don't trust you sorry sons of bitches."

Teddy turned to the woman. "Why don't you go ahead and set up, darling? We should be ready in ten or so minutes."

Teddy said quietly in Daniel's ear: "If you're in the mood for a little distraction tonight, just say the word. She's all yours."

"She's a prostitute?"

"No. Like I said, she's a professional poker dealer."

"Then—"

"Stop being so naive. *Everyone* has a price."

Daniel glanced at Candace and immediately thought of Mia. He wondered if *she* had a price. Was it possible she'd met someone with more money than he had? Was that her secret? He wondered how long it would take to find out.

Half an hour later, drinks were flowing, cigar smoke clouded the air, and cards were being dealt. Daniel was working on his third drink and had already downed three shots with Teddy. The sheer volume of alcohol in his system had been more than enough to put the voice to sleep.

Maybe even in a coma.

He wasn't concerned about getting plastered. Not tonight. After all, being sober wasn't working all that well for him, so at least he could let himself escape for a little while.

Relax.

Unwind.

It would be good not to think about his problems for a few hours. He had no intention of even trying to bring up Respira again. Not tonight. Not after the sting of everyone's disinterest and laughter earlier. He was going to need more time to think. He needed to talk to someone else about this. Someone aside from Mia who was willing to listen and who would do so without bias. Someone in the industry. He remembered that he still hadn't heard back from Andy.

"Come on, Danny. Play a few hands, will you?" Teddy teased. "Don't make me talk to these goons all by myself. It's exhausting."

Daniel checked his phone one more time—in case he miraculously now had coverage.

But he was out of luck.

CHAPTER 26

MIA

AN HOUR AFTER Daniel had left for Teddy's cabin, Mia was folding laundry and feeling lonely, waiting for messages from either Daniel or her friend, Sam Hutchens. She'd reached out to both about thirty minutes ago.

Sam was always the one person she found herself turning to when she was in trouble or needed advice. He'd also been a big part of the reason she'd singled Daniel out that first night at the bar. When she'd seen Daniel sit down that night, her heart had fluttered, and she knew she *had* to talk to him. Not because she'd found him handsome—although she had—but because he'd reminded her so much of Sam. She missed Sam. She hadn't seen him in person since she was fifteen.

He'd been her next-door neighbor and her first and only best friend in the high-rise apartment building she'd lived in with her mother—the first and one of the only men in her life who had been kind to her without expecting anything in return. He'd been almost three years older than Mia and had offered her a much-needed escape from her miserable life with her mother.

After seeing him in the elevator of their apartment building one day, she'd gone to his door and asked if he'd like to hang out, maybe go to the building's rooftop where there were pool and ping-pong tables. Sam had said yes, and almost every day for two years, when she went to his door, he had let her hang out with him. Sometimes she'd just hung out at his apartment, watching television or watching him and his brother, Fred, play video games. Sometimes they'd hang out on the rooftop, playing ping-pong. Sam never seemed to mind her company, and he was kind to her. She'd felt ineffable comfort with him from the very first time they'd met, which had been strange, because she hadn't and still didn't feel comfortable with many people.

They were both children of single mothers who didn't pay much attention to them. Mia's hadn't because she was an addict and emotionally unavailable. Sam's hadn't because she was spread thin working two jobs, and she was always busy with Fred, who was often in some sort of trouble.

Her relationship with Sam had been strictly platonic. He was like the big brother she'd never had—and being with him had been the highlight of her days. But when he'd turned eighteen, he'd joined the marine corps and left for boot camp. She'd been beside herself with grief after he'd left and thought of him every day for years. She'd gotten back in touch with Sam online a few years ago. He was still in the marines and was now stationed in Thailand. They spoke to each other a couple of times a month and messaged each other online sometimes. He was the only person who knew what had happened to her. The only one who knew what she'd done. When she was lonely, she often thought of Sam because he'd been her first escape, her safe haven. Her relationship with him was like a warm blanket on a frigid night. Being with Daniel usually warmed her, too, but he'd been so chilly lately. She needed to figure out how to get them back to their good place.

A text came in. She picked up her phone and saw it was from Elliott, her boss at Jiminy's:

> Hey, wanted you to know someone's been sending you flowers. I'm afraid there was a mix-up and Britt brought one of the bouquets home the other day, thinking they were hers. But the latest bouquet is sitting here on my desk. I've been so busy, it slipped my mind that they were here. Sorry.

Mia frowned and texted back. Who are they from?

The reply came quickly. No card. It was the reason for the confusion.

There were only two people she could think of who would send her flowers. What kind of flowers are they? she asked.

She waited for a reply, knowing Elliott probably knew nothing about flowers and was asking around. After a couple of minutes, she received his response: Britt thinks they're orchids.

Mia thanked him and told him she'd stop by to pick them up, but her mind was already racing. If Daniel had sent them, he had to be wondering why she hadn't said anything.

Crap.

That—and that alone—could explain his strange behavior.

The coldness.

There were only two people who would have sent the orchids. She sent a text to the second possibility.

> Hey, did you send me flowers?

The reply came almost instantly. It always did.

> No. Should I have?

Shit, shit, shit!

Another text came through: Sounds like you have an admirer.

Yeah. My husband, she thought. She hadn't told him about Daniel.

When will I see you again? he asked.

Her heart fluttered like hummingbird wings, and despite herself, she smiled. Watching the play of light and shadow on the curtains, she contemplated the riskiness of seeing him again so soon. It was pretty dangerous, but she was lonely.

So lonely, it hurt.

Maybe she'd go out for just a little while, come back in plenty of time before Daniel returned. He would never know.

She texted back: How about now?

CHAPTER 27

DANIEL

DANIEL WOKE UP to something poking him. He groaned and opened his eyes, surprised to find himself staring at a paneled wall. He wasn't at home. Where was he?

He felt another poke, then heard a deep voice behind him.

"Come on, sunshine. We're burning daylight."

He winced and turned over slowly to see Teddy's big figure towering over him. He sat up, and his head started pounding.

"Whoa. You look like shit," Teddy said.

Daniel rubbed at his temples.

"Damn, kid. I had no idea. You can really put it away."

Yeah, real impressive, Daniel.

"What time is it?" Daniel asked, his voice thick from sleep.

"Nine thirty. I let you sleep in."

Daniel rubbed his eyes. "The guys still here?"

"No. They left this morning."

Teddy walked to the doorway. "Don't go back to sleep. Coffee's downstairs. I'll cook up some bacon and eggs to smother that hangover."

Daniel fumbled for his phone and checked it for messages. Nothing. Still no signal.

Thirty minutes later, after some breakfast and ibuprofen, he felt slightly more human.

"Thought we'd take a little hike," Teddy said.

Outside, the December mountain air felt good on Daniel's face. He inhaled deeply, filling his lungs with the chilled air.

He watched Teddy, who was carrying a water bottle filled with a Bloody Mary as he trudged up the trail. If the man had drunk too much last night, he certainly wasn't showing it today. But then again, Teddy always looked unwell.

"Exercise isn't my thing, as I'm sure you can tell," Teddy said, patting the generous gut that overlapped his pants. "But I've got to take at least one walk while I'm out here. It's just too beautiful not to." Teddy glanced at him. "What did you think of the guys?"

"They were fun."

"Good guys to know."

Daniel wasn't surprised that Teddy had close friends at the FDA. Teddy was well connected and seemed to know pretty much everyone.

"You passed out in the middle of a hand. A pretty big one. Thankfully, Cy let you keep your money."

Shit. "I did?"

"Yep."

"Sorry about that."

"What are you sorry for? You didn't hurt anyone. You let loose. We all need to do that from time to time," Teddy said. "And you've been wound up too tightly lately . . . walking around with that big scowl on your face. Like you're carrying the whole world on your shoulders. You needed last night."

Yeah, like a hole in my head.

They walked in silence for at least five minutes. Daniel wondered whether he should say something or let Teddy direct the conversation.

Deciding to let Teddy take the lead, he pulled his phone from his back pocket and checked for a signal again.

Nothing.

He tried to relax, appreciate the beauty of the forest, but he had too much on his mind. For one, what did Mia do last night? And had she done it alone? Had Billy found out anything?

He tried to engage in some small talk, if nothing else to get out of his head. "How long have you had this place?" he asked Teddy.

"Going on ten years. Bought it with my first wife. Number two hates the woods and wants nothing to do with the cabin, so now I come out every chance I can get."

He glanced at Daniel and winked.

Daniel remembered the female dealer from last night and wondered if Teddy had propositioned her.

Teddy led the way down the dirt path that wound through the tall firs and oaks. The trees were so dense, they almost completely blocked the sun. Daniel saw the two-story cabin in the distance. He hadn't realized they'd walked in a circle.

"So, listen, Chet and Roy don't want you at the monthly brunches anymore. You've been officially disinvited."

After seeing the doctors' reactions to what he'd had to say yesterday morning, he wasn't surprised.

"Those brunches were a privilege. We go there to relax," Teddy continued. "Get away from work. You made everyone uncomfortable."

Daniel nodded.

"Apparently, there's still a lot for you to learn, Danny. But you're in luck because I'm an excellent teacher," Teddy said.

He pushed the front door of the cabin open and walked in. Daniel followed him through the foyer, then Teddy took a right into the living room and slipped behind the bar. "Managed care changed everything for doctors. Now there are all these restrictions on the way we practice. It's more of a big business now than ever." He sighed. "In medical school, you have some noble idea of what a doctor *should* be. Then one day you're smacked with the realization that it's a business. You can't always practice medicine the way you want to. You have to do things according to the rules. You get cynical for a while, but eventually, you have to accept it. I know it's a difficult pill to swallow because I've been there." He held Daniel's gaze. "But I knew if I wanted to continue as a doctor, keep my colleagues' respect, and move up, there were certain rules I had to follow. And, Danny . . . you have to follow them, too."

Daniel listened.

"I'm going to tell you something else now," Teddy said, his eyes locking on Daniel's. "Something I trust that you'll keep between you and me."

"Yeah, sure."

"The practice is in a bit of trouble. Financially speaking. It has been for some time now."

Daniel tried to conceal his surprise. The clinic was always packed.

"I made a few big mistakes."

Daniel was listening.

"I took a big gamble and had the place renovated right before you came on board. Costs started going up: rent, equipment, staff. And don't even get me started on malpractice insurance," Teddy said, shaking his head. "To add insult to injury, when other pediatric practices started turning away patients who weren't getting their vaccinations per the CDC's schedule, I decided not to. I didn't want to turn away families who were concerned about the shots just so I could have a bigger payday. I was feeling a bit like you probably are now. Maybe a little indignant. I wanted to do what I thought was the right thing. Let my families have a choice in the matter, you know?"

Teddy pulled two glasses from behind the bar. "Hair of the dog?"

No, Daniel. Don't.

Daniel nodded. "Yeah, sure."

Teddy grabbed a bottle of Jack Daniel's and began pouring. "But when you allow families to cherry-pick or flatly refuse vaccines, you lose a shit-ton of office visits and the vaccine bonuses. Between those two areas alone, we lose almost two million dollars every year."

Daniel frowned. "I don't understand. Vaccination bonuses. Like what we're getting with Respira?"

"Very similar. We only receive them if a certain percentage of our patient base is current on their vaccines. Anything below that percentage, and we don't qualify for one damn cent."

Teddy mixed another Bloody Mary. "Anyway, I've gotten to the point where I can barely pay the rent or the staff's paychecks. That's why Respira and the sixty other immunoceuticals in the pipeline are such a beautiful gift to us. Not only will these drugs improve the quality of life for our patients and their families, they're going to save the practice."

There was a heavy, sick weight in the air. Daniel opened his mouth to say something, but Teddy held up a hand. "There are doctors. Leadership teams. Experienced medical professionals who are on top of all this drug safety shit. People like Jim and Cy. You have to trust them to do their jobs. You need to let them worry about the safety of these drugs, and you just worry about doing your job. If Respira is as unsafe as you think it is, it will eventually be taken off the market."

"So, you're asking me to administer a drug that I know is hurting patients?"

"Danny, you don't *know* it's hurting patients. And as long as you continue *not* to know, you'll be fine. It's called plausible deniability. It's the way things are done."

Daniel's breath quickened. He'd been right. The financial bottom line was taking precedent over the quality of patients' care at their practice.

Teddy stared at him, his face red. "Don't you understand, Danny? Without Respira, we lose the practice. You lose your job. All the staff loses their jobs. It impacts people's lives. And the patients? They would have to find new doctors. And you know how hard that can be." Teddy snorted with derision. "You don't understand. Pharma is a *multibillion-*dollar game, and you and I are just pawns. There's nothing you can do to stop this drug. Nothing. They won't let you. And if you force it, I'm going to have no choice but to let you go. Good luck paying off your student loans while delivering pizzas. Because if you leave, I guarantee you will never work as a pediatrician in California again. I'll see to that personally. No one can afford to hire a rogue doctor, Daniel."

The threat stung. But Daniel knew what Teddy was saying was true. It didn't matter if what he was doing was wrong or not, the reputation Teddy could give him would haunt him forever. To go against him would be career suicide. But he'd taken an oath to his patients. To do no harm. Not to do what was best for the practice.

"We're talking about kids' lives here," Daniel said.

Teddy's eyes flashed. He spun around and hurled his drink at the wall behind the bar. The glass exploded, and the tomato-red liquid dripped down the wall like blood.

Teddy turned to face Daniel again. A vein in his forehead was jumping. He glared at Daniel and pointed a stubby finger in his face. "Listen and listen closely. This is the last time I'm going to say this to you, so don't forget it: it's never Respira. *That's* all you need to know. Got it?"

Teddy slipped behind the bar and grabbed a stack of bar towels. He took one and wiped his forehead. It was the second time in the last few days that Daniel had seen Teddy lose control. Now he understood why. He was having financial troubles with the clinic. Daniel thought about Chet. "Chet . . . he has seven grandchildren. I wonder if they've gotten Respira."

Teddy's laugh was joyless. "Of course they didn't. I'm sure they don't get half the shit we give kids today."

Teddy went to the wall and started wiping up the mess. "Look, you didn't sign up to be a Boy Scout, Daniel. You signed up to practice medicine. And these days, this is how we practice it. Not only that, but you insist on making more noise about this, unemployment will be the least of your worries."

Least of my worries? What does that mean?

"Oh, that reminds me," Teddy said, turning to face him. "My condolences about your friend."

Friend? "What do you mean?" Daniel asked.

"Andy Cameron, was it? The kid from the clinic you said was asking around about Respira?"

"What—"

"You didn't hear, Danny? He killed himself. Jumped off a cliff in the Hollywood Hills."

CHAPTER 28

MIA

THE MAN'S AWFUL screams sliced through Mia's nightmare and jolted her awake. She tried to shake off the grisly images parading through her brain. Blood everywhere. Spraying on her face, on the leather couch, pouring from between the man's fingers.

Bruce stood from where he'd been curled up at the end of the bed and went to her. He sniffed her face and her hair and whined.

Her heart was pounding. "I'm okay, boy," she said and patted him on the head. She worked to slow her breathing. "It was just a bad dream."

That was only half-true.

The dog stretched his long body, stared at her, then released a big yawn.

It was already 10:00 a.m. She grabbed her phone, checked her texts, and felt a wash of disappointment. She'd texted Daniel several times since he'd left for Teddy's cabin, but he hadn't responded even once.

She'd picked up the orchids last night on the way to the valley, then texted Daniel a story that she'd manufactured about the flower mix-up and had hoped with her explanation the distance between them would disappear. She hoped his behavior—at least where she was concerned—was due to those orchids and nothing more.

Bruce thumped his tail and stared at her.

She forced a smile. "Come on, handsome. I'll let you out."

She crawled out of bed and threw on her robe. By the time she got downstairs, Bruce was already waiting by the door. She let him out, then went to brew a pot of coffee.

She'd driven home from Christian's at 2:15 a.m. and strangely slept like a rock for the rest of the night, which was very unusual for her. This morning, despite the nightmare, she actually felt refreshed for the first time since they'd returned from the Caymans.

Bruce trotted back into the house, barked, and took off across the living room to the foyer.

Weird, she thought. Was someone at the door? She hadn't heard a knock. She followed Bruce to the foyer and watched a shadow pass across the pane of glass to the right of the front door. Then the shadow was gone.

"Hello?" she called out, walking slowly to the front door.

Silence.

She pressed her eye up to the peephole. But she didn't see anyone. Bruce stood next to her, whining and sniffing at the bottom of the door.

She unlocked the door and opened it. Someone had left a brown 9x12 envelope on the doorstep. The words *Dr. Winters* were scrawled across it in thick red marker.

She bent and picked it up, then looked around again. But there was no one in sight. Whoever left it had vanished.

❖ ❖ ❖

A little before 3:00 p.m. Bruce sprinted to the front door again.

Daniel was home.

Mia licked cream cheese frosting from her fingers and grabbed a hand towel as she walked to the door to greet him.

She opened the door just as he was sliding his key into the lock. "Beat you," she said, smiling. But when she got a good look at him, the smile fell from her face.

Daniel was wearing the same flannel shirt as yesterday, only it was now wrinkled. His unshaven face was bloated, his skin was pale, and he reeked of alcohol. Despite it all, it was his eyes that really threw her. They were intense and stormy.

"You okay?" she asked, reaching out to hug him. "I called and texted you. I was worried."

"There was no cell service at the cabin."

He brushed past her and walked to the kitchen, then set his phone on the charging station and opened the wine cabinet. He pulled out a bottle of merlot and set it on the butcher block.

"Want a glass?" he asked.

She shrugged. "Yeah, sure. Why not?"

He was drinking early again. And if his glassy eyes and the stink of alcohol emanating from him were any indication, this wasn't his first drink of the day.

"Did you get my text about the mix-up with the orchids?" she asked, reaching out and fingering one of the blooms. She'd watered them—and placed an aspirin in the water so they'd keep longer—and had arranged them in the center of the island.

He nodded, but his mind was clearly somewhere else.

"Thank you for these. They're really lovely."

Daniel grabbed two wineglasses from the cabinet.

"Are you hungry?" she asked.

He shook his head no and reached for the corkscrew.

"You sure? I baked a cake. Red velvet. Your favorite." She pointed to the cake she'd just finished covering in lemon cream cheese frosting.

"I'm sure," he mumbled.

"So, what did Teddy want to talk about?"

Daniel poured the wine and handed her a wineglass. He took a long sip from his own glass before responding, then rubbed at his swollen eyes. When he opened his eyes, she saw anger in them. "He wanted to let me know that he cares more about his fucking bank account than the well-being of our patients."

"I'm sorry . . . *what?*"

A deep frown creased his brow. "And my friend, Andy?"

"What about him?"

"Apparently, he killed himself."

Shock waves rolled through her body. Her hand flew to her mouth. "Oh, my God, Daniel. I'm so sorry!"

Daniel started pacing the room and told her what he knew. He said that the younger doctor had tried to reach out to him a few days ago. That he'd said it was important, but by the time Daniel was able to get back to him, Andy hadn't responded. And now he was dead. She could see he was torn up about it.

He took another long sip of his wine, then set the glass down and reached for the bottle again. "Suicide," he said, shaking his head slowly. "It just doesn't sit right. I can't wrap my head around it."

Mia reached in the cupboard and grabbed a dessert plate and a knife while Daniel talked. A ray of afternoon sun filtering in from the kitchen window glistened on the sharp blade of the knife, and remnants of her nightmare came flooding back. Trying to shake it from her head, she sliced the cake. Then she remembered Daniel telling her that Andy had been asking him about Respira. She thought about the Hemsworths. "Wait. Do you think it was possible he was murdered?" she asked. "For asking around about Respira?"

Daniel turned toward the ocean. He stared at it and rubbed the back of his neck. "It sounds pretty far-fetched, but honestly . . . at this point, I don't know what to think."

Daniel told her some of the things he and Teddy had discussed at the cabin. About the practice being in financial trouble. About Teddy's threats. "He made it clear that I prescribe Respira or I'm out of a job. Maybe even a career."

Mia noticed his left hand was shaking. He seemed to notice it, too, because he stopped talking for a moment and stared at it. She also noticed that he kept checking his phone.

Since waking up this morning, she'd been doing more research on Respira, curious to find out more about the drug. She'd read that there was a huge push to get it on the shot schedule. Quickly. Much quicker than any other drug that had been awarded a spot. They wanted to establish a precedent with it. "If they get it on the schedule, parents will be forced to give it to their kids if they want them to have access to public schools. Even day cares," she said.

Daniel raked his hand through his hair and stared out the window at the ocean again. "Yeah, I know."

❈ ❈ ❈

Several hours later, they made it to bed. They lay silently, Mia's head resting on Daniel's chest. They didn't talk. Didn't turn on the television. They just lay, listening to the waves lap the shore outside. They'd talked about a lot, and Mia wondered how much of their conversation Daniel would remember tomorrow.

He'd almost singlehandedly polished off two bottles of wine. She knew he was hammered, but she was relieved that he had warmed up toward her again. He wasn't shutting her out or being cold, like he'd been yesterday. It was a step in the right direction. She only hoped he'd continue to let her in once he sobered up.

She wondered again if Daniel would be in danger if he continued to question Respira. Continued to talk to people about it. If *she* would be in danger. If what Hemsworth's father was saying was true, they both could be. She would need to talk to Daniel when he was sober. Figure out what they should do to protect themselves.

Daniel's phone lit up and started dancing across the nightstand.

He turned away from her and fumbled for it. She lifted her head and watched his eyes move across the screen. A peculiar expression flashed across his face.

"Daniel?" she asked. "Is everything okay?"

He ignored her, jumped out of bed, and staggered from the room.

CHAPTER 29

DANIEL

DANIEL BARELY HEARD Mia's voice behind him asking what was wrong as he stumbled his way into the hallway. He reread Billy's text, and his breath caught in his throat.

> You were right to be suspicious. Mikey had an emergency, so I had to bail, but we should meet in the morning.

You were right to be suspicious? What the hell did that mean?
I've been telling you this all along. She's—
Anger flooded his belly. "Shut. Up!" he said, his voice shattering the silence of the house.
Shit. He hadn't meant to shout. What the hell was happening to him?
For one, you're drunk. You're also—
He shoved the voice away. He had no idea how it was even still awake. He'd had a lot to drink.
Daniel called Billy, but the call went directly to voice mail.
Shit!

He typed: Answer your phone!

He pressed redial, shuffled into his home office, and slammed the door. Again, Billy didn't answer. *Dammit!*

He typed: WHAT did you find out?

He sat down, stood back up, paced the small space of the room. Why the hell wasn't Billy answering?

He contemplated driving to Billy's place, but he'd had far too much to drink. Besides, he had no idea where Billy even lived. All he knew was that it was somewhere in the San Fernando Valley.

He tried to call again.

Once more, he got Billy's voice mail.

He felt his mouth tighten. *Shit!* Fine beads of sweat sprung from his forehead, and he glanced wildly around his office. There were printouts strewn across his desk. Research. A couple of sheets of paper had fallen to the floor. Two cans of Dr Pepper were on his credenza, both empty, one crumpled.

He was never untidy like this.

Deciding to make use of the adrenaline pumping through his veins, he began straightening up his mess. He tried pulling the paperwork together, but his hands weren't cooperating. They were shaking badly now. He glanced at his phone and saw thought bubbles had popped up. Billy was finally typing a reply.

He picked up the phone and waited for the reply to come through. Billy seemed to type for ages. But then the ellipses vanished.

Shit!

Daniel typed again: Where are you? Give me your address. I'll come to you.

He would get an Uber or a Lyft or something. There was no way he could wait until the morning to find out what Billy had discovered.

Shit, Billy! You can't leave me hanging like this. Pick up your damn phone! Mia *was* cheating, wasn't she? He should've known. He should have trusted his instincts that first night at the bar. Why hadn't he trusted them? He'd started drinking, that's why. He'd started drinking while he was talking to her, and it had made him stop thinking.

He'd been such a fool. He thought again about how Mia didn't have an internet footprint. That wasn't normal. Even he had a Facebook account. He didn't really use it, but at least he had one. Mia, on the other hand, was a ghost. He wondered if maybe cheating wasn't all she was doing. If there was something more that he didn't know.

A message finally came through: Meet me at that diner in Brentwood at 6 a.m. tomorrow. The one we saw Matt Damon at last year.

Daniel stared at the message, wondering how the hell he would be able to wait until six in the morning. Thought bubbles appeared again. Then: UR old lady is not to be trusted.

CHAPTER 30

DANIEL

WHEN DANIEL WALKED into the diner the next morning, the sky was still the color of ink, and the wine he'd drunk yesterday was still pumping through his bloodstream.

Arriving half an hour early, he slid into a booth and texted Billy to let him know that he'd arrived.

A middle-aged waitress walked over. She looked tired, as though she was on the tail end of a graveyard shift. Daniel tried not to stare at the red smear of lipstick on her front tooth. "What can I get you, sugar?"

"Coffee, please."

"That all?"

"Yes."

"We have fresh doughnuts."

"No, thanks."

"And cherry turnovers. They just came out of the oven. They're real good."

"Just the coffee."

She nodded and walked off.

Daniel scrolled back through his and Billy's conversation.

You were right to be suspicious . . . UR old lady is not to be trusted.

The words had haunted him all night. What had Billy found out?

Rage ballooned in his chest. It had *all* been a lie. Since the night they met. Hadn't it?

The waitress placed a coffee cup on the table and filled it with hot coffee.

"Sure you don't want something to eat?"

"I'm sure."

"Okay, then." She motioned to the plastic creamer and sugar packets that were in a bowl on the table. "Help yourself."

She walked away again, and Daniel took a sip.

He peered down at the brown envelope in front of him. He'd discovered it this morning on the island in the kitchen. It had his name on it. He was just about to tear it open when a text message came in.

He set the envelope down and picked up his phone.

It was Mia.

What's going on? Is everything okay?

He'd left early this morning without telling her.

Ignoring her message, he propped his elbows on the table and held his head between his palms. He was so disappointed, so disillusioned, so angry. He'd wanted so badly for Billy to say that Mia had a good explanation for everything so that they could go back to the way they'd been. All he had to hang on to now was the possibility that Billy had gotten something wrong. Or that he was exaggerating. After all, both scenarios were possible.

He wasn't going to talk to Mia until he knew. Until he finally knew what he was dealing with. He had slept—if you could even call it that—in his home office last night, not wanting to see her again until after he and Billy had talked.

He set the phone down and drummed his fingers on the table. The diner was old and had clearly seen better days. It smelled like a combination of bacon and Pine-Sol. Someone had carved the name *Jenna* in both the table and the red vinyl seat. He noticed dust had gathered in the corner of the seat, and someone had stuck some pink gum into a hole in the vinyl. *God knows the last time this place had a proper cleaning,* he thought. But the coffee was decent.

The coffee.

He couldn't believe he was thinking about coffee at a time like this.

He rolled a small tub of half-and-half between his palms and focused on breathing.

His phone buzzed again. Another text from Mia.

I'm worried. Let me know you're okay.

Worried about what?
What I might have found out about you?

He was feeling sick just thinking about her. He decided it would be best to redirect his thoughts until Billy showed up. He texted Collin, the young doctor who had been at brunch. Since he'd been the only doctor who had shown at least a morsel of interest in what Daniel had said, Daniel wanted to talk to him. He hoped that what he'd seen the young doctor throw away when he left the brunch hadn't been one of his packets.

Wanted to see if you had time to go over the information I shared at brunch. Would love to meet and see if you have any thoughts.

He shot the text off and set his phone down. It was 6:02 a.m., and he realized that if he moved his eyes too quickly to the left or the right, the room slanted a little. Maybe he should order some food to help soak up some of the alcohol.

At 6:10 a.m., he ordered a doughnut and a second cup of coffee.

Anger simmered deep inside. *Come on, Billy. Where are you? How the hell can you be late for something like this?*

At 6:20 a.m., he ordered a cherry turnover.

At 6:25 a.m., he realized his head was beginning to clear a bit. He drained his second cup of coffee and motioned to the waitress for another cup.

At 6:30 a.m., a text came in. It was from Collin.

Sorry, but I can't get involved. Family to feed. Good luck.

He stared at the message. Had he read that correctly?

Can't get involved?

The air stalled in his lungs. What the hell was with these people? How could doctors, *doctors*, turn their backs on their patients?

It's called self-preservation. Something you should also be concerned with. But we both know how terrible you are at that.

Daniel glowered, sweat now soaking his armpits. Everyone was falling short of his expectations: Mia, Teddy, Chet, Roy . . . now Collin.

He tapped a foot on the sticky floor.

Where the hell was Billy?

His phone buzzed again. Another text. He picked it up but this time didn't recognize the number.

Hi. My name is Gail Whitman. I'm a medical journalist and run GetTheFactsAboutRespira.com. I need to talk to you ASAP. Call me when you can.

He was very familiar with the website. He'd found a lot of his research on it. But how in the hell did she get his number? And why did she want to talk to him? He stared at her message for several seconds, then realized that maybe this was a good thing. She might be the perfect person for him to talk to. He would definitely call her later.

The little bell above the diner door jingled, and Billy came swaggering in.

Finally.

"Sorry I'm late, bro," he said, sliding into the cracked booth.

"What did you find out?" Daniel interrupted, his words rushed.

Billy sighed. "Sorry, man," he said. He leaned forward and punched something on his phone. He slid the device across the table to Daniel.

Photographs.

Daniel's jaw tensed. The first photo was Mia's red Jetta parked in front of a house he didn't recognize.

He glanced at Billy. "This was two nights ago?"

Billy nodded. "Yeah. When you were on your camping trip."

The next photo showed Mia standing next to the car, and Bruce jumping out.

"Christ, she took my dog with her?"

"Yeah, man. She did."

A chill started at Daniel's head and spread all the way down his back as he looked at the next photo. A well-built shirtless man meeting Mia and Bruce at the door of a small ranch-style house. Mia and the man hugging.

"She left the house about an hour after you left with your boss. She jumped into her car with the dog, then drove straight to the valley, to this guy's house. They stayed inside the house the entire time. Ordered a pizza a couple of hours later. And she left at 2:15 a.m."

She stayed there until 2:15 a.m.?

Daniel felt like he'd been kicked in the gut. Tears burning his eyes, he studied the picture of his wife hugging the man again as she left. The man was now wearing a sweatshirt. He was quite a bit taller than Mia. Probably around six feet or a little taller.

"You don't know him?" Billy asked.

Daniel shook his head.

"Sorry, man. I was hoping I wouldn't find anything."

"What's his name?" Daniel asked.

"Christian. Christian Davis."

Daniel felt nauseated. Even though he had expected the worst, it didn't make it hurt any less. First his career, and now this?

There was a final picture. Christian and Mia, standing outside Mia's Jetta. Bruce stood at Mia's feet, staring up at them.

"That one was taken at 2:15 a.m., right before she left. Sorry, man."

Jesus.

Daniel stared at the final photograph.

"Want me to make him go away?" Billy asked. "Just say the word, bro, because I do that, too."

Make him go away? What did that even mean? Daniel's hand trembled as he swiped back through the pictures again.

"Send me these."

"Sure. You got it, man."

Daniel's phone buzzed. It was Mia.

Fuck you, Mia.

He silenced the call.

"Where does he live?" Daniel asked. "I want his address."

CHAPTER 31

DANIEL

IT WAS STILL fairly early when Daniel reached Pacific Palisades and turned onto Entrada Drive. He was stuck so deeply inside his head that, at first, he didn't even register the people standing outside of the practice holding signs.

Frowning, he pulled into the parking lot and slid into his usual parking space. He got out of his car and headed toward the office. As he approached, he realized the group was picketing.

What the—?

One of the protesters pointed at him. Everyone turned in his direction, and the chants grew louder.

The group was fairly small. Ten people at the most. He recognized a few of them as parents he'd seen at the practice. Patients of Teddy's and Dr. Thornton's, though, not his. As he walked past, they all waved signs in his face, their chant erupting into a unified yell: "STOP POISONING OUR KIDS!"

He saw two young children were also holding signs that read:

The Doctors Here Hurt Us!

One young boy, maybe seven or eight years old, was sitting on a curb, his sign resting in his lap. Daniel stopped in his tracks and stared at him. The boy looked so much like his late brother. When the kid noticed Daniel staring, he held up his sign:

Stop Sacrificing My Health So You Can Send Your Kid To Private School!

Daniel squeezed his eyes shut for a quick moment.

The protestors' words stung because they were blaming him. Even worse, they had every right to. He was part of the problem. He wanted to talk to these parents. Tell them that they had every right to be concerned. To picket. That he agreed with them. That they were doing the right thing: spreading the word.

But he couldn't say any of these things.

At least not yet.

He pushed through the glass front door of the office and felt as though he'd stepped into an alternate universe. Everything seemed normal inside the building. The chanting outside quickly becoming just a distant hum. The blinds were closed. The air was heated and smelled of their signature antiseptic cleaner. A handful of children were there for early Respira appointments. They sat with their parents, watching a cartoon on the overhead monitors. Margy was sitting at the front desk as usual. The only thing out of the norm was Teddy standing next to her, staring at the protesters outside. His face was flushed, his hands planted on his generous hips.

When Daniel approached, Teddy glared at him. "Did you do this?"

"What?" Daniel asked.

Teddy pointed toward the front door. To the protesters outside.

Daniel shook his head. "No, Teddy. I didn't."

Teddy stared at him as though contemplating whether to believe him.

Daniel walked past him to his office. As he shrugged on his lab coat, he realized the practice no longer felt like a second home. And he was pretty sure it never would again.

He was putting his things away when he realized he still hadn't opened the brown envelope. Pulling it from his bag, he tore it open and pulled out two 9x11 sheets of paper. The first was a news story that had been printed in the *Los Angeles Times*:

PEDIATRICIAN'S FAMILY SLAIN IN MURDER-SUICIDE

Frowning, he scanned the story. It was consistent with what he'd heard on the radio. That the doctor and his family had been found dead from gunshot wounds, and that the deaths were suspected to be a murder-suicide. No mention of Hemsworth's father suspecting foul play from an outside source. Also, nothing about the private pathologist.

His heart thudded in his chest.

The second was also a *Los Angeles Times* piece, but this one was only a small paragraph:

SUICIDE SUSPECTED IN DEATH OF MAN, 30, FOUND AT BOTTOM OF GORGE IN HOLLYWOOD HILLS

The short article read: *The death of a man found Thursday at the base of Mount Lee just below the world-famous Hollywood sign landmark has been ruled a suicide, the Los Angeles police said. The man, 30, has been identified as Andy Cameron of Encino.*

Daniel bristled.

Who the hell sent him these?

Someone was trying to scare him.

CHAPTER 32

MIA

MIA GUNNED THE accelerator and sped toward the valley, wondering who had texted Daniel last night and what that person had said. After receiving the text, he'd sequestered himself in his office and hadn't wanted to talk. She'd spent most of the night awake and worrying, but she must have fallen asleep for a few minutes, because at some point before dawn, he'd slipped out of the house. She'd tried checking his computer again for possible clues, but he'd installed a password on it.

Once she reached the house, she killed the engine and jumped out of the car. She yanked her hoodie up over her head and hurried up the sidewalk. Just as she was about to knock, the door opened. Christian was wearing an undershirt and had shaving cream slathered on his face and a razor in his hand. He smiled. "Well, this is a nice surprise."

"I needed to get out of the house," she muttered. Maybe Christian had been a mistake, but being with him soothed her, and right now, she desperately needed soothing. She was starting to freak out. With Christian, she felt the acceptance she'd once felt with Daniel. With Sam.

She walked past him into the small living room. Like always, the place reeked of pot. It was also a mess. Dirty dishes littered the coffee table. Clothes were flung on a chair, and the worn carpet needed serious vacuuming. It was clear that Christian was far from perfect, but even so, there was no doubt she had begun to feel something for him. The more time she spent with him, the more she trusted him. Believed what he told her.

She noticed he was staring at her. "Are you okay?"

"I'm fine."

He looked skeptical. "You sure? Because you don't *look* fine."

She smiled. "I'm sure."

He still didn't look convinced. "Okay. Give me a few minutes. I'll be right back," he said and disappeared into the short hallway that led to his bedroom.

She walked around a little more. Maybe she'd offer to clean the place. It would help her keep her mind off her problems with Daniel. She checked her phone to see if she'd missed any texts.

Nothing.

She stuffed her phone into her back pocket, pulled off her hoodie, and tossed it on the couch. In the small kitchen, a protein shake canister sat uncovered. A glass with the remnants of a shake sat next to it. She found the lid to the canister and was wetting a paper towel when she heard laughter outside.

Curious, she walked to the living room window and pushed the curtains aside. Two little dark-haired girls wearing backpacks were heading down the sidewalk. Mia watched them until they were out of view. She was about to leave the window and return to cleaning when something else caught her eye.

She froze.

Parked two cars behind her Jetta was an older-model black Suburban. A man was sitting in the driver's seat. She could only see his profile, but she was pretty sure she'd seen him somewhere before. She racked her brain, trying to place him. She narrowed her eyes, trying to see the man more clearly.

Christian poked his head into the living room, buttoning his shirt. "Want to go grab breakfast somewhere?" he asked.

No, completely out of the question.

"I have training today for the new job. But I can make it work if we are quick," he said.

No, she just wanted to be with him. In this house. Even if it was just for a few minutes. Being with him calmed her. But she couldn't go out in public with him.

"If you don't mind, I'd rather stay here."

"Okay. Whatever you want. Give me a sec. I'll be right back."

"Take your time."

She peered out the window again and studied the guy in the car. Then she realized who he looked like.

Daniel's friend, Billy.

She frowned, wondering if it was possible. She was squinting, trying to see the guy more clearly, when the guy suddenly turned his head toward her.

It *was* Billy.

She wasn't being paranoid at all.

"Oh, no."

As if the man sensed he'd been spotted, the SUV roared to life and shot down the street.

Mia grabbed her hoodie. "Oh, shit. Oh, shit!" she whispered, her lungs heaving.

Christian walked into the living room, smelling of spicy aftershave. "Hey. What's going on?"

She grabbed her purse, gave him a quick kiss, and hurried to the door. "Sorry. I've got to go."

CHAPTER 33

DANIEL

DANIEL HIT MIA on speed dial and waited for her to pick up. She answered on the third ring.

"Hey," she said, sounding out of breath.

He tried to ignore the anger and hurt he was feeling toward her, to compartmentalize for now. To focus first and foremost on finding out more about the brown envelope. "I found a brown envelope in the kitchen this morning," he said. "Where did it come from?"

"I found it on the doorstep."

"Did you see who left it?"

"No."

He quickly explained what he'd found inside and told her that it was probably just a ploy to scare him, nothing to be overly concerned about, but to keep the doors locked just in case.

"Jesus," she replied. "Yes. Of course."

Daniel ended the call without saying goodbye, then slipped his phone into the pocket of his lab coat.

For most of the morning, his patients asked about the protesters. Teddy had instructed the staff to say very little. To tell only the parents who asked that the protestors were misinformed, that Respira was completely safe and to leave it at that.

Behind the closed doors of the examination rooms, though, Daniel urged his patients to do their own research before making a decision about the drug. He encouraged them to start at GetTheFactsAboutRespira. com since the webmaster had curated so much helpful information. But for many parents that wasn't enough. They didn't want to read the information. They wanted a professional recommendation. He told those parents that his recommendation would be to skip it. He knew that if word got back to Teddy about what he was doing, he'd be fired on the spot. But as scary as that was, he had no choice. If he lied and another child was injured, he wouldn't be able to live with himself.

He was going to put in his resignation, but it needed to wait another day or two. It was a difficult thing to do after all the hard work and sacrifice he'd put in over the last several years, but he couldn't—wouldn't—inject another child until he had sufficient evidence that it was safe to do so. He needed to come up with a plan before resigning.

Between aggressively paying off his student loans the last two years, what he'd spent on his recent honeymoon, and the loan he'd let Mia have for her "friend," he wasn't very liquid. He'd have to sell the house, but that would take some time. Plus, if he didn't line up another job quickly, he could lose even more. Everything he'd worked so hard his entire adult life to build was on the line.

He was with a patient when he heard Teddy's voice from the front of the office. He was screaming at the top of his lungs at someone.

"I'll be right back, okay?" Daniel said to his patient's mother and hurried from the examination room.

As Daniel weaved through the patients and practitioners peeking out from the various examination rooms, he saw Teddy charging toward a redheaded woman, his arm thrust forward. "Get the hell out of my practice. Now!" he screamed.

What the hell?

What was going on—and why was Teddy behaving this way, especially in front of a clinic full of patients?

Daniel watched the redheaded woman push the heavy glass door open and disappear. The big man was shaking, and sweat glistened at his temples. Everyone was staring at him. Daniel, parents, children, the medical staff.

Daniel placed a hand on Teddy's shoulder. "You okay, Ted?"

The big man's eyes stayed locked on the front door.

"Who was she?"

"A piranha," he spat. Teddy's eyes flitted to his. They were full of accusation. "She was looking for you. Have you been talking to the media, Dan?"

Daniel remembered the messages he'd received from the medical journalist. Had it been the same woman? "No. Someone left me a couple of messages, but I haven't responded."

Teddy clenched his jaw. "What was her name?"

"Gail something or other."

"That was her," Teddy said. "Whatever you do, don't talk to her. And if you hear from her again, let me know."

He walked past Daniel and bumped his shoulder hard.

❖❖❖

Later that afternoon, Daniel peered into Margy's office and found her working on her computer.

"Got a second?" Daniel asked.

Margy waved him in. He shut the door behind him and sat down in the chair across from her.

"Do you know if the parents of any of our patients have complained about their kids experiencing severe adverse reactions after Respira?"

Her smile faded. She folded her arms over her chest. "Why do you ask?"

"Just curious," he said.

She stared at him for a moment, then glanced past him to make sure the door was shut. "Yes, some have."

"Have there been many?"

"If when you say *many*, you mean *too many*, the answer is yes."

"Does Teddy know about these complaints?"

"Of course. He knows about everything that goes on around here."

"Can you give me the exact number?"

She looked hesitant.

"Whatever you tell me won't get back to Teddy. You have my word."

"I don't know off the top of my head. But I can find out."

"Thanks, Margy."

She nodded.

At her office door, he turned. "Also, are you familiar with the VAERS database?"

Margy nodded. "Yes, a little."

"Do you know if any of the reports have been filed with VAERS?"

"I doubt it, but let me check. Give me an hour, and I'll get you that information, too."

❀❀❀

An hour later, Daniel took advantage of a patient cancellation and stole away to his office to do some research on Christian Davis. Finding his Facebook page was easy. The guy was apparently very active on social media.

He was good-looking and young. Late twenties? Midtwenties? He thought about the young server who had placed his hands on

Mia's shoulders the night he and Billy were at Jiminy's. He had been young, too.

He clicked through the guy's photographs. He was in immaculate shape, and his stomach looked like a rock. The guy probably spent most of his waking life in the gym. Watched everything he ate. Unlike Daniel lately, he probably never skipped a run.

Most of his pictures were of him at the gym, going to the gym, or leaving the gym. All his posts were equally inane: *Getting pumped up!* or *Feeling the burn!* How could Mia have fallen for a gym jock like this? She was smarter than that.

Where had they even met? He remembered her talking about a yoga class she'd been going to, but this guy didn't look like he'd be into yoga. Plus, he'd assumed she was taking yoga someplace close. Why go way out to the valley? Was it possible they'd known each other before Daniel and Mia had even gotten married?

There was a soft knock on the door. He quickly minimized his browser. "Come in," he called.

It was Margy. She walked up to his desk and handed him a sticky note with the number *36* written on it.

Daniel stared at the number.

"Only one report was filed with VAERS," she said quietly. "The one you filed for Suzie Jacobs."

Daniel nodded. "What were these complaints for?"

She pointed at the sticky note. "Turn it over." He did and saw that on the other side she'd printed the words *seizures, migraine headaches, changes in personality, motor regression, sleep apnea.*

"Why weren't more reports filed with VAERS?" he asked.

"Our practice has never reported to VAERS. And in case you don't already know, Teddy's outright discouraging it for this drug."

"And everyone's just been going along with it?"

Margy looked pointedly at him. "Well, yes. We all need our jobs, Dr. Winters."

CHAPTER 34

RACHEL

SUZIE STILL WASN'T well. Rachel glanced at the clock on the wall. She had one more hour. One more hour, then she would break it to her boss that this was going to be her last day, and she was going to beg for him to cut her a check. He owed her for Monday through Wednesday of last week plus today. The four days of work would give her enough money to rent a U-Haul and drive to Minnesota. She'd have to figure out everything else once she got there.

Originally, she'd planned to finish out the full week. But just being away from Suzie for almost eight hours so far today was killing her. She didn't want Suzie out of her sight again until she was back to her old self.

Sunlight streamed in through the window next to her, stinging her eyes. She hadn't gotten much sleep the last several days and probably wouldn't until Minnesota.

But that was okay.

That's what the Adderall in her pocket was for.

She thought about her meeting with Gail. The woman took down her story but warned Rachel that she wouldn't be believed by most who read it. At least not at first. It would take a lot more parents telling the same stories over and over for a long period of time and for more doctors to go public before she would really be heard. When she asked why people would find it so hard to believe that her little girl had gotten injured from Respira, Gail had said because it challenged people's belief systems to think that anything their doctors might have encouraged them to do could be so dangerous. That people like her were simply written off . . . at first.

She'd just finished typing a memo for Jeff and was saving the file when her cell phone rang.

She looked at the screen. It was Martha.

Oh, my God.

Was it Suzie?

Her fingers trembled as she picked up the phone. "Is everything okay?" she asked into the receiver.

There was silence on the other end.

Rachel's pulse pounded in her ears. "Martha?"

She heard sobs from the other end of the line. Then it sounded as though Martha was trying to say something but couldn't get it out.

Goose bumps broke out along Rachel's arms. "What? What did you say?" she asked.

More sobbing sounds.

"You're scaring me, Martha. Tell me what's going on!"

Martha's voice was small, quiet. "I kept trying to get up the courage to . . . to call. I'm so sorry."

She had to be dreaming. There was no way this was real. No way. Rachel pinched her forearm, and pain seared up her arm.

"What's going on? Where's Suzie?"

"She just stopped breathing in her sleep. I don't know why," Martha said. "I told the police where you work. They should be there soon. I'm so sorry, Rachel."

❀❀❀

The double doors to the emergency room flew open, and Rachel rushed into the hospital, leaving her car sitting halfway on the curb behind her, the engine still running.

She hurried to the reception desk. "My daughter! Where is she?"

The heavyset woman behind the desk looked up from her glasses, and her brow furrowed. She said calmly, "I'm going to need more than that, hon."

When Rachel told her who she was and that she was there to see Suzie, the woman's features softened. She told Rachel to take a seat; then she picked up the phone and spoke quietly into the receiver.

Rachel was too nervous to sit. She paced across the room for what seemed like forever, replaying the awful phone call from Martha.

A doctor walked in from behind the reception counter. "Ms. Jacobs?"

"Yes," Rachel said, out of breath, and hurried to him. "Where's my baby? Where's Suzie?"

The man introduced himself as Dr. Rowdy. The way he was looking at her made her heart thunder even louder in her chest.

"Where is she?" Rachel asked.

The doctor stepped toward her. "I'm so sorry."

The air left her lungs. Fear trickled like ice water in her veins as she followed him down the corridor.

CHAPTER 35

DANIEL

DANIEL SAT PARKED across the street from 333 Reseda Lane and stared at the small ranch house. His pulse pounding in his temples, he picked up his phone and pulled up the photos Billy had sent him.

The house was small, in ill repair, and located in a questionable neighborhood. From the looks of the place, the guy didn't seem to have a lot of money. But Mia was seeing him, anyway. So, what was the deal? Was she with Daniel for the money and with Christian for love? And how long had this been going on?

Mia. Just thinking about her made his blood boil. Was he naive to think it had been good at one time? Magical, even? Had there been signs he hadn't noticed? Had he done something wrong? Something to drive her into another man's arms?

His phone dinged. He grabbed it from the passenger seat and looked at the screen. It was Mia. He ignored her message and looked out the window. Darkness was falling fast. The sky was streaked with clouds, and the shadows were getting longer.

He wasn't leaving until he saw the guy. Although he'd learned plenty from the man's social media accounts, he wanted to see him in person. Another ding. Mia again.

I see that you're reading my messages. Why aren't you replying?
We need to talk.

Yes, we do. But not yet.

Billy had sent him a text message with yet another photo just before lunchtime. Apparently, Mia had visited the guy again just this morning. *Unbelievable.* He'd thanked Billy and told him there was no reason for him to continue following her.

He tossed the phone back on the passenger seat, popped open the glove compartment, and stared at the flask of whiskey he'd stored. He contemplated taking a swig.

Don't you dare.

Just two. He desperately needed his thoughts to slow down. To line up in single file. If he kept it to two, he'd still be okay to drive.

He amended his rules yet again.

Three drinks maximum while out.

Three drinks at home.

Two shots while driving.

He reached for the flask, unscrewed the top, and took his first gulp. He winced as the liquid carved a fiery but pleasurable path down his throat. Exhaling loudly, he sank lower in his seat and stared at the house again.

What did Mia see in Christian, anyway? Well, of course, he knew what she saw. A young guy with a flawless physique. He probably had better stamina. Probably never had trouble getting it up in his life. He winced as he remembered the other night when he couldn't.

She'd spent six hours at the guy's house.

What did they talk about for six hours?

Or *had* they talked?

Daniel couldn't compete with guys like Christian in the age department. Hell, he didn't want to compete with him. Shouldn't have to. He shouldn't have to compete with anybody, dammit. It wasn't what he signed up for. None of this was.

He'd been right about beautiful women. They were manipulative, and Mia wasn't any different. She was just very skilled at it. A skilled con artist.

Six hours!

Just thinking about the amount of time made him feel sick. And where had Bruce been when all this was going on? Daniel took swig number two, despite the voice's protests.

The whole thing had probably just been a setup. She was just trying to get his money somehow. She hadn't asked for much yet, just $5K, but that had probably been a test. And the friend who was in a bind? No doubt he was staring at the asshole's house right now.

What exactly was her endgame? God, he was so confused.

And pissed.

He glanced at his reflection in the rearview mirror. There was a fine sheen of sweat on his forehead. It was damn hot in the car. As he lowered the window, it began to drizzle.

As he waited for Christian to come out of his house, he replayed the entire relationship with Mia in his mind. Even in hindsight, he couldn't see the signs. Not until he'd caught her in that lie after her shift at Jiminy's.

I hate to say I told you so.

Shut the hell up.

You've been so naive.

Yes, he had. If he weren't so angry, he'd be embarrassed right now.

"Shit!" He slammed his fist into the steering wheel.

Kick her to the curb, and apologize to Teddy. You can go back to the way life was before you met the tramp. Your life was so good just a year ago. Remember?

Like it was that easy. Especially now that everything, *everything*, was crumbling down all around him.

Listen. All you have to do is—

"Shut *up!*" he shouted, slamming his fist against the steering wheel again, the intensity of his voice surprising him. Pain flared in his knuckles and wrist.

The front door to the house swung open, and Christian walked out. Daniel leaned forward to get a good look at him in person. Although it was December, the guy was wearing a sleeveless shirt that showed off his biceps. He had the enviable build of a fitness model. Well-muscled, toned. The kind of physique Daniel had always aspired to have and had fallen just short of.

The guy leaned against his garage, a phone pressed to his ear. He was laughing. Who was he talking to? Was it Mia?

Blood roared in Daniel's ears.

Want me to make him go away? Billy had asked. *Just say the word, man. I do that, too.*

Again, he wondered what Billy had meant. It sounded violent—and violence in his book was out of the question.

Or was it?

Maybe the guy had earned it.

He was sleeping with his wife.

His goddamn wife, for Chrissake.

Now you've seen him, Daniel, the babysitter in his head said. *Go home.*

He shook his head. "No," he said, staring hard at the younger man, his head filling with fantasies of things he'd like to do to the guy. Things that would quickly wipe the smile off his handsome face.

CHAPTER 36

MIA

THAT EVENING, BRUCE ran to the door and whined. Daniel was home.

Mia froze, unsure of how to play her hand.

This morning she'd been convinced Billy had been sitting outside of Christian's house, but as the day had progressed, she'd become less certain and wondered if she might have just been paranoid. After all, she hadn't gotten but maybe an hour of sleep again.

The ceramic tile was cool beneath her bare feet as she approached the foyer. Hearing the key slide into the lock, she took a deep breath and tried to center herself. The door opened, and Daniel appeared, the chilly night air rushing in with him.

She wrung her hands together and watched him as he shrugged out of his jacket and hung it on the coatrack. "I made dinner. Earlier. You want me to heat you up a plate?"

"No. Thank you."

He walked past her without even looking at her.

She'd left the television on for background noise and saw that he was staring at it. On the screen, protesters were chanting and carrying signs outside an office building. A man she recognized was being interviewed.

She stepped closer to the television. "Isn't that your boss, Teddy?"

Daniel nodded, watching the images on the screen.

"I know these parents are well intentioned," Teddy was saying into the microphone, "but so much goes into the approval of a drug. I assure you, these drugs are rigorously and painstakingly studied. Even more so because they're given to children. And it's not only important that kids get Respira. It's actually dangerous for them not to. For both the child and our public's health."

The camera pulled back to reveal the reporter, an attractive Asian woman in her early twenties dressed in a black suit.

"Is it true that the CDC is thinking of adding Respira to the schedule of required vaccinations for kids to attend school?" she asked.

"Yes, it's true. Immunoceuticals like Respira will certainly be added. It's not a question of if but when. And, frankly, it can't happen soon enough. When a drug like this is available, every child deserves to benefit from it. Whether parents want it or not."

"Thank you, Dr. Reynolds," the reporter said. She turned back to the camera and signed off, then the news went to commercial.

"Parents were picketing outside your office today?"

Daniel nodded.

"Sorry. Is that what's bothering you?" she asked.

Daniel's face seemed to darken. His eyes bore into hers. "And why would you think something's bothering me?"

"Because you slept in your office last night. And you didn't answer my calls or texts."

If it had been Billy this morning, then Daniel might know about Christian. But if he did, why wasn't he saying anything? Or maybe

Daniel had found out about something else somehow. Something far worse.

Her heart beating wildly, she stepped closer to him, slipped her arms around his waist. "Did you find out anything else about who left those news articles?" she asked, breathing him in. He once again smelled of alcohol. When didn't he these days?

He peeled her arms away. "No. Not yet." He mumbled that he was going to his office and headed for the staircase.

"Daniel?" she called.

He turned and looked at her. She recognized the look on his face. Anger. Maybe even hate. Still, she tried. There was so much to lose, and she was scared to lose it. She had to do something to clear the bad energy between them. To help preserve their relationship. She'd do just about anything.

"Daniel," she pleaded. "Please. Let's talk."

He stared at her. "Later."

"Okay," she said. "I love you."

She watched him clench his jaw; then he walked up the stairs. A moment later, she heard his office door slam.

CHAPTER 37

RACHEL

RACHEL SAT IN a dimly lit hospital room with her lifeless daughter. The room was bland and sterile and contained only a gurney, a couple of chairs, a stainless-steel table, and a box of crisp tissues. She'd been sitting in the room for hours when there was a soft knock on the door.

A tall, thin man wearing a button-down shirt and a lab coat stepped in. Flanking him was an orderly and the nurse she'd been turning away all day. When the man in the lab coat laid a hand on Rachel's shoulder, her panic ratcheted up another notch. They were going to make her leave.

"Good evening, Ms. Jacobs. I'm Dr. Howard," he said, sitting in one of the room's two chairs. His forehead creased. "I'm so very sorry for your loss."

Rachel stared at the man through her tears and nodded. Or at least she thought she did.

"I understand you've spoken with Suzanne Whitney, one of our grief counselors," he said. "Suzanne is great at what she does. She'll help you coordinate the funeral arrangements for your daughter, and . . ."

Funeral arrangements.

Please . . . let me be dreaming.

Martha said that Suzie had stopped breathing. Dr. Rowdy told her that her little girl had been declared DOA: dead on arrival. *Dead on arrival.* Rachel asked if Suzie had another seizure, but no one seemed to know at this point. How could Martha have let this happen? How could *she* have let this happen? It felt like someone was standing on her chest. The bottom of her rib cage burned from the many hours of crying.

She was vaguely aware that the man was still talking. But his voice sounded far away. His words pointless. *Everything* was pointless, surreal. "Is there someone we can call? Someone who can drive you home?" the man was asking.

Home.

There was no home without Suzie.

CHAPTER 38

DANIEL

DANIEL CALLED IN sick for the first time in his two-year career as a doctor.

He isolated himself in his office most of the day, figuring out his finances and typing his letter of resignation, still unsure of what the hell he was going to do with his life now that the one he had so carefully built was coming apart at the seams.

He squeezed the bridge of his nose. There were so many things he needed to do and think about. It was difficult to prioritize everything.

Mia had knocked around 6:00 a.m. to tell him she'd made him breakfast. A few hours later, she slid a note beneath the door to let him know she had left lunch for him and was now going out.

Tell her you know about Christian. Tell her to pack her stuff. To get the hell out of your house! the voice roared in his head. Lately, it had become louder, more insistent. He cracked open the seal of a bottle of Jameson and poured a drink in an attempt to shut it up.

He didn't have the mental energy to make a decision about Mia just yet. There was still a part of him that didn't want to see her go.

Daniel . . . No.

He was going to take care of one thing at a time. Shift his focus back to Respira and the children it was harming. His relationship issues would have to take a back seat . . . for now. He'd just put one foot in front of the other and take things at a reasonable pace or else he feared he would snap.

He searched for the number of that medical journalist. He wanted to meet her to see what she wanted. He would also reach out to Rachel. To apologize for not giving her concerns more attention, and he'd ask if there was anything he could still do to help her and Suzie.

❖ ❖ ❖

An hour later, Daniel turned off San Vincente Boulevard onto Montana Avenue and found New World Grill, the farm-to-table-themed restaurant where he and Gail Whitman had agreed to meet.

He handed his keys to the valet and walked in, inhaling the sweet scent of cedar. He told the hostess he was meeting someone and wandered through the restaurant looking for the redhead whom he'd seen Teddy chase out of the office. He found her sitting in a booth toward the back of the restaurant. She was dressed crisply in a blue jacket over a white blouse.

She stood up when she saw him. "Thank you so much for meeting me," she said, smiling warmly. She held out her hand. As he shook it, he noticed the right side of her face was bruised, and there was an inch-long cut across her forehead.

The waitress stopped by the table, and he ordered a whiskey. After she'd walked off, Gail regarded him. "Like I said on the phone, everything we talk about today is off the record."

If Teddy could only see you now, Daniel. For God's sake, get out of here. This woman isn't to be trusted. She's a hack reporter!

The voice had screamed at him the whole way to the restaurant. He continued to ignore it. He wanted to hear what this woman had to say.

"Why did you want to talk to me?" Daniel asked.

"Rachel Jacobs told me about you. She said it was fine to mention her name."

He'd suspected it had been Rachel. "If this is about Suzie, you need to know that I didn't know—"

Gail shook her head. "I'm not here to attack you, Doctor. Quite the opposite. I'm here because I think you want the same thing I do."

"Which is?"

"To raise awareness about Respira. To get it taken off the market until it can be studied properly."

How did Rachel know he had concerns?

As though reading his thoughts, Gail said, "Rachel Jacobs isn't the only person I've spoken to. I've heard you've been raising concerns."

"Who—?"

"The source asked for anonymity. I'm sure you can understand."

He nodded but was still very curious.

"So, am I right to assume you have concerns?" Gail asked.

Leave, dammit. You're making your situation even worse!

"Yes. I do have concerns."

Gail nodded. "Then we'll have a lot to discuss."

Gail explained that her nonprofit, Help Our Kids, provided parents, other caregivers, and medical practitioners unbiased information on pharmaceuticals commonly prescribed to kids. "When Respira hit my radar, I became especially concerned and launched a sister site called GetTheFactsAboutRespira.com, and it's been my focus the last two months."

"I'm familiar with the site. Impressive resource when I'm not getting 404 errors," Daniel said.

"Yeah, that." Gail sighed. "It gets hacked often, despite having both browser and server-side validation, remote file upload denial, and HTTPS encryption."

Daniel's forehead creased. "Your site's being hacked?"

"Multiple times a day."

"Do you know who's doing it?"

"My guess is it's someone who's profiting handsomely from Respira's sales," she said. "We maintain a bank of mirrored servers, so we can usually bring the website back online within a few minutes. But now with the big push to get Respira on the shot schedule, I can barely keep it up."

"I'm sorry to hear that," Daniel said, studying the bruising on the side of her face. Wondering how she'd gotten it.

The waitress set Daniel's drink on the table. Daniel took a long sip, then set the glass down. "What I don't understand is how Respira received approval in the first place. I mean, for one, it contains an exceptionally high amount of aluminum. For two, there've been no long-term studies. Our kids *are* the long-term study. That doesn't sit well with me. Hell, it shouldn't sit well with anyone."

Gail nodded. "Yes, it was certainly fast-tracked like other drugs of its kind, not studied nearly as long or as rigorously as most other pharmaceutical products. In terms of aluminum, it meets the FDA's guidelines but only when it's broken into the three doses. It seems it was carefully designed so that each dose hits just at the maximum allowable dose. But inject three doses over a period of six days, and kids are dealing with a shitstorm of aluminum. It appears some kids can tolerate it in the short-term. But some kids can't. It's like a lottery of sorts; we don't know who will be injured until after the kid is injected. Then there are the doctors who are telling everyone that the kids' adverse reactions are not connected. They're underreporting the reactions, if they even report them at all. Not only that, but aluminum is only one of many concerning ingredients," Gail said. "This drug contains three known carcinogens, but no one's talking about that, either. That or the fact that Respira hasn't been tested for carcinogenicity and probably never will be."

He thought about how the other doctors at brunch refused to even look at the information he'd compiled for them. Didn't want to hear his concerns. Teddy's rant about plausible deniability. He decided to talk to Gail about all of it.

When he was done, Gail nodded. "Willful ignorance. It's almost impossible to get someone to understand something when his or her livelihood depends on them *not* understanding it, isn't it?" She sat back in her chair. "Immunext and the industry as a whole are doing everything in their power to control the conversation right now. There are over sixty more immunoceuticals being rushed through the pipeline as we speak. If they let parents question one, they'll be much more likely to question the others, which would be disastrous to sales."

Daniel sipped his drink and listened.

"A lot of folks want to see this medication succeed despite its medical value. Then there are people like your boss, Dr. Reynolds, who have even more riding on it winning a coveted spot on the shot schedule."

"What do you mean? Because of the incentive bonus?"

"Well, there's that, which of course is rather significant and difficult for a lot of doctors to say no to," Gail said. "When promised a juicy piece of a multibillion-dollar pie, people, doctors included, will justify doing things they never thought they'd ever stoop to doing." She tilted her head and watched him. "But it appears Dr. Reynolds has gone an extra step. While digging through Immunext's SEC filings, I made an interesting discovery. Large blocks of stock were purchased by a fairly new offshore trading company named Teddy Bear Trading. The owners of the company? Dr. Reynolds's wife, his sister-in-law, a brother-in-law, and a cousin."

Daniel's breath caught in his chest. "Wait. Teddy bought stock in Immunext?"

"It appears so."

"How did you find that out?"

"SEC filings are a matter of public record, Doctor. When Respira makes it onto the schedule, shares of their stock will explode, and Reynolds will be financially set for life."

Daniel was speechless.

"People do dark, despicable things when it comes to money," Gail said.

There was a heavy, sick weight in the air. The puzzle was finally coming together. *Now* Teddy's behavior was starting to make all the sense in the world. Daniel shook his head. He'd looked up to Teddy. Had thought he was an excellent doctor. But that was before. "So, why me? Why did you want to meet with me?"

Gail leaned forward and clasped her hands together. "I'd like to do an interview with you. To go public with your concerns." She was silent for a moment, as though letting what she'd said sink in before going further. "Of course, it'll be risky for you, so I understand if you decline. But I hope you won't because our children need your voice, Doctor. I've published stories from several parents of kids who were injured by Respira . . . and while it helps raise awareness, at the end of the day, parents can scream until they're blue in the face that this drug is hurting their kids, but most people won't listen. Most will quickly write off parents without even taking the time to hear them out."

Daniel's phone buzzed. He looked at the screen. It was the office. Probably wanting to find out if he would be in tomorrow. He silenced it, deciding to call back in a few minutes.

Gail continued, "But it's different when a doctor speaks up. What a doctor says carries a lot of weight. I've spoken to half a dozen doctors and nurses over the last month who tell me behind the scenes that they are concerned about Respira, but they aren't willing to go public because they know they will face backlash that could cripple their careers. Although there are physicians in Europe and Japan who have been speaking out for months now about their concerns, our media has failed to cover any of it, so the American public has no idea. We need more American doctors to speak up."

Daniel nodded. "Okay. Give me some time to think about it."

"Fair enough."

Daniel decided to tell her about the brown envelope and its contents. While he talked, she seemed to listen intently.

"So, you're already on their radar."

Daniel knitted his eyebrows. "I guess so, but I don't understand why. Only a few people know that I have concerns."

"Well, *I* knew, didn't I?"

Good point.

"Word travels fast in these circles, Doctor," she said. "Of course, if you *do* decide to go public, you're going to have to take safety precautions."

He thought of Dr. Hemsworth. Also the possibility, however small, that Andy's death might be connected, too. "So, I don't understand. If doctors who speak out about this are in danger, then why not you, too?" Daniel asked.

Gail's laugh was bitter. "I get death threats all the time. I can't even step foot in my own house or drive my car right now. Not to mention stay in the same hotel more than one night at a time. Three weeks ago, I was working in my living room when someone unloaded five rounds into the bay window. The police never came up with any leads. Then, a week later, the brakes in my car were cut. Hence the bruise, the gash," she said, pointing to her face. "Three nights ago, when I returned to my hotel room, I found it ransacked, and my laptop was gone. Trust me. I'm always, *always* watching my back."

"That's . . . unbelievable."

"Believe it. It's true," Gail said. "But I'm not going to let them frighten me. I'm not going to stop spreading the word about this drug. They'll have to kill me first."

Another call was coming in. It was the office again. Daniel frowned, wondering why they were being so persistent. Maybe something was wrong. "Excuse me. I need to take this," he said and stood up.

"Dr. Winters here," he said, walking toward the bathroom.

"Hey, Doc." It was Margy. Her voice was muffled, as though she was covering the phone with her hand. "I'm afraid I have some bad news."

"What is it?" he asked, pushing open the door to the men's room and walking in.

"We received word that one of your patients passed away."

"What? Who?"

"Suzie Jacobs."

It took Daniel a second to process the words. When he did, his vision began to tunnel. He leaned against the long counter and fought to breathe. "What?"

He realized Margy was still talking, but he heard the rest of her words through a fog.

"I'm really sorry to have to relay such bad news."

"What happened?"

"All we know at this point is that she died in her sleep."

He squeezed his eyes shut, thinking about the kid who died of respiratory arrest during the drug's remarkably short drug trial. "Jesus."

After ending the call, Daniel dropped his phone on the counter, whirled around, and punched one of the metal stall doors. A stinging pain shot through his knuckles and up to his elbow.

He punched it again.

CHAPTER 39

DANIEL

SOMEONE SLID A shot glass in front of Daniel. He looked up and saw it was from a man about his age with a large mole in the middle of his forehead. He'd been so deep inside his head, he hadn't even noticed the guy was sitting next to him. "You looked like you needed one," the man said. He held up his own shot glass. "Cheers."

"Thanks," Daniel said. He toasted the man, his words wobbly. He tipped his head and downed the liquor. Even though it had been tequila—he usually couldn't even stand to smell the stuff—he didn't so much as wince.

He'd had a lot to drink.

Way too much.

But at this point he didn't care.

He needed to unfurl the knots in his stomach.

Suzie.

He couldn't stop seeing her face. Rachel's. He wished he'd done things differently. Rachel had trusted him, and he'd been wrong. He knew he'd never be able to forgive himself.

He'd told Gail that he would go on record. That he was going to help in any way he could to get Respira off the market until proper safety testing could be conducted. Gail said she would call him again tomorrow to talk about their next steps.

Gail. He had so much more to tell her. And he was going to tell her everything. Everything that—

He lost his train of thought.

He peered down at his drink. He was staring at it when a large pair of hands appeared in front of him. He looked up to see the bartender. "It's last call."

What? But it was just the afternoon a few minutes ago.

He looked around. All but one of the tables flanking the bar was empty. In the distance, a band was tearing down. He picked up his phone to see the time. It was late. He must have lost track of time.

The bartender lingered.

"How much do I owe you?" Daniel said, reaching into his wallet to pull out some money.

"You have a tab going. I'll just close it out."

"Okay. But put one more on it. I'll drink it fast."

Bad things, Daniel.

Daniel wondered how the hell the voice could still be awake after everything he'd drunk.

You're really screwing up, you know.

"Shut the hell up," Daniel seethed.

"Sorry?" the bartender asked.

Daniel looked up at the young man. His head was cocked, and his brows were knitted together.

"Oh, nothing. Just thinking out loud," Daniel said, chagrined that he was starting to get more and more mixed up between the voice and his own voice.

The bartender nodded and walked away.

Since hearing the news about Suzie, Daniel had also begun thinking about his brother, Jason. Of those last weeks that he had been in the hospital, dying from leukemia. He remembered it like it was yesterday. The dusky tone his brother's face had taken. How frail and weak he had become.

The girl wasn't your fault. You were simply doing your job.

No. That's not true. I should have known.

You were just doing your job.

That's a cop-out, and you know it.

No, this . . . turning to this poison is the cop-out.

I said shut the hell up. He tried to fling the voice back into its little room, but it dug in its heels.

You'd be dead without me. You know that.

When Daniel closed his eyes, lights flashed behind his eyelids. He was going to have to figure out a way to get home. Driving was out of the question. So was calling Mia.

Home.

Mia.

Neither word sounded warm or comforting anymore.

Maybe he'd call an Uber. He picked up his phone and was searching for his Uber app when someone placed a hand on his back. He turned to see who it was, and the room tilted.

It was Billy. No, two Billys.

"Jesus, Dan. You look like shit."

Yeah. He'd been hearing that a lot lately.

"What are you doing here?" Daniel asked, his words bouncing into one another.

Billy laughed, then stared at him. But the grin quickly slipped from his face. "You're kidding, right?"

Daniel blinked.

"You seriously don't remember calling me? A couple of hours ago. You said you needed a ride home."

Daniel nodded. Or at least he thought he did.

Billy . . . both of them . . . laughed. "Damn. You really don't remember, do you?"

"I've had a pretty shitty day," Daniel mumbled, but getting his tongue to land in the right places so he could make the appropriate sounds was much more difficult than usual.

Billy patted him on the shoulder. "Come on, let's get you home."

When Billy touched Daniel's hand, it screamed with pain. He yanked it away.

"Jesus, man. What'd you do to your hand?"

❖ ❖ ❖

Daniel sank into the passenger seat of Billy's car and plunged his feet into a graveyard of trash. Discarded fast-food bags and other items sat almost a foot deep on the floorboard. He trained his gaze on the glove compartment so the world didn't tilt. If he closed his eyes, looked out the window, or even at Billy, he knew he would vomit.

Everyone around him was failing him. Teddy had failed him, his colleagues, Mia, his father. Strangely, Billy, of all people, had been there for him more than anyone in his entire life. Billy, who was never on time, always screwing something up, and couldn't keep a job for the life of him. If it hadn't been for Billy, Daniel was pretty sure he never would have applied for medical school and would probably be working as a computer repairman now, which is what he'd originally set out to do. He laughed out loud at the realization, and the sound sent pain knifing through his head.

"What's so funny?" Billy asked.

Funny? He didn't remember. "I don't know."

"You're a mess, dude. How long were you in there?"

"Hell if I know."

"How about some tunes?" Out the corner of his eye, he saw Billy fidget with the car's stereo. Suddenly, Iron Maiden began blasting from the speakers.

Daniel's brain rattled. He winced and brought his hands to his head to hold his skull together. To keep it in one piece.

"Can you turn that off?" he asked.

The music vanished.

"Sorry, man."

Snippets of the conversation from his meeting with Gail ran circles in his head. Then the fact that Suzie had died. His throat tightened, and tears filled his eyes. "A little girl died," he said. The tears slipped down his cheeks before he could bring his swollen hand to his face to wipe them away. "She was only eighteen months old. A patient of mine. And it was my fault."

"Holy shit."

More tears fell. He wiped them away with the back of his hand, and his knuckles stung.

"Dude. Does your boss know?"

"Probably."

"Shit. You gonna lose your job?"

Daniel laughed grimly. "Only if I stop administering the drug that killed her."

A pause. Then: "Dude, you're drunk. That makes no sense."

Billy was right. It didn't make sense. None of it did.

Blood surged through his veins as he thought about the stock Teddy had bought in Immunext. The man was a crook and a pathetic excuse for a doctor.

He straightened a little in his seat, still careful to keep his eyes on the glove compartment. He thought about going home to Mia in the shape he was in. What would she think? Well, to hell with her. She was part of the reason he was drinking so much. If it hadn't been for—

A thought flickered in his mind. He stewed on it, turning it around in his head. "You said you could make Christian go away. What did you mean by that?"

The car was silent. He could hear only the sound of rubber on pavement. "You know," Billy said. "Scare the living shit out of him. Make sure he stays away from your old lady."

Daniel thought about Christian's model-perfect face. His disgustingly hard body. Mia's arms flung around him. The guy probably had pet his dog when Bruce was over at his house with her. More anger bloomed inside of him. An anger bigger than he'd ever felt before. "I want you to do it."

More rubber on pavement, then: "You sure?" Daniel could hear a little excitement in Billy's voice.

Daniel nodded. "Rough him up—and make sure it hurts."

"Yeah, sure. You got it, man."

Daniel's phone rang. He fumbled for it and checked the screen, expecting it to be Mia again. She'd been blowing up his phone with calls and texts all night. But the screen read: *Unknown Number*.

Frowning, he answered the call. "Dr. Winters," he said, trying to keep his words from tumbling into one another.

"Call and retract any statements you made," said a deep, gravelly voice on the other end of the line. "If anything you told that bitch reporter goes public, I'll make sure you and your ex-con wife live to regret it."

What the hell?

"Who is this?"

"Call off the reporter. Immediately," the man said, then the line went dead.

CHAPTER 40

MIA

IT WAS LATE when Mia heard a car pull into the driveway.

Daniel was finally home.

She lay on the couch, listening. But instead of hearing his key slide into the lock, someone knocked. She thought about how heavily Daniel had been drinking lately, and her heart beat like a drum in her chest.

Had he been in an accident?

She rushed to the front door and peered through the peephole but couldn't make out the man on the other side. "Hello?" she called. "Who's there?"

"It's Billy. Daniel's friend. Daniel's here with me, but he's . . . he's obviously had a lot to drink."

She hesitated.

"I'm telling the truth, lady. Please hurry up. Your husband isn't exactly light."

She opened the front door to find Billy propping up a very drunk Daniel. She stepped aside to let Billy help her husband inside.

"Where should I put him?"

She pointed to the staircase. "Upstairs."

With one of Daniel's arms flung over each of their shoulders, they walked a barely conscious Daniel up the stairs. Mia stole glances at Billy. Was he the guy she'd seen at Christian's? If so, what had he seen? Why had he been there?

A few minutes later, they had Daniel in bed. Bruce sniffed at him and whined. Sensing Daniel was in bad shape, he jumped up on the bed and curled up next to him.

"If I were you, I'd get a bucket or trash can or something to keep over here," Billy said, pointing to the floor beside Daniel. "He's been fine so far, but you never know. And you might want to put something on those knuckles."

Mia looked at Daniel's knuckles. They were swollen and crusted in blood. What the—? "Did he get into a fight?"

"I have no idea what he did tonight. He was pretty out of it by the time I got there."

Mia nodded. "Thanks for bringing him home."

Billy's eyes lingered on her. He clenched his jaw and stared at her with such venom in his eyes she was certain it *had* been him she'd seen parked outside of Christian's house. Startled, she took a step backward.

"I'll see my way out," he said.

She nodded. Then she listened to his footsteps as he walked from the room. They stopped when he got to the staircase.

"Mia?" he called.

She went to the doorway. "Yeah?"

"Make sure you lock the door behind me. I know this sounds strange, but I think someone might have followed us here."

Followed them?

Monte's face flashed into Mia's mind. Then Dr. Hemsworth and his family. An icy sensation raced through her. "Okay, I will," she said.

She followed Billy down the steps and to the front door. Once he was outside, she locked up. Then she walked around the interior of the house and made sure the other doors were locked. The windows, too.

She grabbed a large bowl and filled it with water, then went upstairs and cleaned Daniel's knuckles while he lay in bed. She noticed for the first time that he seemed thinner. He also hadn't shaved today. As she was bandaging his hand, his eyes fluttered open.

She smiled at him. "Looks like you had quite a night, mister."

He blinked at her. "You remember that question you asked me that first night at the bar?" he asked, his words horribly slurred.

"Which one?"

"If I thought I was destined for happiness."

Mia nodded. "Yes, I remember."

He shot her an icy look. "I've been thinking about that the last couple of days—and the answer is no."

Mia opened her mouth, but nothing came out.

Daniel's eyes seemed to glow. "I should have known better than to trust someone like you."

CHAPTER 41

DANIEL

WHEN DANIEL WOKE up, he felt like someone had pounded on his head with a hammer. Everything ached. Even his skin.

He cringed at the harshness of the morning sun streaming in through the window next to the bed. The ceiling fan above his head rotated in slow circles, and its repetition nauseated him.

He familiarized himself with his surroundings, relieved to find himself at home, in his own bed. He turned his head to the side, his vision taking a second to catch up with the motion. The other side of the bed was empty and didn't look as though it had been slept in.

What day was it?

What time?

It was a weekday. He grabbed his phone and realized it was after 8:00 a.m. He was already late for work. There were several messages in his text message in-box. Many of them from Teddy. *Fucking crook,* he thought. He wasn't interested in reading anything Teddy had to say, so he ignored the man's messages and texted Margy letting her know he wouldn't be in again.

He slowly reconstructed last night. His meeting with Gail. He struggled to remember everything that had happened and what had been said. Some of it trickled slowly back to him. Some of the things Gail had told him about Respira. The fact that he'd agreed to go public about his concerns. He'd told her she could write about everything he'd shared with her last night if she thought any of it would help.

Then he remembered the phone call from the office.

Suzie.

Oh, God. No.

Bile slid up his throat.

Every inch of his body screamed as he dragged himself out of bed and staggered to the bathroom. He barely made it to the toilet before he lost last night's alcohol. As he gripped the toilet's porcelain rim, he noticed his right hand was bandaged. He tried to remember why, but he had no recollection.

When he was finished vomiting, he went to the sink and flipped the light switch on the wall. The fluorescent light overhead flickered off and on as he splashed cold water on his face.

You're going to kill yourself, Daniel. You know that, right?

He stared at his reflection, the water dripping from his bloated face. He looked like shit. He squeezed some toothpaste on his toothbrush. How had he gotten home? He hadn't driven, had he? Had Mia been awake when he got home? Had he spoken to her? Was she at home now?

After brushing his teeth, he shuffled to the guest room to look out the window. His car wasn't there. He tried to think. Then he remembered Billy. Billy had driven him home. His car had been filthy.

He and Billy had talked. About what, he couldn't remember. He felt like it was about something important, though. Something he *should* be remembering. It was just on the edge of his recall.

What the hell was it?

An even greater sense of unease overtook him.

In the shower, the water pelted his skin like thousands of tiny razor blades. It was too painful. He turned the water off and stood there, dripping, freezing, and just as filthy as before.

No more damn drinking, Daniel. You're going to—

"I *know*, dammit!" he said, his words reverberating painfully in his skull. But he agreed. The drinking had gone too far again.

He was done with it.

He couldn't go on like this.

He was going to get help.

You mean it?

"Yeah. I do."

Good. Now tell Mia you know about Christian, and kick her ass to the curb.

He nodded. "I will."

But first, he had questions for her. He wanted to know why. Ask her how she could look him in the eyes and tell him she loved him while she was screwing some other guy. Ask if she'd ever really loved him.

Suddenly, too exhausted to even stand any longer, he lumbered back into the bedroom and, still wrapped in the towel, crawled back into bed.

Bruce's ears pricked, and he whined, staring at the bedroom door. Daniel figured someone might be at the front door, but there was no way he was going to go downstairs, no way he was getting out of bed right now. His body felt like a huge boulder, too heavy to move. He needed some rest.

"No, buddy. Stop," he muttered.

Bruce continued to stare at the door, panting.

He'd sleep for another hour, then get up. Read Teddy's texts. Figure out what his next steps were. Just as he was closing his eyes, his phone dinged on the nightstand. A text from Billy:

Just brought your car back to you. The keys are under the
driver's seat. About to head out now. I'll let you know when it's
all done.

Daniel's brow creased. *When what's done?* he wondered, and he
dozed off again.

CHAPTER 42

MIA

MIA SAT OUTSIDE of Pavilions, an upscale grocery store in Malibu, waiting for the store to open. When she'd left the house, Daniel had still been in bed, sleeping.

His words last night frightened her.

I should have known better than to trust someone like you.

What hurt the worst about his words was that he'd been right. She wasn't someone worthy of his trust. Their relationship had been based on lies. He'd never known the real her. The person she'd been most of her life. Also, she'd gotten the news she'd been waiting for. Now she had to tell him—and she'd tell him not just the truth about that, but everything. The whole sordid story. She'd tell him when he woke up. Then she'd pack.

She wondered what he already knew. Had he somehow traced the money back to Christian? No, that was impossible. She'd been careful and had given Christian cash. When Christian had first asked for the money, she had cringed. At that point, she still hadn't known if she could trust him, thought he might be taking advantage of her, but she hadn't had much of a choice. She felt she had to help him. He'd been behind on his rent and was going to be evicted.

When they'd first started dating, she'd told Daniel that she'd had a troubled past and that she didn't like to think about it, much less talk about it. She had told him how she'd been an only child of a single mother. How her mother hadn't been much of a mother at all. She'd told him a little bit about her friend, Sam. How he'd been the only person who had ever been there for her, and how the US Marine Corps had whisked him off. But she hadn't told him any of the important stuff. Luckily, Daniel had been laid back and hadn't pried.

"Take your time," he'd said. "When you're ready to tell me more, I'll be here."

The idea of being able to start over with a blank slate had felt wonderful at first. She'd have time to figure out what to tell him and how to tell him. On her terms. When she was ready. But then Christian happened.

The store's double doors opened, and an employee in a Pavilions uniform walked out and signaled to the people who were sitting in their vehicles that the store was now open to the public.

Mia climbed out of her car and walked toward the supermarket. She noticed a poster for Respira as she walked in. On it was an image of a mom and a little boy. They were gazing into each other's eyes. The words below them read:

YOU WANT THE BEST FOR ME, DON'T YOU? SHOW ME YOU DO
BY GETTING ME RESPIRA TODAY.

Apparently, the drug was being offered in the supermarket's pharmacy. She literally couldn't go anywhere without seeing or hearing an ad for it. There were the television commercials, ads plastered on the sides of city buses, bus stops, taxicabs, cash registers, on the radio, on websites. She couldn't recall a bigger push for a single drug.

Inside the supermarket, she found a cart and pushed it across the polished floor to the produce section. The market smelled like freshly baked bread and made her stomach growl.

She thought back to how all the pivotal things had unfolded in her life. Two weeks after Sam left for boot camp, she'd met Monte at the Laundromat. The next day, he took her on her very first date at an Applebee's restaurant. She had been only fifteen, but her mother hadn't paid much attention to her whereabouts. Two weeks later, Monte had convinced her to run away from home to live with him. He said he'd take care of her, and she had believed him. It took her only a week to realize that he was able to afford their nice apartment and his shiny black Lexus because he was dealing drugs, but at the time, she hadn't cared. What had mattered most to her was that she wasn't lonely any longer. A week after she'd moved in with him, he'd begun hitting her and playing mind games.

"Can I help you with anything, ma'am?" a teenage employee wearing a white apron asked, yanking her from her memories.

She smiled tightly. "No, thanks. I'm fine."

Listening to the classical music playing from the speakers overhead, she rolled her cart to the meat section and picked out two porterhouse steaks for tonight's dinner. Then she chose potato salad, coleslaw, and in the bakery, freshly baked sourdough bread.

Buying this much food was ridiculous. Daniel was going to be too upset to eat any of it, anyway. But she had to keep moving in order not to break down, so she just kept grabbing food and placing it into the shopping cart.

CHAPTER 43

RACHEL

RACHEL WALKED INTO Healing Hands Pediatrics, her right hand buried in her jacket pocket. Clutching her handgun, she asked for Dr. Winters.

"He's out of the office right now. Can I help you?" the woman at the desk said, her voice sounding far away. In fact, everything had sounded strangely distant since Suzie had passed.

Rachel blinked, trying to grasp the woman's words.

Dr. Winters wasn't in?

That had been the last thing she'd expected.

"Ma'am, are you okay?" the woman asked.

"Is that other doctor here? The big one?" she asked.

The woman regarded her for a moment, then said, "Dr. Reynolds is in a meeting off-site at the moment. Perhaps someone else can help you?"

Rachel turned and faced the lobby, where a sea of parents and children were waiting. A mother bounced a little girl with blonde hair who looked a little like Suzie on her knee. A father in a dark-colored business suit was talking on his cell phone, absently watching his son tap on the glass of the practice's aquarium.

Blood pounded in Rachel's ears as she stepped toward them. "They killed my daughter," she said.

The mother stopped bouncing her daughter on her knee.

Rachel took a deep breath. She said it again even louder. "They killed my little girl. They said Respira was safe, but they lied. It killed her. She stopped breathing in her sleep."

"Ma'am?" the receptionist said behind her. "You can't—"

"They kept telling me it was safe. But my baby is dead now. Because I believed them. I don't want that to happen to you."

"Ma'am, sorry, but you need to leave," the woman behind her was saying.

But Rachel continued talking. Continued telling these parents what had happened to her little girl. Someone needed to tell them the truth. "Don't trust them," she said.

The father in the business suit was off his phone now, standing by the aquarium, his hands pressed to his little boy's shoulders. He was watching her carefully.

"Ma'am, we called 911," the woman behind her said.

Someone gently clutched Rachel's arm just above the elbow and tried to guide her toward the clinic's double doors. She yanked away. "Let go of me!" she screamed. She turned back to the parents and said, "I'm not crazy. I'm not. I'm telling you the truth."

A man in a white lab coat and green tie was now standing in front of her. "Ma'am, please come with me."

"Are you a doctor?" she asked, her hand gripping the gun more tightly.

"Yes, ma'am. I'm Dr. Thornton. Let's take you to the back, where we can talk."

The doctor had a kind face. Maybe he'd listen. Maybe he'd care. She nodded and let him lead her into the hallway. He guided her to room six and motioned for her to step in. She did so, then turned to him and watched him hold up a finger.

"Wait right here. Let me go grab you a glass of water, okay? Then we'll talk."

He walked out of the room and closed the door behind him.

She heard whispering in the hallway. She grabbed Fluff Fluff from her pocket and started to cry. She had been waiting by herself for what seemed like an eternity, smelling the stuffed animal and clutching it between her hands, when she heard police sirens in the distance.

She went to the door and tried the doorknob, but it wouldn't turn. Was someone on the other side holding the knob? She tried again to open the door. And again, the knob wouldn't turn.

The doctor . . . he'd lied to her. He'd never come back.

He hadn't wanted to talk to her, had he? He'd lied, like the other doctors.

Her whole body trembling, she took the gun from her pocket and flipped the safety.

CHAPTER 44

MIA

WHEN MIA RETURNED home from the grocery store, she tiptoed up the stairs and opened the bedroom door a crack. Daniel was still snoring. She went back downstairs to put the food away and marinate the steaks.

When she finished and he still hadn't woken, she lay on the couch and waited. After hours went by and he still wasn't awake, she decided to take a walk on the beach. Although it was freezing outside, she walked barefoot in the sand, letting the cool grains sink between her toes.

She let her thoughts loop back to Monte. She'd wanted to leave the moment he'd first hit her, but he'd threatened her. Told her that if she ever tried to leave him, he'd come after her. That he'd kill her. And she'd believed him. She'd endured beatings, belittling, and malicious pranks for six years before mustering the courage to try to leave. The day she finally decided to do it, he'd been at a casino with his buddies. She'd thrown some of her belongings in a large suitcase, then grabbed some of his meth in hopes of selling it for enough money to get her far away. She drove to the apartment of one of his longtime buyers with hopes of selling the meth to him at a fraction of the price Monte would have charged.

But as soon as the man answered the door, she realized he was high and that she'd made a big mistake. Before she could turn away, though, he grabbed her by the hair and yanked her inside. While she screamed and fought, he pulled her to the living room and yanked her jeans down. Panic ripped through her because she knew she was about to be raped or maybe even worse.

There'd been a knife on the coffee table, its blade glistening beneath the warm glow of a lamp. Next to it were two small mounds of white powder, a credit card, and a half-eaten cheeseburger. As the man slid her panties down, she grabbed the knife and slashed the air with it, hoping to hurt him badly enough that he'd let go so she could run. She wanted only to get him off her so she could escape. But when the blade made contact, it severed an artery in his neck, and blood had spurted everywhere. In her face, on the couch, between his fingers.

She'd called 911 immediately, but the damage had already been done. She stood motionless, screaming inside, as she watched his skin grow pale and bleed out right before her eyes. He was dead when the paramedics arrived, and with no witnesses and no physical evidence of a rape, getting off on self-defense hadn't been a sure thing. Her mother hadn't had the money or desire to hire a lawyer, so she'd been given a public defender who had advised her to take a plea bargain, and she did—and she'd spent the next ten long years behind bars in an Arizona state prison.

While in prison, she'd dreamed up the perfect person. One she'd fallen in love with and wanted so badly to one day become. When she got out, she'd used the money she'd earned in prison to assume a new identity. It was important to her to hide from Monte as well as from what she'd done. She'd quickly changed her name from Amy Bishop to Mia O'Brien, then took a bus to California and found a job at Jiminy's.

She spent the next few years working quietly, rebuilding her life, a simple one that hadn't felt dangerous.

When the loneliness got too bad, she'd let herself date a little, but nothing serious. Her contact with men had been just for the physical intimacy. From time to time, she'd needed someone to take away the crippling loneliness at night. After Monte, she'd sworn to herself that she'd never let a man into her heart. And she hadn't . . . for years. But then she'd met Daniel. After their first night together, her gut had told her he might be different. When he kept asking her out, she'd decided to give it a chance, but she knew it was critical to keep her past from him. Daniel was a decent man. A respectable professional. If he'd known whom she'd been, what she'd done, he never would have been able to see past it. Never would have been able to let himself love her. Besides, Amy Bishop was gone. She'd become Mia O'Brien, who was so much more together and mature and much worthier of love than Amy could have ever been.

The first several months, she'd felt as though for the first time in her life, she was getting things right. She knew she'd lucked out to finally find a good man, and she'd wanted nothing more than to be a good partner for Daniel. But the day Daniel returned to work after their honeymoon, she'd received a call from Christian. And that had changed everything. Now, for a woman who had vowed to never give her heart to a man, she was sharing it with two.

And it was tearing everything apart.

She returned to the house and was heading to the stairwell to check on Daniel again when she heard movement upstairs.

He was finally awake.

And she was finally going to tell him everything.

She ran a finger beneath her eyes, clearing away smeared eyeliner, and finished her dinner preparations. She set the table, lit the candles, threw the steaks on the grill, and poured wine. When she was done, she went back to the living room. As she waited, Christian's handsome face flashed in her mind. His bright blue eyes, the musky, masculine scent of whatever cologne it was that he wore, and she felt her heart fill up.

The timing was so horribly bad, but wrong or right, she couldn't say that she regretted him. If Daniel left her, at least she'd still have him. Yes, she'd be devastated at losing Daniel, but if she still had Christian, maybe she could learn to be okay again.

She turned toward the staircase, straightened her spine, and waited for Daniel to walk down.

CHAPTER 45

DANIEL

THE SUN WAS in its death throes when Daniel finally woke up. He'd slept the whole day. He sat up, still wrapped in the damp bath towel from earlier, and now it stuck uncomfortably to his sweat-drenched body.

He could hear music playing downstairs—"Margaritaville" by Jimmy Buffett. A song he and Mia had listened to a lot while in the Caymans. The scent of steak grilling wafted through the air vents.

Noticing he was awake, Bruce stood up, whined once, and licked his face. Feeling queasy and disoriented, Daniel climbed out of bed. He went to the toilet and hurled again. Then he returned to the bedroom, pulled some clothes out of his bureau, and carefully dressed. Grabbing his phone, he headed for the stairwell.

When he reached the stairs, he saw Mia standing in the middle of the living room, her arms folded across her body. She was smiling, but it was a sad smile. Her eyes were red, swollen. It was apparent she'd been crying.

His eyes flitted to the dining room, and he noticed the table was set.

"You haven't eaten all day. You must be hungry," she said, her voice breaking a little.

"No," he answered and walked past her into the kitchen. He set his phone on the counter and grabbed a glass from the cupboard. He filled it with water and gulped it down.

"Can you sit with me?" she asked. "We need to talk."

They sure as hell did.

He nodded and refilled his glass. Then he went to the table and sat down.

Mia followed a minute later, carrying a platter of steaks and a bowl of potato salad. She slid a steak on his plate, then one on hers.

"Potato salad?" she asked.

He shook his head.

He noticed her hands trembling when she placed the bowl in the center of the table. She sat and stared down at her plate for a long moment, silence filling the space between them.

She took a deep breath. "There's something . . . well, a lot of things . . . a lot of *important* things I need to share with you."

He nodded so she would know he was following.

She wrung her hands, then bit into her lower lip. "There are things about me. Things you don't know."

He knows more than you think.

His phone dinged in the kitchen. He'd set it down when he'd poured his glass of water and had forgotten it on the counter. It was probably just Gail. They'd planned to talk again today. Or maybe it was Teddy. Whomever it was, he would call them back. He nodded for Mia to go on.

"I've done some things that I'm not proud of," she said. She took another deep breath and exhaled hard. "Things I never wanted you to know about because I knew that if you knew, you wouldn't want me."

He saw a vulnerability in her eyes that he had never seen before and enjoyed the fact that this was hard for her. He was so angry with her that he *wanted* her to hurt. Maybe needed her to hurt. Like he did.

Tears glistened in her eyes. "I lied when I said that my parents were dead, although they might as well be. I never met my father, and my mother was never much of a mother. When I was fifteen, I met an older man. His name was Monte. When I turned eighteen, we got married."

He stared at the glass of wine she'd poured for him.

Don't even think about it, Daniel. You've reached your ninth life. You realize that, don't you? There will be no more chances.

He didn't argue this time. The voice was right. He needed to be sober for this conversation. No, he needed to stay sober—period. Drinking was not working for him. He knew this logically, but dammit, the wine was flirting with him. Feeling agitated, he tapped his foot on the floor, wondering if maybe he could just wean off alcohol. Drink one glass tonight. Quit for good tomorrow.

You can't. You're an alcoholic.

No. This time I will.

What's it going to take, Daniel? Think about it. Haven't you lost enough?

Mia was talking in the background. "Monte was involved in some things. Cocaine. Meth . . ."

Daniel's phone *dinged!* again.

It kept dinging.

Mia stopped talking and watched him.

Someone obviously wanted to get hold of him badly. He wanted to give Mia his undivided attention, but it was going to be impossible if his phone kept going off.

"Let me see what they want, and then I'll turn my phone off," he said.

She nodded.

He excused himself and went to the kitchen. He picked up his phone from the counter and looked at the screen. There were sixteen text messages and five missed calls. Most were calls from the office and Teddy's cell phone. The most recent messages and calls were from Billy. One had been left less than a minute ago.

Something went wrong. Answer your phone.

Went wrong? What did that mean? He read Billy's previous texts, realizing he'd been trying hard to get hold of him. One of the texts confused him: Will call when it's done.

He'd read that last text earlier, before falling back to sleep. He asked himself again what it meant. When *what* was done? A sense of dread fell over him. He hit Billy's number, and his friend picked up on the first ring.

"Jesus, Dan, where have you been?" Billy asked, sounding out of breath. There was a tremor in his voice Daniel had never heard before.

"What are you talking about?" Daniel asked.

"I went to Christian's. To do, you know, what you asked me to do."

Daniel's pulse sprinted. "What? What are you talking about?"

There was silence on the other end of the phone. "You don't remember?"

"No."

More silence. "To make him go away," Billy whispered into the phone.

Fragments of their conversation started trickling back.

Yes. He had asked him to make Christian *go away*. He remembered now. *But what was Billy talking—*

"Daniel?" Mia asked softly. She was standing in the living room, her arms crossed. "Is everything okay?"

Daniel held his finger up, indicating he'd just be a minute.

She disappeared back in the dining room. Billy was still talking, but his voice was muffled.

"I can't hear you," Daniel said.

"I said I brought a gun. I was just trying to scare the guy, but he came at me," Billy said, his voice clearer now. "He moved so damn fast. I . . . shit, man . . . The gun went off before I even realized what I was—"

Daniel went cold all over. "What?"

Silence.

"Billy? What happened?" he asked, more loudly.

"He's dead. The guy's dead."

Daniel's heart stuttered.

Dead?

Oxygen fled his brain, and he clasped the back of his neck and tried to understand the meaning of Billy's words.

"It was a total accident. Self-defense," Billy said. "Look, I'm freaking the hell out. I'm heading out of town for a little while. I'll call you in a bit."

"No, Billy. Don't! I need to know—"

The line went dead.

Bruce, sitting at his feet, looked up at him and panted.

Sweat trickled in his armpits. *What did you do, Daniel?*

His mind spinning, Daniel stumbled back to the dining room.

"Are you okay?" Mia asked, a frown creasing her brow. "You're white as a ghost. Who was that?"

"Just work stuff," he said, shivering on the inside. He sat down. "Go ahead. Finish what you were saying." Anything to get her to stop staring at him like that.

Mia started talking again, but his heart was pounding so loudly in his ears, he could only hear snippets of what she was saying. He was in total disbelief.

Why the hell did I ask him to go and scare the guy? Jesus. If he'd been in his right mind, he never would have done it. But he hadn't been in his right mind, had he?

Bad things, Daniel. I've warned you so many damn times. This wouldn't have happened had you listened—

Shut the hell up!

He blinked himself back to the present. Mia was talking about doing time in an Arizona prison now. Ten years. He'd missed what she'd done to get there. In fact, he'd missed a lot of the conversation. But he couldn't think about that now. His brain wasn't capable of comprehending anything else.

He looked down at his steak. It was medium rare, the way he usually liked it. But the bloody juice that was pooled beneath the meat made his stomach turn inside out. He pushed the plate away.

"Daniel?"

Raking his hand over his mouth, he looked up at Mia. "What?"

"Are you even listening to me?"

Mascara was running down her cheeks now. At some point, she'd started crying, but he hadn't even noticed. The tip of her nose was bright pink. She wiped at it with her napkin.

He nodded, still not completely sure what she was saying. He just remembered the name Monte. That they were together. That he used to beat her. Something about drugs. Prison. She started talking again, and he tried to focus on what she was saying this time. He knew it was important. But there was no way it was as important as what Billy had just told him.

"When we got back from our honeymoon, Daniel. That first day that you went to work. It was a Monday. That's when I got the first call." Fresh tears sprang into her eyes. She wiped at them with her napkin and sniffed. "I was skeptical at first. I didn't want to say anything to you until I knew. But the test results came back." Her chin was trembling. "Monte and I had a son, Daniel. I gave him up for adoption, but he contacted me the day we got back from our honeymoon."

She took a deep breath. Exhaled.

"I have a son, Daniel. He's twenty-one. His name is Christian."

CHAPTER 46

DANIEL

DANIEL'S TEETH CHATTERED as he sped down the Pacific Coast Highway, but it wasn't due to the cold weather.

I have a son, Daniel. He's twenty-one. His name is Christian.

He could barely breathe as he tried to grasp the horror of it all. "Oh, my God! What have I done?" he muttered aloud, sweat trickling down his temples.

Calm down!

Focus on the road.

You keep veering out of your lane.

Daniel nodded and swiped at his nose with the back of his hand.

He thought about Mia lying about being at Jiminy's. She said it had been because she'd been meeting Christian. Trying to get to know him. That she'd given him up for adoption, but a private investigator whom he'd hired had found her right before they'd returned from their honeymoon. She said she wasn't sure at first that he was who he said he was . . . She'd had suspicions that Monte had found her, and that this was one of his sick pranks. But they'd gotten their DNA tested, and the results had come back. She knew 100 percent that he was hers.

The texts she'd deleted, the photos Billy had taken of Mia at Christian's house. The hugs. It all made sense now. Mia hadn't been cheating on him at all. Christian wasn't her lover. He was her son.

I told you something like this was bound to happen.

The drinking, Daniel . . .

Nothing but bad things . . .

"Shut up!" he shrieked.

He clutched his throat and stared at the highway in front of him. How could he have possibly done something so horrible? But he'd never wanted Christian killed. Just roughed up. It had been an accident. That's what Billy had said.

He tried Billy's cell again. His fingers were trembling so badly, it took him three tries to get him on speed dial . . . and Billy didn't answer.

Oh, my God! He was her son. Her *son!* A chill crept up Daniel's spine and skittered across the tops of his arms.

Daniel swerved back into his lane, replaying Billy's call in his mind. Bruce whined loudly in the passenger seat.

Mia's words had hit him like a bullet to the chest. He remembered getting up from the table and leaving. Mia had called out to him, saying she was sorry, begging for him to come back. To forgive her.

This . . . can't . . . be happening.

God, please. Please. No. Please, please no.

His phone dinged.

It was Mia.

No, he couldn't talk to her now.

He had no idea where he was going. He just knew he had to get away. As he rounded the next corner, panic ripped through him.

Speeding away from Malibu, he began to scream.

CHAPTER 47

MIA

MIA KNEW DANIEL would take the news badly. She'd been prepared for that. But she hadn't expected him to just leave without saying a word. Now she wasn't sure what to do.

Should she pack?

Yes, she probably should . . . but she didn't have the energy.

She could still see Daniel's face. How it had twisted in disbelief, how his skin had gone white. The fork that he'd been using to move his food around hit his plate with a loud clink. Then he'd stood and, stumbling a little, made his way to the foyer and staggered out of the house, as though he were drunk.

She went up to the bedroom and grabbed two sleeping pills, washed them down, then slid beneath the covers. She reached for her phone and texted him.

I'm so sorry I lied. I love you. I understand if you don't want me anymore, but I do love you. I always have. That wasn't a lie.

And she did love him. More than she'd ever loved anyone else.

She'd told Daniel everything tonight. Left nothing out. She wondered what part bothered him the most. That she'd killed a man? That she was a convicted felon? That she'd been involved with a drug dealer? Had an adult son he hadn't known about? Or the fact that she'd lied to him all along? That she'd never really been the person she'd portrayed herself—but very much wanted—to be?

She could tell he'd been distracted during the conversation. Distant. He'd had such a weird look on his face the entire time. There were many times during the conversation he seemed as though he wasn't even listening to her. But once she'd started talking, she hadn't been able to stop. In a way, she was relieved to just get it all out there. For once in her life, she wasn't hiding anything. Not one thing. It made her feel different, lighter.

She'd told him that there'd been the possibility that Monte had tracked her down and was playing head games with her, but the first time she'd met Christian, something inside of her knew. Maybe a mother's intuition? The DNA results that had come back yesterday had only confirmed it.

Now she was frightened and had no clue where Daniel had gone. The loneliness was closing in again, and she desperately needed comfort.

She texted Christian: I love you, Christian.

It was the first time for her to ever say she loved him—and it was about time.

She waited for him to reply.

But for the first time since they'd reconnected, there wasn't an immediate response.

Fifteen minutes later, with no response from either Daniel or Christian, and feeling lonelier than ever, she clicked the light off, and the room went black.

❖ ❖ ❖

Later that night, Mia was roused from a deep sleep. Her eyes shot open, her mind fuzzy from sleep and the pills.

Her eyes were raw from crying, and she felt hollow inside. Remembering that something had woken her, she strained her ears, listening for any strange sounds in the house. But all she heard were the gentle sounds of waves hitting the shore outside.

Normally, the sounds of the ocean soothed her.

But not tonight.

She closed her eyes and tried to go back to sleep, but the memory of her conversation with Daniel kept churning around and around in her head. Feeling the darkness in the room pressing down on her, she pulled the cotton sheets tightly around her body and watched the shadows crawl across the ceiling. She lay in silence until her mind finally began to drift inward, more deeply inside itself. Until the sleeping pills took over again, and her muscles began to relax. Until sleep began to beckon her back into its dark sticky web.

There was a thud downstairs.

Her heart jackknifed in her chest, and she shot up, knowing for certain she hadn't been dreaming this time.

Someone was inside the house.

Was it Daniel?

Had he already come home?

Her eyes darted to the bedroom door. If it was Daniel, he would have turned on at least a lamp by now—and light would be drifting up from the stairwell. But there was no light. The house was pitch-black.

A stair creaked.

Her scalp prickling, she threw her legs over the side of the bed and fell to her knees. She felt for the bottom of the bed's frame, but it was closer to the floor than she'd expected.

Find somewhere else!

Whoever had broken in was probably halfway up the stairs by now. The panic room!

Move! Hurry!

She darted to the bedroom's spacious walk-in closet, stepped in, and carefully closed the door. Then she felt her way through the darkness to the back, feeling for the full-length mirror at the far end that concealed the entrance to the panic room. She found it and pulled the door open, then she slipped into the dark space and carefully pulled it closed until she heard the soft click. She quietly engaged the deadbolt, then, with the cement floor chilly beneath her bare feet, backed her way deeper into the 5x4-foot space, until her backside hit the far wall. She crouched down. The room was empty except for her and the shoebox she'd been storing her waitressing tips in for the last several months.

Her heart was pounding so hard, she could barely breathe. Who was in the house? Was it a robbery? Or, she wondered, cold dread curling in her belly, something more sinister? An image of Monte flashed inside her head. His mean eyes and twisted mouth. Had he found her? Could he be making good on his promise?

Then the Hemsworth family flickered into her brain, the death of Daniel's friend Andy.

Teddy's warning to Daniel to stop talking about Respira.

A thousand needles pricked her skin.

She heard heavy footsteps moving around the bedroom, then the bathroom. A moment later, she heard the closet door open and the light flip on.

The air squeezed from her lungs when the person stepped into the closet, and her heart hammered in her chest so loudly, she was afraid the intruder would hear it.

Please, no. She prayed silently that whoever it was wouldn't think to look behind the mirror. But as she prayed, she heard the sound of a gun cock and the footsteps draw closer.

CHAPTER 48

DANIEL

DANIEL PARKED IN the driveway and sat in his SUV. He'd driven around for three hours, hoping that it had all been just a bad dream and that eventually he would wake from it. He'd pinched his arms, slapped himself across the face. But it hadn't been a dream. It was real.

All of it.

How could he have let any of this happen? All his life, all he'd wanted were two things: to help people and to not end up anything like his father. But not only had he turned out like his father, he was worse than his father had ever been. His father had killed only himself, whereas Daniel was responsible for the death of a little girl and Mia's son . . . *his own stepson.* Maybe he hadn't asked Billy to kill Christian, but he was the impetus to him doing so. It had been the result of a very bad decision . . . the result of drinking too much.

He sat slumped in the driver's seat, fear coming off him in hot waves, his soul black and dying. When had he veered so off course? He had no idea what he was going to tell Mia. He had no idea what he was going to do—period . . . about *anything.* Between the lingering hangover and the terrible things that were happening all around him, his mind still wasn't working well. All he knew was that he was remorseful and wanted more than anything to rewind everything. Take everything back.

I had such high hopes for you.

Just think . . . you were just beginning to actually become someone.

"Shut the hell up!" he screamed, his voice so loud and shrill, he was certain all of Malibu had heard it.

One more chance, he pleaded. To whom, he wasn't sure. He hadn't prayed for years, since his brother had died.

I'll never drink a drop of alcohol again.

Please.

Just one more chance.

Losing his career and house certainly paled in comparison with the loss of a life. He also now had no reason to think Mia had been unfaithful to him.

He opened his text app and deleted the incriminating texts from Billy, then climbed slowly out of the SUV, still unsure of what he would say to Mia. Maybe he wouldn't say anything. Maybe he'd just hold her tonight. Lay with her head on his chest. Connect with her for what could be the last time.

Then tomorrow . . . *tomorrow* . . . maybe he'd tell her the truth of what he'd done. He'd beg forgiveness, then figure things out from there. If he could just have one more chance, he'd clean up his life. Do better. Hell, he would do whatever it took.

There were so many opportunities he hadn't seen before. He'd do something outside of the medical field. Or maybe go to work with Gail. Help children by outing Respira. Maybe by helping more kids, he could right some of the things he'd done wrong.

He dragged himself out of his vehicle, to the front porch. When he went to unlock the front door, he discovered it wasn't locked. Panic clawed at his throat.

He threw the door open, and Bruce bounded ahead of him into the house. An unfamiliar odor lingered in the foyer, and the hair stood up on the back of his neck. Something was wrong.

Get out of the house, Daniel, the voice said. *Now. Get out!*

Daniel ignored it and walked deeper, past the foyer and into the living room. The first floor was dark and smelled like grilled meat. He felt for a light switch, and, finding one, the living room lit up. He watched Bruce in the distance hobbling up the staircase, looking for Mia.

Daniel flipped on another light and scanned the dining room. Their dinner plates were still on the table. Both still full of food. The big bowl of potato salad sat untouched in the middle of the table. Mia never went to bed without clearing their dishes, cleaning the kitchen. But tonight hadn't been an ordinary night.

Upstairs, Bruce started barking. Then he heard a door slam.

What the—?

If Bruce was barking, it meant something was wrong.

Mia! Adrenaline roaring through his body, he ran to the staircase and took the stairs up two at a time.

No! Get out of the house! the voice screamed as he reached the upstairs landing.

At the bedroom door, he saw movement in the hallway. He whirled around, and it took him a moment to register the man standing outside his office. He was holding a gun and it was pointed at him. Daniel's blood ran cold.

What the hell?

The hallway was dimly lit, and he couldn't make out the man's features.

"Billy?" He could only hope.

The man didn't answer.

Fear inched from his stomach into his throat. He could hear Bruce behind him, whining and sniffing at the bedroom door.

His mind went into overdrive. Images flashed into his mind. Dr. Hemsworth. Andy. Gail. The articles in the brown envelope. Chet's threat at brunch. Teddy's words: *If you insist on making more noise . . . unemployment will be the least of your worries.*

Mia. Where was Mia? Her car was parked in the driveway. Was she safe?

He threw his hands up in the air, his throat so dry he could barely swallow. "You can have whatever you want."

"I'm not here for your money," the man said.

The skin on Daniel's scalp pulled tight. "Then what are you here for?"

The man nodded to Daniel's office door. "Is this your office?"

"Yes."

"Let's go inside."

Daniel stared at him.

Run, Daniel!

"Move it!" the man snapped.

Daniel did as the man instructed and walked into his home office, a ball of terror forming in his middle.

"My wife," Daniel said, panic zigzagging in his stomach.

Something passed behind the man's eyes: a question mark. Then he pointed to Daniel's office chair. "Sit *down!*" he commanded.

Daniel did what the man instructed.

"Now. Where's your wife?" he asked, staring at Daniel.

Daniel tried to think. Was Mia not home? But her car was outside in the driveway, so she had to be. But then again, someone—not Christian, obviously—could have picked her up. Then it hit him that she could be hiding. He remembered her mentioning the panic room. *Oh, God. Please let her be okay,* he pleaded silently, his second prayer tonight.

"Where is your wife?" the man asked, more loudly this time.

"I think she's out with friends," Daniel said.

The man stared at him as though trying to get a read on him, but he looked confused. Unsure whether to believe him.

"What are you here for?" Daniel asked, wanting to change the subject. "You said you're not here for money. So, what do you want?"

The guy pointed the muzzle at Daniel's head. "To do my job."

Daniel's heart thundered in his chest. A million memories floated to the surface of his mind, then scattered like leaves. He thought of his childhood, his sister, his nephews, his first day working as a doctor, meeting Mia, the Caymans, Respira, Dr. Hemsworth, Andy, Suzie. He held his breath, praying for Mia to be protected. For her to somehow get out of this okay.

When the gun went off, he felt his head snap back. Then he realized he was looking down at his lap. He watched blood drip off his nose onto his tan pants. Then he felt his shoulders sag; his world gradually darkened until it went black.

CHAPTER 49

MIA

A FEW SECONDS after hearing the sound of a gun being cocked, Mia heard a vehicle pulling into the driveway. The intruder's footsteps retreated away from the closet and toward the bedroom.

The house was quiet for several minutes. Then Mia heard the front door open and Bruce's claws scrabbling on the hardwood.

Daniel was home.

And the intruder was somewhere in the house.

"This . . . can't . . . be . . . happening!" she shouted inside her head, sweat dotting her forehead. She swore silently at herself for not bringing her phone into the room with her. She could be calling 911 right now. Getting help.

It all happened so quickly. The sound of Bruce bounding up the stairs, the bedroom door slamming. Bruce's whines, then Daniel and another man's muffled voices in the hallway. Then . . . the horrific sound of a gun going off.

She began to shake.

No.

She buried her face in her hands and tried to block out Bruce's howls. *No, no, no!*

She sat in the dark, cold space, listening to the man moving around the house. Then what seemed like hours later, she heard footsteps receding down the stairs and the front door open and close. She quietly unlocked the deadbolt and pushed on the door. It slowly yawned open, and Bruce hobbled into the closet, panting, worry in his big brown eyes.

She stepped down into the closet, then tiptoed into the bedroom. Soft light streamed gently through the bedroom window. Morning. She glanced at the alarm clock and saw it was 5:55 a.m. The man had waited for her all night. She listened to the other side of the bedroom door for a long while, making sure no one was still there. When she felt fairly certain, she opened it and peered down the dimly lit hallway. The door to Daniel's office was closed.

The odor of gunpowder filled Mia's nostrils, and fresh tears burned her swollen eyes. Bruce pushed past her, down the hallway and whined at Daniel's office door.

"Daniel?" she whispered.

There was no answer.

She drew closer, chills chasing up her spine. Bruce whined louder.

"Daniel?" she called again.

Again, nothing.

She reached his office and hesitated, not sure she was ready to see what was on the other side of the door. Then finally, with a shudder, she pushed his door open wider and saw him slumped over in his office chair.

She got a good look at him and stepped backward. She covered her mouth with her hands. *Please, oh, my God, no. Daniel!*

A large chunk of his scalp was gone, and blood was splattered on the side of his face, his desktop computer, his desk, and the wall behind him.

"No, no . . . no!" she sobbed, and the world shimmered in front of her eyes. "Oh, Daniel. No," she whispered. "No."

She didn't have to search for a pulse to know he was gone. Grief welled up in her so big she thought she might suffocate. She stood there, blinded with the sting of hot tears, sobbing until her rib cage ached.

She realized that whoever was behind this might want her dead, too . . . and that she had to get out of there. Tears burning a path down her face, she reached into Daniel's jacket pocket and found his phone. She pressed her lips to his cool cheek and held them there for a long moment, knowing it would be her last time to kiss him. Then she ran back to the master bedroom and threw a bunch of her things into a suitcase.

Not five minutes later, she and Bruce were in her car, speeding toward the valley. "This . . . can't . . . be . . . happening!" she screamed over and over inside her head. She didn't feel safe going to the police. She knew all too well how easy it was to buy off law enforcement. She'd seen Monte and his dealer friends do it several times over the years she was with him. Also, if Hemsworth's father's story were true, she knew that medical examiners could be bought, too. The fewer people she trusted, the better.

Thirty-five minutes later, she turned onto Christian's street and was startled to find two police cruisers outside and the house cordoned off with yellow crime scene tape.

What the hell?

Her blood ran cold.

What was going on? Was Christian okay? She parked across the street a few doors down and watched as a cop walked out of Christian's house and climbed into his vehicle. He drove off, leaving the other cop car in Christian's driveway and the front door wide open.

Mia's hand froze on the door handle. Her first instinct was to jump out of the car and run up his sidewalk to find out what was going on, but after what she'd just witnessed, she was afraid.

Was it possible this was connected to what just happened to Daniel?

An elderly woman was walking a small dog on the sidewalk next to her. As she started to pass Mia's car, Mia lowered her passenger window. "Do you know what happened?" she asked, pointing to Christian's house.

"The young man who lives there was shot yesterday."

A shock wave rolled through Mia's body. "Wha-at?" She worked to catch her breath. "Is he . . . is he okay?"

The woman shrugged. "I don't know. But a couple of my neighbors saw them bring him out and said he didn't look good."

The old woman's words stabbed Mia's brain like an ice pick.

"Is he a friend of yours?" the woman asked.

Mia ignored the question, her gaze flickering back to the house. "Do you know where they took him?"

"I'm not sure, but I'd imagine Valley Presbyterian."

Mia nodded. She took one last look at the house, then threw the Jetta into gear and sped off. Bursting into tears, she headed east, leaving a bloody wake behind her.

❖ ❖ ❖

After putting a hundred miles between her and the San Fernando Valley, Mia stopped at a gas station and dipped into her stash of waitressing tips to fill up her tank. Her cheeks stained with tears, she slid the nozzle into her gas tank and set it to automatically pump, then reached back into the car and grabbed Daniel's phone. She checked the call log and jotted down the last several numbers he'd called, then removed the battery in both of their phones so the devices couldn't be traced.

A few hours later, running on pure adrenaline, she crossed the Nevada state line and stopped at a Walgreens drugstore to purchase some supplies, including a disposable prepaid phone, hair dye, a screwdriver, and dog food.

At nightfall, she exited the interstate again and pulled into the parking lot of a seafood restaurant. In the lot, she switched her license plates with those on an old pickup truck. She tried to call Christian, but she got his voice mail. Then she called the last few phone numbers

Daniel had dialed in hopes of talking to someone who could help her make sense of Daniel's murder.

In the last thirty-six hours, there'd been several calls from the office, Teddy, Billy, and someone named Gail Whitman. She ignored the calls from both the office and Teddy and called Billy. She received his voice mail as well and left him a message to call her back, saying it was urgent and that something had happened to Daniel. The next number she called was Gail Whitman's. The woman answered on the second ring.

"My name is Mia Winters," she said, trying to keep fear out of her voice. "I understand that you spoke with my husband recently."

"Yes. Hi, Mrs. Winters," the woman on the other end of the line said. "Is everything okay?"

Mia debated how to answer the question. Finally, she said, "No. It's not. It's not okay at all." She asked Gail who she was, and Gail explained she was a medical journalist and filled her in on the conversation she'd had with Daniel, explaining to her how he had agreed to go public with Respira. She asked if Mia was calling because Daniel had been hurt.

"He was . . . shot, Gail. Killed," she said, tears spilling down her cheeks.

"Oh, my God," the woman said. "What happened?"

Since Daniel seemed to have trusted the journalist, Mia decided to tell her everything. She told her about the break-in and everything she'd heard while she was hiding in the panic room. Then about the gunshot and finding Daniel's body.

"I am *so* sorry," Gail said. "Are you in a safe place?"

"I . . . I think so. I'm on the road."

"You need to be very careful. They are probably looking for you right now."

Bruce whined from the passenger seat.

Gail told her she had no doubt that Daniel's murder was connected to Respira—and that she believed the people behind it were also connected to the Hemsworths' murders and maybe even Andy's.

Mia told Gail about Christian. Asked how Gail thought he might fit into everything. Gail said she had no idea. Daniel hadn't mentioned him during their conversation. Gail asked what she could do to help. Mia told her how concerned she was about Christian, and before getting off the phone, Gail promised to find him. She said she'd call Mia tomorrow with news.

At 11:00 p.m., Mia checked herself into a roadside motel. She told the desk clerk that she'd lost her driver's license. When he said he couldn't rent her a room without identification, she slipped him a fifty-dollar bill. He pocketed the money, jotted something into the computer, and gave her a room key.

After walking Bruce, she grabbed her things from her car and found her room. It was small and smelled of stale cigarette smoke. Cigarette burns pocked the carpet. She threw her backpack on the queen-size bed and unpacked her items from the drugstore, then got to work cutting and dyeing her hair.

While waiting the thirty minutes for her hair to bleach, she tried calling Christian again. She checked the local crime section of the *Los Angeles Times* online and saw that they'd reported a shooting in the 300th block of Reseda Drive, but there was no news on the status of the victim. She checked Christian's social media accounts and saw nothing had been updated for over a day, and no friends had posted any news. She hoped Gail was having better luck.

Her adrenaline beginning to wane, she closed her eyes and listened to her neighbor watching *Jeopardy!* on the other side of the wall for a little while, then she pushed herself off the bed and went to the window and looked out. Everything looked just as it had when she'd arrived. No new vehicles. No one wandering around looking as though they were searching for someone.

She picked up her phone and placed a call to her friend Sam.

CHAPTER 50
TEDDY

Two Days Later . . .

TEDDY SAT AT home, nursing a bottle of scotch.

His thoughts circled back to Rachel Jacobs killing herself in one of the examination rooms in his clinic, and he shook his head. The suicide had forced him to close the practice for a few days. The police had needed some time to conduct a quick investigation, and the cleaning crew had needed time to clean the woman's blood and brain matter from the walls and furniture.

Margy and Deepali had also asked for a couple of days off to recover from witnessing the carnage. He planned to give them a generous bonus, considering what they'd gone through. Hell, he'd be more than generous. He sure as shit could afford to now.

It still gave him chills to wonder how differently things would have gone down if he had been in the clinic when Rachel arrived. He knew he'd just narrowly dodged a bullet with that one.

He was in one of the guest bedrooms right now, waiting for the news to come on. As he waited, he grabbed a vial of OxyContin, screwed off the lid, tossed two to the back of his tongue, and chased them with the scotch. He glanced around the room. The curtains were closed tight, and the large room was dark and cool. His wife constantly complained about how cold he kept the house and was always turning up the temperature while he was at work, but he was uncomfortable sleeping with the air at anything above 62. To remedy this, he kept a separate floor AC unit in this room, and right now it was blowing out highly chilled air to the tune of 50 degrees.

The news came back on. A young Latina woman was reporting outside of Immunext's headquarters. The caption *Talks Underway on Respira Being Added to Shot Schedule* was splashed across the bottom of the screen.

Teddy strained to get his eyes to focus on the screen.

"Immunext's shareholders are celebrating a major windfall today as Respira shares jumped sharply from its open of $69.96 to a closing price of $78.96 per share, representing a gain of almost ten percent in a single day—something not seen often in even the most volatile of trading."

Teddy's pulse sprinted, just as it had when he'd heard this news the first and second times. But he couldn't fully enjoy his win yet because there was still a loose end. Teddy hated loose ends.

"The jump came on the heels of an announcement that discussions are underway about the corporation's new pharmaceutical Respira being added to the CDC's shot schedule as early as next year. Pediatric clinics and chain drugstores across the country have been administering this drug to children as a part of an important nationwide public health campaign."

The news cut to a prerecorded interview set in front of the California Department of Education headquarters. The same reporter asked a spokeswoman, "What exactly does this mean for parents in California?"

The DOE spokeswoman answered, "If Respira is added to the schedule, children will be required to get their full complement of Respira before they can be admitted to day care or public school."

"No injection, no school, or are there exemptions available? Religious? Philosophical?"

"No injection, no school. The State of California no longer offers exemptions. It's a move other states are sure to follow."

The reporter continued, "Respira could be added as early as ten months from now, despite parent protests against the drug around the country. What do you say to these parents' concerns?"

"I say we appreciate and understand parents' concerns for any new drug," said the DOE spokeswoman. "But these drugs are rigorously studied and have been proven to be very safe. Parents need only to talk to their pediatricians for assurance."

"Reporting from Immunext Corporation's headquarters, this is Carmen Flores for KTLA Channel Five News."

Teddy picked up one of his burner phones and texted his broker again.

The sale went through, right?

His broker replied: Yes. All the shares have been unloaded.

"Good, good," he whispered. The gamble had paid off, and now he could breathe again.

The stock would only continue to rise, but he wasn't going to take any chances. After all, Respira was bound to be pulled from both the shot schedule and the market at some point. Although it would probably take several months, maybe even years, before it happened, he was done taking risks.

In fact, the faster he could extricate himself from this drug and the people involved, the better. This whole ordeal was giving him an ulcer, and he was glad it was almost over with. If any of the others got caught, he sure as hell wasn't going down with them. He was a highly respected physician, not a criminal. He'd just done this one thing so that he could save the practice. After all, this drug was going to be forced on kids whether he made money from it or not. The people who wanted it to succeed were much too powerful for it not to. But now he was done. Respira could go to hell for all he cared.

When he'd first become involved with Respira, he'd had no clue it would injure so many children. But by the time he understood what he'd gotten himself into, it was too late. He had already dumped the practice's money into it, and he needed the drug to fly under the radar at least for now . . . to do well enough to be considered for a coveted spot on the schedule. If Respira went down, he went down.

He swallowed another mouthful of whiskey, rubbed his puffy eyes, then switched the television off. He sat in the dark, the only sound in the room his shallow breathing.

His burner phone rang.

He accepted the call.

"I'll make this short and sweet," the caller said. "It's about Mia Winters."

The loose end.

Teddy had been furious at the caller's incompetence when he'd first heard that Mrs. Winters was still alive. Now not only was she still breathing, she was unaccounted for.

"What do you have?" Teddy asked the caller.

"We got a lead on Mrs. Winters's whereabouts. She's in Mobile, Alabama. We have guys heading there now." The caller paused for a moment. "As promised, there will be no additional mistakes. She'll be taken care of immediately."

"Taken care of?" Teddy asked.

"Eliminated."

"Make sure you get rid of the body. We don't need any private investigators meddling or goddamn pathologists conducting private autopsies."

"Don't worry. There won't be a body once we're done with her."

"Call when it's done."

"Will do."

"And the Jacobs girl?"

"The medical examiner's office will be releasing Suzie Jacobs's autopsy report in the morning. It's going to say she had a mitochondrial defect that no one knew about. A combination of different medications caused the respiratory arrest. Hell, the girl could have just *sneezed* the wrong way, and it would have happened."

"Perfect."

"I'll keep you updated."

Teddy hung up and took another long swig of scotch, even though his stomach was turning a little. He picked up the handgun on his night-stand and twirled it. The dead kid had been a little difficult for him but certainly survivable. And while Ms. Jacobs's suicide had brought some negative attention to his practice and Respira, they were able to easily explain her actions away by painting her as an understandably distraught but misinformed mother. But Danny. *Dammit, what a waste.* Teddy had really liked the man. Had begun to see him as the son he'd never had.

"Shit, Danny," he whispered now. "How many times did I try to warn you?" But the younger doctor had been so naive. He thought by speaking up he'd make a difference. He had no clue just whom he had been dealing with. How big all of this was. This industry was a machine . . . and a very powerful one at that.

Teddy tried to redirect his thoughts back to his recent win. He'd just made a ridiculous amount of money. Much more than he'd ever had before. He'd never have to worry about money again. Not in this lifetime. But the adrenaline was quickly dying off, leaving a dull numbness. He wondered how difficult it would be to get to sleep tonight.

He tried to smile again. After all, everything was good now. *Better* than good. It was the best it had ever been.

CHAPTER 51

MIA

Four Days Later . . .

MIA PARKED THE Jetta behind a surf shop in Clearwater Beach, Florida, and climbed out. It was a little past 9:00 p.m., and the air smelled of salt and marijuana smoke. She clipped Bruce's leash to his collar, locked the car doors, and headed toward the small strip of storefronts.

As she rounded the corner, a street musician began performing a cover of Jimmy Buffett's "Margaritaville." Mia's insides untethered all over again, and tears welled up in her aching eyes. She and Daniel had listened to that song so many times during their happier days.

A huge part of her heart had died back in California, and she knew she'd never get it back. She also didn't think she'd ever get over the overwhelming sorrow. *Oh, Daniel.* She missed him so much. And she was beside herself with worry about Christian.

Her world had tilted on its axis yet again. She'd spent the last few days lying in the fetal position in a motel room bed, seesawing between feelings of grief, anger, and fear . . . vacillating from pain to numbness and back again all in a moment's notice.

Gail had made good on her promise and had found Christian. He was alive but barely. She'd found him at Valley Presbyterian in the intensive care unit, having suffered a gunshot wound to the chest. Under the guise that she was Christian's aunt, Gail had visited him twice so far. The bullet had collapsed a lung and ruptured his diaphragm. He was on a respirator in critical condition, and the doctors said it was still touch and go. At this point, it was fifty-fifty whether he'd recover. At Mia's request, Gail had whispered in his ear that Mia had to go away for a little while, but that she loved him and was thinking about him every moment of every day. And that she'd contact him soon. That she'd be back once all this blew over. To stay strong and hang in there. Gail said she wasn't sure how much he'd heard or understood because his nurse had said he was heavily sedated and he'd been unmoving, his eyes glazed and half-closed. Gail promised to visit him again tomorrow and give her another update.

Mia wanted more than anything to drive back to California to be with Christian, but it would be too dangerous—plus, it would likely put him in harm's way. She'd been racking her brain trying to figure out how he'd possibly been connected to any of this but hadn't had any luck. Gail said she was working on it, and if or when she found out, Mia would be the first to know.

Not wanting Daniel's death to be in vain, Mia had given Gail her story. She told her everything she'd witnessed inside the house that night and everything Daniel had told her about Respira and what Teddy had told him. Gail had planned to publish a story about it this morning, but someone had hacked into her server, and her site had been down all day.

The strip of storefronts was bustling with teenagers and young adults, some of them swaying to the street musician's music. With Bruce's leash in her hand, Mia tucked her chin and hurried toward the beach. She heard several female voices *ooh* and *aww* over Bruce, but she pretended not to hear.

When she'd called Sam and told him what had happened, he'd given her the number of his older brother, Fred, and told her to call him immediately. Apparently, Fred was still caught up in illegal dealings after all these years and was now well connected in the underground world. Fred had instructed her to lie low for the last few days, then show up at this beach in Clearwater tonight.

Mia stepped from the sidewalk to the sand and stared out at the moonlit ocean. She pushed off her flip-flops and tossed them in the backpack, then let Bruce off the leash. He darted toward the water. Tonight was the first time since the night of Daniel's murder that the animal wasn't actively grieving, searching for his owner, his ears pressed against his skull.

She folded her arms across her middle, the sound of the surf and the scent of the salty sea making her feel closer to Daniel. The breeze picked up, whipping her hair into her face. She buried her feet in the cool sand and watched Bruce in the distance, digging at something. Then she caught a glimpse of someone up the beach about fifty yards away, heading toward her. Her heartbeat stuttered as she watched Bruce eyeball the man and bound up to him.

The guy knelt and pet the dog, and she wondered if the man was Fred. She figured it had to be. After all, besides the two of them, the beach was deserted. The big crowds were back at the strip. The guy straightened and started walking toward her again. She shivered as he got closer. At this point, it was difficult to trust anyone.

"Mia?" His voice was deep. Different than it had been all those years ago.

"Yeah," she said, her muscles relaxing a little.

"It's me, Fred."

He stood across from her now, a backpack of his own slung over one shoulder. "Man, it's been a long time, hasn't it? Over twenty years. You're all grown up now, and you . . . you changed your hair," he said, gesturing to his own hair.

Back at the motel room, she'd cut her hair into a pixie cut and dyed it blonde.

Fred looked different, too. The last time she'd seen him was right before he'd gotten busted for trying to rob a convenience store. He'd been only twenty.

"A lot of people are looking for you right now. You know that, right? Your photo is everywhere."

"Yeah, I know."

The news outlets were reporting her as a person of interest in Daniel's death. Her image—the photo her coworker had posted to Facebook—was splashed across media outlets all over the country. They were claiming she was armed and dangerous.

"Did you do what I suggested about the motel in Alabama?"

She nodded. "Yeah, thanks for that." Back in Mobile, she'd pulled off the highway and rented a motel room for a week using her real identity, Mia Winters. She'd stayed in the room for fewer than five minutes, only long enough to leave some clothes and a notepad with a note that indicated she was planning to meet someone at a restaurant in Mobile at the end of the week. Fred thought that this extra step would help buy her some time to get safely out of the country. After leaving the note, she'd lifted another pair of license plates and driven to Clearwater.

Fred grabbed the backpack and unzipped it. "It's all here," he said. "New Social Security number, passport, driver's license, and birth certificate."

"Great, thank you." She took the phone and envelope and slid both into the main holding area of her backpack, then grabbed the money to pay him.

Fred shook his head. "Keep it. Sam said this is on him."

Tears welled up in her eyes at Sam's continued kindness. "Thank you."

"You heading out tomorrow?"

"Yeah."

"Good, good. Do you need anything else?" Fred asked. "Have a place to stay tonight?"

"I'm good, thanks."

Bruce whined at her feet.

Fred's gaze went to the dog. "So, is this the big guy you were talking about?"

Mia swallowed. "Yes, this is Bruce."

She knelt and massaged the scruff around Bruce's head, and tears spilled down her face. She was leaving Bruce with Fred. She hated to do it, but it would be too risky to fly anywhere with a three-legged dog right now, especially internationally. Like Fred had said, a lot of people were looking for her.

Sam assured her that Fred would give Bruce a good home. But God, she would miss him. He was the only piece of Daniel she had left. Maybe someday when . . . *if* . . . she was able to come back . . . But it was way too soon to think about the possibility of that now.

"Goodbye, handsome," she whispered. Bruce stared at her and panted, and his tail wagged back and forth.

A sob erupted from the back of her throat.

"Thanks for taking him in," she said, still looking at Bruce.

"Absolutely."

She scratched the dog behind the ears and gave him a long kiss on his moist nose. Then she said goodbye to both of them and headed back toward her car.

As she walked, she stared up at the moon. She thought about Daniel and Christian again, and the moon started sliding in and out of focus. She rubbed the tears from her eyes and took a deep breath.

Daniel had been flawed, but he was also warm, loving, and honest, and he was only the second man she'd ever known who had treated her well. Sam being the first. Christian had been messy, smoked too much weed, was funny and caring. He also had loved and accepted her. Even though she had given him up, he hadn't given up on her.

God, it was all so unfair.

She didn't think she'd ever get over the heartbreak.

She exhaled gently; then tucking her chin to her chest, she pulled her jacket closer to her body and walked back toward the strip.

Her mind looped back to the choices she'd made, all the secrets. She couldn't help but wonder if she'd done anything differently, if Daniel would maybe still be here. There was no way of knowing for sure. She thought about their conversations about being destined for happiness or not. They'd both been right. Neither of them had.

Reaching the parking lot, she hit the unlock button on her key fob and slipped into the car. When she pulled onto the main drag, an electronic billboard caught her attention, and anger flared in her belly. Another ad for Respira. Although she'd just lost nearly everything, the machine would keep marching on. It wasn't right. She averted her eyes and watched the road.

She was driving to Tampa tonight and was going to fly to Thailand in the morning. She'd stay with Sam until she could fully process everything and figure out her next steps. If Christian pulled through, she was going to help him in every way possible from Thailand until things died down and she could figure out a way to safely get back to the States. She'd also reach out to Claire and explain what had happened. Although she wasn't a fan of Daniel's sister, the poor woman hadn't deserved to lose her brother. She also deserved the truth.

When she got a second wind, she was going to finish what Daniel had started and was going to help Gail as much as she could to bring about awareness of Respira's dangers. The way she saw it, she now had a purpose bigger than herself for the first time in her life. Maybe she wasn't destined for happiness, but maybe she could help someone else live a happily ever after. Maybe her life could mean something.

Tomorrow she would be going underground indefinitely—and Mia and the life she'd created for herself would disappear forever . . . and someone else would be born.

ACKNOWLEDGMENTS

I HAVE SEVERAL incredible people to thank for supporting me during the writing of this novel. Jessica Tribble, thank you for both your belief in this book and your patience. This novel was by far the most challenging to write for various reasons. I want to thank Gracie Doyle, Sarah Shaw, and all the other *incredible* people at Thomas & Mercer . . . the publisher of my dreams. I can hardly believe this is already my *sixth* thriller with you!

A huge thanks to my first readers, Jennifer LeBlanc, Roger Canaff, Izabela Jeremus, Tim Welch, Bruce Gardner, Sara Koelsh, and Bevin Armstrong. You guys are wonderful. Thank you for being so generous with your time.

A very special thank-you to Deanna Finn and David Wilson, who both read probably the first twenty drafts of this book and gave me excellent feedback. I'm so very grateful for you two for many reasons. This book wouldn't have been the same without your help.

Thank you to Charlotte Herscher for being the best developmental editor ever. I hope you stay in this industry for many, many years to come. Working with you is always an incredible experience.

Dr. Shobhit Aurora, Dr. Genevieve King, Dr. Leanne Davis, Dr. Jocelyn Stamat, and Cynthia J. Ward, MSN, RN, thank you for answering my medical questions. Heather Turano, Jessica Fitch, Nikie DesRoches, Cher D'Beck, Robert Meyers, and Brandi Lewis, thank you for sharing your stories with me. You are such *amazing* parents. ❤ Also, a huge thank-you to JB Handley, Del Bigtree, Brittney Kara, Elaine Shtein, Mary Jo Perry, and Shawn Forshage for tirelessly spreading awareness about the many different categories of drugs parents might want to take a closer look at.

Last but certainly not least, I owe a great deal of gratitude to my husband, Brian, for being a first reader, giving me constructive notes, and, most of all, for helping with the twins and the household so I could write. I love and appreciate you.

ABOUT THE AUTHOR

Photo © 2014 Alan Weissman

#1 *USA TODAY* AND internationally bestselling author Jennifer Jaynes graduated from Old Dominion University with a bachelor's degree in health sciences and holds a certificate from the Institute for Integrative Nutrition. She made her living as a content manager, webmaster, news publisher, medical assistant, editor, publishing consultant, and copywriter before finally realizing her dream as a full-time novelist. Jennifer is the author of six thrillers, including *Disturbed, The Stranger Inside, Never Smile at Strangers, Don't Say a Word,* and *Ugly Young Thing*; and the children's book *I Care About Me.* When she's not writing or spending time with her husband and twin boys, Jennifer loves reading, cooking, and studying nutrition. Visit Jennifer at www.jenniferjaynes.net.